Praise for

"I'm reading a fantastic nov[...] *Lucky*. It's suspenseful and [...] going to like this a lot, and I think a lot of you are going to like it. It has that *Where the Crawdads Sing* vibe."

—Stephen King

"An absorbing thriller with heart." —*People*

"What's more thrilling than a fictional character speaking to us in a voice we haven't heard before? A voice so authentic and immediate—think Huck Finn, Holden Caulfield, Mattie Ross—that we suspect it must've been there all along, that we somehow managed to miss it. Daniel, the protagonist of Will Leitch's smart, funny, heartbreaking new novel *How Lucky*, is just such a voice, and I'm not sure it will ever completely leave my head, or that I want it to."

—Richard Russo

"Not many writers can shift gears from hilarious to heart-rending to harrowing, all on the same page. Will Leitch does it again and again. *How Lucky* is one of the most original thrillers I've read in years, with an improbable hero that no reader will ever forget." —Carl Hiaasen

"It's a testament to Will Leitch's ability that he can blend seemingly disparate elements—mystery and illness and humor and football—and come away with something so winning. *How Lucky* asserts that 'the world is a terrifying place these days' and the novel explores those terrors quite convincingly, yet I was heartened by the depth of Leitch's writing, his obvious love for the world and what it could be. He imbues his hero with a kind of hopefulness that comes from seeing the worst and finding some way to keep living."

—Kevin Wilson, *New York Times* bestselling author of *Nothing to See Here*

"*How Lucky* is a gem: a riveting plot and a narrator who is charming, engaging, and downright inspiring. Will Leitch brilliantly juggles hilarity and horror. I loved this novel—every page."

—Chris Bohjalian, #1 bestselling author of *The Flight Attendant* and *Hour of the Witch*

"A lovely book. Set in Athens, Georgia, the novel is a model of verisimilitude. It is also beautifully written and suspenseful, at the same time being all about goodness and caring without once being sappy or, well, sentimental. And that is a rare feat in fiction."

—*Booklist* (starred review)

"A touchingly imagined portrait of friendship and community."   —Sam Sacks, *Wall Street Journal*

"Witty, vigorously written. . . . *How Lucky* succeeds on more than just luck. . . . Leitch builds his cast beautifully. . . . Gives us an authentic, compelling portrait of a narrator who motors through the obstacle course of his life with grit and grace."

—Hamilton Cain, *Washington Post*

HOW LUCKY

ALSO BY WILL LEITCH

Life as a Loser

Catch

God Save the Fan

Are We Winning?

HOW LUCKY

A NOVEL

WILL LEITCH

HARPER PERENNIAL

NEW YORK • LONDON • TORONTO • SYDNEY • NEW DELHI • AUCKLAND

HARPER PERENNIAL

A hardcover edition of this book was published in 2021 by HarperCollins Publishers.

HarperCollins books may be purchased for educational, business, or sales promotional use. For information, please email the Special Markets Department at SPsales@harpercollins.com.

FIRST HARPER PERENNIAL EDITION PUBLISHED 2022.

Library of Congress Cataloging-in-Publication Data has been applied for.

ISBN 978-0-06-307305-0 (pbk.)

22 23 24 25 26   LSC   10 9 8 7 6 5 4 3 2 1

To Alexa

HOW LUCKY CAN ONE MAN GET?

—*John Prine*

HOW LUCKY

My life is not a thriller. My life is the opposite of a thriller. What a relief. Who wants their life to be thrilling? Don't get me wrong. We want our lives to be *exciting*: we want them to inspire, to be surprising, to provide us a reason to get up and experience something new every day. But thrilling? No way, man. Everything that happens in a thriller would be completely fucking terrifying in real life. You've seen a million chase scenes in movies, so many that you barely even look up from folding laundry when one happens in whatever you are watching on Netflix at that particular moment. They are dull; they are rote and boring. But if you were *in* one of those chase scenes, it would be a nightmare. You'd be running . . . for your life! If you survived it, you would spend years trying to get over it. You'd shake and cower about it in therapy, you'd have nightmares reliving it from which you woke up screaming, you'd have trouble developing any sort of human connection with another person. It would be the worst thing that ever happened to you.

Real life, mercifully, isn't a thriller. Those things don't happen to you, and they don't happen to me. My life is nothing but small moments, and so is yours. We don't live in a series of plot points. We should be thankful for that. We should realize how lucky we are.

When I say that I know that she got in the Camaro at 7:22 a.m., trust that I know this for certain. My certainty is a result of my routine. You might not think so, but my routine really isn't that different from your routine. I am certain because the day was an ordinary, pedestrian morning like every other one. I am certain because I saw her like I always see her.

Marjani woke me up at 6:00 a.m. We had a silent breakfast. I answered emails and scrolled through Instagram until the *Today* show came on and alerted me to all the fresh horrors that had taken place in the world the night before. After Hoda cheerfully ran down how everything's falling apart, Al explained that it was going to be 106 in Las Cruces today, hoo boy, and then he grinned and threw it to 11Alive, the local affiliate in Atlanta, like he does every weekday at 7:17. Weatherman Chesley McNeil, which is somehow his real name, grinned like *he* always does every weekday at 7:17. Then it was WIZometer time. Every television station should have a WIZometer. It's just a number between 1 and 11, 11 being the platonic ideal of weather on this planet and 1 presumably being a meteor shower that will kill us all, that sums up the weather for that day. Chelsey McNeil has exactly four minutes to tell us the local weather and get to the WIZometer before he has to throw it back to Al in New York.

Those four minutes can be agony. It is worrisome how much of my emotional well-being I sometimes wrap up in the

WIZometer. I work out of my home. I'm here all the time. "Outside," beyond my front porch, is a place I visit only sporadically. The WIZometer is my invite to see the world for a few minutes. You give me an 8 or more on the WIZometer, like we got today ("You're gonna like the way your weekend is shaping up, Atlanta!"), I'm scooting out the door to the front porch posthaste. More to the point: I'm scooting out at 7:21 a.m. It was the case this day, it will be the case tomorrow, it will remain the case as long as I'm able to get out there, and as long as the weather report is good.

Marjani walked to her Honda Civic and waved goodbye, *See you tomorrow Daniel.* Our routine now is a wordless dance, forged from years of practice, Marjani the Astaire, me the Ginger Rogers, doing what she does but backward and in heels. Her English is really good now, but the years in which she spoke so little taught us this silent tango. Sometimes we talk. Sometimes we don't. I watched her old car groan and groan before starting. She's had that thing since I've known her, and I have no idea how it's still running.

Marjani drove down Agriculture, toward Stegeman Coliseum, where she had to help clean up after an athletic booster event the night before. There was a University of Georgia home football game coming up, which meant all sorts of big events during the week, which meant more work for Marjani. She helps me in the morning, and then it's off to a series of odd jobs, cleaning, babysitting, house visits, occasionally cooking. That's what she did the day before, and that's what she will do for hundreds of tomorrows. If that sputtering car can make it, anyway.

I took a sip from my water straw and watched her leave from my front porch. She had to slam on the brakes as some kid with a Misfits backpack absentmindedly waded into the middle of the street, and he raised his hand, partly out of apology, mostly out of obliged apathy, and shuffled off into the woods. The road was otherwise clear, a quiet type of morning when all of Athens is hungover. Everyone seemed to be sleeping an extra hour. Even the student family housing building, which is usually clattering with dutiful doctoral students, was sluggish and dim. I took a deep breath and tried to absorb a rare moment of silence outside. How often is it just me out here? How often am I outside with no one else?

Then I saw her. I am making it sound, as I describe it to you now, as if it were a big dramatic moment, like she jumped out at me, like I couldn't miss her, like she was wearing a bright red coat in a black-and-white world. Like I was in a thriller. But it wasn't like that at all. She was just walking like she always walks. She is usually not the only person out this early but was the only person that day. I had seen her every day at this time for the last three weeks, prompt, right on the button. A sophomore college student, maybe, carrying a blue backpack and walking on the sidewalk in the same direction Marjani had just driven. She was meandering up Ag Drive at 7:22 in the morning on a beautiful fall day, an 8, maybe 9 on the WIZometer, easy, just another kid walking to class.

As usual, the only thing different about her was that she wasn't staring at a phone. She never even had headphones in. She doesn't look up, she is always by herself, she blends into the sidewalk. She has never seen me out here, and frankly, I would never have thought to notice her either if she weren't out here the same time as I am every day. She just walks. That's all she ever did.

Until that day. That day, she stopped for a second. No reason: no car pulling in front of her to get out of the way of or anything. She just stopped, looked up, and for the first and only time made eye contact with me. It was a clear accident; her eyes darted away faster than they'd landed on me. But she saw me. And I saw her. She then stopped again, glanced back up at me, closer this time, with a little smile. She raised her right hand. *Hello.* Then she went back on her walk.

The Camaro turned left off Southview Drive onto Agriculture. It was a drab tan one that needed a new paint job and a lot more tender loving care than it was currently receiving. I'd guess it was late '60s, vintage—back when the Camaro was considered a classy sports car rather than something you tried to go parking in with Sally or Betty back in the 1970s. It is a car worthy of the work you'd need to put into it to restore it to its former glory, work it wasn't currently receiving.

The car pulled beside her and stopped. She looked inside. She seemed to shrug. I couldn't see what was happening inside the car. She shook her head once, seemed to laugh lightly, then shrugged again. The driver then opened the passenger door. I couldn't make out his face, but I caught two things: a glimpse of a shiny, almost translucent boot tip on his left foot—it shone like chrome—and a blue Atlanta Thrashers hat on his head. I remember finding the Thrashers hat strange, even in the moment. There was an NHL team here called the Atlanta Thrashers back ten, fifteen years ago, but no one in the South likes hockey, so they moved to Winnipeg. Who wears an Atlanta Thrashers hat?

She paused and looked slightly to her right, as if she were making sure no one was watching. Then she looked to her left and saw me again. She quickly looked away, as if embarrassed, or maybe just searching, as if she were looking for . . . what? My permission? Maybe she was just glad someone was looking. Maybe she wished no one was. I have no idea. It was just another fall morning. There was no reason to think about it the rest of the day, and I didn't. You wouldn't have either. It was nothing.

But she did get in the car. It was 7:22 in the morning. I am certain of it.

TUESDAY

1.

At 11:13, I'm called "zombie intern cocksucker" for the first time by a stranger, and all told, that's not a bad little run for a sleepy Tuesday. Midweek travelers are mostly business travelers, who are on the average nicer than tourists but much more devastating and furious when wronged because They Have Status. But today's an easy Tuesday. It's another good WIZometer day, which must have everyone in a better mood.

"Zombie intern cocksucker" is, I assume, a reference to my soullessness, my lack of power and influence in society, and my general odiousness, respectively. (The latter is too crude and too irrelevant to the pertaining conversation to refer specifically to what may or may not be my sexual orientation.) The instigating incident is a minor storm, the only one I can see on my Weather Underground radar, that is apparently keeping the airplane @pigsooeyhogs11 is hoping to take to Nashville grounded in Little Rock, Arkansas. While I can appreciate the unfortunate situation of being stuck in Arkansas, there is not much I can do for him, being as I am sitting in this chair and this desk in Athens, Georgia. But he doesn't want me to do anything for him. He just wants me to sit and take it. I possess a unique set of skills for this job, and sitting and taking it is foremost among them.

> @spectrumair sitting at LIT for 25 minutes now no updates WTF?
> @spectrumair 35 minutes now still waiting #fuckspectrumair
> @spectrumair i know you dont give a shit but im still here

We are trained not to respond to every single tweet. It might be possible for us to do so—Spectrum Air is a regional airline that only flies back and forth between eight different airports, three times a day; there aren't enough passengers to overwhelm us even if every single one of them were pissed off—but responding to each one would give them the illusion that we actually cared about their complaints, which we do not. Sure, we have to *look* like we care: the last thing any brand wants, even a tiny regional airline based in a field in Alabama, is to appear as if it does not value each and every one of its loyal customers. But they do not care. If they cared, they would hire a full-time public relations staff, and a social media coordinator, and I dunno, maybe get some planes that don't have to be grounded because a couple of clouds were spotted fifty miles away. That is not what kind of airline Spectrum Air is. Spectrum Air is the sort of airline that pays me twenty-five bucks an hour to blandly respond to "dissatisfied" tweets. At $79 one-way from Little Rock to Nashville, you get what you pay for.

Of course, this is not what I tell him. After his third tweet, and an alert from the home office that the flight is on an indefinite hold until the "weather incident" has resolved, I respond. It takes me a little longer to respond than it might take other people, which I suspect is another reason they like me at this job.

@pigsooeyhogs11 We apologize for the inconvenience. Weather has delayed your flight. We have no further info at this time but will update as soon as we know anything. 🤙

Always use the hang loose emoji when responding to angry people. How angry can you be at an emoji? If we communicated solely with emojis, there would be no wars.

Turns out, @pigsooeyhogs11 can be quite angry at an emoji: the zombie intern cocksucker line comes out two tweets later. Once a customer becomes obscene or abusive, there's nothing you can do with them, so they tell us to just mute them on Twitter right then and there. You aren't supposed to block them—that lets them know you heard them—you are instructed simply to mute them, turning all their screams and complaints into empty wails into the ether. They are simply shouting into space.

I'll confess there is a certain lonely justice to the idea of pissed-off people pounding insults into their phone that literally no one will ever see because they've been muted. In this way, my job is almost a public service. Everybody has their demons, and in your daily life, it's difficult to find places to vent all those frustrations. You can yell into your pillow, or take it out on your dog, or just let it all build up until it explodes at the wrong time, hurting yourself or someone you care about. Expressing rage online toward a discount regional airline, I'd argue, is in fact one of the most productive, healthy ways to express your rage. People have to get it out somehow. Might as well get it out at us.

But, still, I never mute them. Right now they're furious travelers, but outside our plane they're just sons and daughters and moms and dads and coworkers and bosses and the fifth guy in line at Publix and worried hospital visitors, and eventually they're just the guy lying in the coffin that everybody sitting in the fold-up chairs feels guilty they didn't spend more time with. They are working through something, desperate to be heard, and it feels churlish to deny them that. Once he threw out the "cocksucker," the conversation was over. But shutting someone up, someone in pain, feels cruel. Company policy is to mute them. But I just can't do it.

One of the things I do like to do, when someone has crossed the line and company policy says I'm not allowed to interact with him anymore, is to look for other people who are on the same flight, who have complained about their flight in less vulgar ways, and give *them* information. Maybe they're sitting near the angry person, and they can tell him. That's what I want to believe. I like to imagine that when a stranger on the flight of a person who called me a cocksucker learns that the flight is taking off in twenty minutes, she'll walk over and let that person know. The angry person puts down his phone, forgetting he was ever angry in the first place, smiles, and says, "Oh, thank you." The other person smiles back. Two strangers have exchanged information in a pleasant fashion, and each has made the other's day, in a small but not inconsequential way, a little bit better. We have these sorts of interactions all day. Someone opens the door for us. A man picks up the glasses we dropped in the checkout line. No one remembers these quiet, passing, minor acts of banal kindness we see every day. We only remember the guy who called us a cocksucker on Twitter. People are kind to one another in the real world, even if it's a meaningless kindness. It goes unremarked upon. But it shouldn't. We are always much angrier on our phones than we are in the real world.

I'm either terrific at this job, or horrible at it. I haven't figured out which. But it's a job, and to be honest, there aren't that many jobs that would have me. I'm certainly not going to complain about this one. Even if @pigsooeyhogs11 just told me he hopes I get brain cancer and die in a fire. Come to think of it, I am not sure why having brain cancer would make the fire any more painful or fatal.

The doorbell rings, and as usual I've been online for so long I haven't noticed that the entire morning has passed. I log out and make my way over to the front door. Travis is making his Tuesday lunchtime visit, and he brought Butt Hutt BBQ sandwiches. I've already forgotten @pigsooeyhogs11 and every other interaction I had this morning. Funny how that works. 👊

2.

So, crazy shit about your girl, see," Travis says. "I gotta theory about her, yep."

Travis is wearing a Daniel Johnston T-shirt that hangs off him, a size small that he could still tuck into his socks, and his blond hair keeps falling into his eyes; he blows it off his nose in a cartoonish way, like he's blowing out a birthday candle. I'm always afraid that if I bump into him, I will break him in half. He's like a stoner Ichabod Crane. I've known Travis longer than I've known anyone in my life other than my mother, and one of the reasons we get along so well—and the primary reason I think he loves hanging out with me—is that he never shuts up. He is a wiry, sly talker with a lopsided laugh that makes him sound a little like the son of Woody Harrelson and Jesse Eisenberg raised by a stoned Foghorn Leghorn. He goes on long, rambling soliloquies about politics, or sports, or music, mostly music, that are impossible to follow even if you are paying close attention. I've seen people slowly stand up and leave in the middle of one of his monologues, not out of anger or annoyance but mere fatigue, the way you wait for an elevator too long, realize it's never coming, and just take the stairs. When they come back, he's still talking.

Before hitting the only topic anyone in town wants to talk about, "the girl," today's topic had been the band Wilco. Travis is exactly my age, twenty-six years old, and thus far too young to have ever enjoyed Wilco in their prime. Their first studio album came out before we were born. The lead singer is old enough to be our dad. But he's obsessed with them now.

"The thing is, he was the second guy in a band everybody loved, see, and they thought he was the lame one," he says, spooning out a massive pile of barbecued chicken onto a Styrofoam plate, spilling half of it on my kitchen table. "But he wasn't, see? He was the genius all along!"

I'm condensing what was an extended discussion about Jeff Tweedy's warmth and humanity for your benefit. Just trust me: Travis has a lot to say on this topic. He has a lot to say on every topic, and those topics are always directly related to whatever he has going on at that particular moment. There's a woman who works at the 40 Watt Club downtown that he likes, she's into Wilco, so there you have it: Travis is a Wilco guy now. It'll be something else next week. Travis wants a little bit of everything so he doesn't have to choose a lot bit of one thing.

But now he's talking about "the girl." Everybody's talking about the girl. The first sign that something was up was an Athens Reddit thread I came across two nights before while clicking around to see if anyone was selling tickets for the game against Middle Tennessee State this weekend. Scanning the ticket market for Georgia football games is an excellent way to make some extra cash, particularly when your job is just to sit on the internet all day; there's always someone selling them for less than they should, and that's when you pounce.

There wasn't much happening on Reddit that night: a bridge flooded off Lake Road, a tree was down in Five Points, someone on Barnett Shoals wanted to sell a chair. I'd been about to sign off for the night when I noticed a new thread appearing at the top of the page:

ROOMMATE MISSING. LAST SEEN IN FIVE POINTS.

Five Points is my neighborhood. I clicked.

Urgent: Student missing. My hallmate, Ai-Chin Liao, left for class last week and hasn't been back in our apartment since. She is never late and not irresponsible and we are very concerned. She speaks very little English but answers to the name Ai-Chin. Was last seen walking down Southview Drive. Police looking but we're trying everything. Please email me at stephanie2001@gmail.com if you've seen her. VERY WORRIED.

There was a picture attached, but it was blurry and she was looking the opposite direction. It could have been anyone. My synapses briefly fired, regardless. But only briefly. Marjani was ready to go home, and I was very tired myself. I didn't think any more about it.

Over the next two days, the disappearance of Ai-Chin has become the number-one topic in town, and Travis, being Travis, is brimming with theories.

"I bet I know where she is, see," he says, and I know he's about to go on another of his rants. I'm always here to listen and indulge. I'm not going anywhere, and he isn't either. Travis has always been there.

Travis and I were born within eleven days of each other at Sarah Bush Lincoln Health Center in Charleston, Illinois, a sleepy town that's the home of Eastern Illinois University, a fantastic record store called Positively Fourth Street Records, and not a helluva lot else. His mom was a philosophy professor at EIU, and my mother, Angela-don't-ever-call-her-Angie, worked as her secretary. (Technically she was the "executive assistant" for the whole philosophy department, but the only other philosophy professor was an elderly man named Ed who never left his office and might have actually died there in 1983.) Even though his mom was ten years older than mine and lived in one of the biggest houses in Coles County, one of the fake-marble-porched ones out by the country club, with her doctor husband and Travis's four older sisters, while Mom and I had a cramped row house in neighboring downtown Mattoon, they became best friends in short order. My dad left before I ever knew him, and Travis's dad was always working at the hospital, so our moms were both used to being lonely and exhausted and overwhelmed with nobody around to either help out or complain to. The school had a lousy family leave policy, so after giving birth they were both back at work before they were ready, and they discovered quickly that the path of least resistance was just to take us to work with them. You could say that we were raised right there in Coleman Hall, listening to frantic students try to get Travis's mom to change their grade for them while my mom worked the phones and occasionally checked to see if Ed was dead yet.

Travis and I napped in the same pack-and-play together, crawled through the same dusty hallway together, took countless baths together, and sat and cried to the same teaching assistants brought in to give our moms a break together. There aren't many memories of Illinois that don't involve Travis in one way or another. We even had our first birthday party together: Travis's mom had a huge shindig out at their house, with clowns and a bouncy castle and even some sort of train that drove everybody around their massive yard. We slept through the whole thing, but when I woke up, Mom says I refused to stop crying until Travis woke up and we could get back to crawling all over each other. She says we ended up staying there for a week. They had the space.

When you are the same age as someone you spend that much time with, you're inevitably compared to one another, and Travis's mom was always worried how much faster I seemed to pick things up than he did. I napped better, I cried less, I even figured out how to use a spoon, though the mess that resulted hardly made the discovery worth much. And man, could I *move*. Mom always said that if she looked away from me and Travis for no longer than a second, she'd turn back around and I'd be halfway down the stairs, scooting away to wherever, while Travis just sat in the middle of the floor, laughing, egging me on. Mom called me Trickle back then, *my little Cole Trickle*, and she still brings up that name sometimes today. She once joked that she thought she was going to have to put barbed wire around my crib. Travis, though, he just sat there and laughed.

One day, when we were about eighteen months old, on a lazy Saturday with the four of us lolling around Travis's mom's house while the sisters sprinted around and screamed at each other upstairs, my mom noticed something odd. When Travis's mom picked him up by his hands and tried to guide him across the linoleum floor, he stumbled right along, left foot, right foot, eons of Darwinian muscle memory and instinct working together to create . . . walking! Movement! Autonomy! But me? I couldn't do it. Not only could I not start to work my legs in concert, my legs in fact couldn't hold any weight at all. Pull me up, and I flopped right back down. Every time she lifted me up, I collapsed to the floor again. Here was Travis, usually the one lagging, starting to pull himself up and lurching himself forward. But not me. I couldn't seem to figure that part out.

The weeks went along, with Mom growing increasingly concerned. She had heard about "floppy leg syndrome," which is a sign of toddlers having low muscle tone, and I wasn't getting any stronger, so she thought that might be it. Once Travis started legit walking while I still lay there, she couldn't wait any longer. She never liked calling and bothering doctors every time I had a runny nose. She didn't want to be one of *those* moms. But this was strange. If there was a problem, she wanted it fixed.

Ai-Chin has been gone for seventy-two hours.

The initial story was in the *Athens Banner-Herald*.

CHINESE UGA STUDENT MISSING

by Matthew Adair

University of Georgia police are asking for help finding a missing Athens woman. Police department spokesperson Michael Cetera said friends notified police this weekend that Ai-Chin Liao, 19, was last heard from about 6:30 a.m. Friday. Multiple attempts to contact her at her home and on her cell phone have been unsuccessful, Cetera said. Police have also talked to friends and checked local hospitals, routine in missing persons cases.

Liao is a visiting scholar from China studying veterinary medicine. She lived at the Family Housing Complex on Agriculture Drive in Five Points and was last seen leaving for class Friday morning, Cetera said. Family friend and local resident Melissa Lei is the woman who first alerted the police. She has been putting up posters with Liao's picture across Athens. Lei told the *Banner-Herald* that Liao had only moved to Athens in mid-August. Lei says she was recently introduced to Liao through relatives in China and had planned on introducing her to her Christian youth group on campus. "She doesn't know anybody else in town and I have no idea where she possibly might have gone."

The Chinese embassy in Washington, D.C., has been informed of Liao's disappearance.

"We've exhausted all our options, so we are asking the public for help. We're not ruling anything out," Cetera said. Police ask Athenians to call the Ai-Chin Liao tip line at 706-234-4022 if they possess any information.

I have only one detail of her, and it is a big one: I have seen her every weekday for the last two months, at the same time, at the same place. She only waved to me once, that one day. The last day. I only realized this last night, before sleep, when they showed her picture on the news. Ai-Chin looked like her. She sure did. I immediately texted Travis to say that the lady from the news used to walk by my house every morning. It wasn't until later this morning that I remembered the Thrashers hat and the boot that shone like chrome.

That is the girl. And that was the car.

"So let's talk about the girl, see," Travis says. His theory, as he scoops BBQ pork into my mouth: Ai-Chin Liao is a stoner.

It was inevitable that Travis would come up with a theory like this at some point, though I'll confess I'm a little surprised it's where he went first. The idea: she's in a new place. She doesn't know anyone. She has all this pressure on her to succeed academically. She's never had any freedom in her life. She's a little bit more interesting, more rebellious, than anyone thinks, and now, for the first time, she can express it. Her new roommates are stodgy and repressive. They just want her to study—but she doesn't want to study! America isn't about studying! It's about pop music and Netflix and weed. Definitely weed.

According to Travis, she probably sneaked away from her fellow Chinese nationals one night and got invited into a frat party. ("She's cute," he says, shrugging.) She ends up meeting some kids and smoking weed with them, which just opens up her mind further. Why is she spending all this time working so hard? Why is she so far from home? Why does everyone want her to be a vet anyway? Vets have to put animals to sleep, like, *all the time.* Why would anyone want that shit job? She realizes that her whole world has been a lie, that she doesn't want to be part of the *system,* that she's gotta be Ai-Chin, ya know? So she says fuck it. She finds a weed friend whom she runs off with— "Maybe she's gay and never knew until now!"—and she's hiding in a Normaltown apartment ordering takeout, taking bong hits, and binge-watching every episode of *Black Mirror.* She doesn't even know people are looking for her. She's just living America, see.

It is possible that Travis is projecting a bit with this one. But I note his theory for the historical record.

He pauses to shovel more BBQ in his mouth, and I wait for him to finish chewing so he'll go on, but then he spoons another massive wad of pork butt in, and kindly one more into mine, so I have to wait a little longer to hear about his theory. I begin to struggle a little bit, the pork heading down the wrong hole, so Travis walks around the table and lightly taps me on the back. He thinks I'm having breathing issues, but I'm not, so, face still full of sandwich, I growl at him. He snorts, "Sorry, jeez," and leaves me alone. I'm fine.

Twenty-five minutes later we're back to the girl who works at Wuxtry Records downtown who has an eyebrow ring and a tattoo of Kurt Cobain on her back that Travis hasn't seen but wants to and how she told him to listen to Wilco, and then we're back on Wilco and I honestly could give two shits about Wilco but this is what you sign up for when you hang out with Travis and I don't mind, I'm glad he's here, and the BBQ is aces.

I look him in the eye so we can talk.

We should pause for a moment here. If you and I are going to be able to travel this little journey together, you're going to have to meet me halfway. You see, I can't . . . well, I can't talk. At least not like you and most of the people you know can. There's a whole story behind it, and we've got plenty of time to get into all that, but just because Travis and I can't talk to each other doesn't mean we can't *talk to each other*. I have known Travis my entire life, and we can communicate without words—sort of like twins, but not creepy like twins. He can look at me and I can look at him and we can each understand what the other is saying without speaking a word. I'm oversimplifying it, it's more complicated than it seems here in two-dimensional prose; you just sort of have to trust me. I can do it with my mom too, and Marjani has also picked it up over the last couple of years. It would be incomprehensible for you if you were to watch it happen, but it works for us. So go with me on this.

OK? We cool? You with me?

All right. So. As I was saying: I look him in the eye so we can talk.

I think that girl is the one who walks by my place all the time.
Who, the stoner girl?

I don't think she's a stoner, Travis.

Are you bullshitting me? If you think that might have been her, we need to say something.

I can't tell. But it's weird that I saw her every day, and then she wasn't there yesterday, and this girl who looks like her has disappeared, isn't it?

Fuckin' weird. Really fuckin' weird.

What should I do?

Want me to call that tip line? I can do that. Later. Later? Tonight. Maybe tonight.

I think I am going to have to remind you.

Hell yes you are.

He shrugs the definitive Travis shrug and says, aloud, "Crazy shit. I gotta get to work." He wipes my chin with a napkin, tosses the plastic Butt Hutt bags in my trash, and pulls his backpack over his left shoulder. "Your mom's on that vacation right now, yes?" he says, moving on as usual. "My mom said she's going to pick her and her boy toy up at the airport when she gets back."

He pops one last piece of toast in his mouth and jiggles his keys. "I'll be by tomorrow, 'kay? I'll text you when I'm on my way over. You still got my special ringtone?"

I grin at him. Of course I do.

"And we got game day this weekend, baby. Game day! WOOLLY MAMMOTH! WOOOOOOOOLLY MAMMOTH!" He throws his arms in the air in triumph. The Woolly Mammoth is his proudest achievement. He's already counting down the minutes until he unleashes the Mammoth.

He asks me if I need to piss, I shake my head no, and he moves out of the way so I can wheel back into my office, in front of my computer. Twitter is open. Travis reads the message off my screen.

> @SPECTRUMAIR HONESTLY, FUCK YOU AND YOUR SHITTY AIRLINE.
> I MEAN IT. GO FUCK YOURSELF. RIGHT NOW. #late

He bends down and whispers in my ear, like he has a secret to tell me. "Your job sucks, dude."

Travis's visits are always over too quickly.

3.

His name was Dr. Morton, a neurologist called in by Mom's pediatrician to explain what was happening to her son, but my mom, after that day, referred to him only as Asshead Ned. I don't even know if his name was actually Ned. She might have just liked the way it sounded. Mom has told the story of that day so many times that she knows exactly when to stop for every desired effect, each laugh, each gasp, each tear wrung out for maximum impact. Asshead Ned gets a roar every time.

Two weeks after Mom took me to the doctor because I was having a hard time standing, she went into a sad office in the bowels of Sarah Bush Lincoln Health Center, three doors down from the chapel and four doors down from the morgue, to meet with Asshead Ned. Asshead Ned drove down from Champaign for the meeting and immediately apologized for the fact that he would have to head back soon, that he was only down here as a favor to Dr. Gallagher, who he'd known for years, that he ordinarily didn't have time to talk to every single patient, as if Mom cared about any of this, as if any of this had any possible connection to her or her son's life. I was still sitting in my car seat, still strapped in, right there in Dr. Gallagher's office, chewing on a squeaky plastic giraffe.

"Anyway," Asshead Ned said, "I'm also here because what David has—"

"Daniel," my mom interrupted. "His name is Daniel."

"Yes, sorry, Daniel," Asshead Ned went on, only barely noticing Dr. Gallagher and my mother both glaring at him. "I'm here because what Daniel has is extremely serious, I'm sad to say." He said "I'm sad to say" in a way that did not sound like he was all that sad, or all that particularly interested. He said it like a schoolkid saying the Pledge of Allegiance: it's just the thing you're supposed to do. "We couldn't figure out what was going on at first, so we ran some genetic blood tests, and then ran the EKG and the CPK tests, that's what that was all about. We had to be certain. We are certain now."

And then Asshead Ned introduced my mother to the world of spinal muscular atrophy.

He went on for a long time about it, but Mom always skips over this part of the story, at least when I'm there, because everyone listening always knows what SMA is already. She'll only mention that she was barely listening to any of his explanations or descriptions—"I didn't give two Irish shits about the details," is the phrasing she uses, and a quarter century later I'm still not entirely sure what the difference is between an Irish shit and any other shit—because all she wanted to know was, "Is he going to be OK?" She kept trying to interrupt him, to break in with this essential question, the only question that mattered, but he blew right past her, like the professor who insists that his students save their questions for the end of class. She was trapped once again by another man who wouldn't listen to her, who wouldn't even notice that she was trying to talk, until he decided he was finished.

She then pounded her fists on the table, knocking over the picture of Dr. Gallagher's wife and three fat children, and glared at him.

"Is. He. Going. To. Be. OK?" she screamed through her nostrils.

What Asshead Ned said next is what drove my mother for the next twenty-five years. You could argue that her life was instantly divided between what happened before that, and what happened after. It gave her life purpose, and it ruined it at the same time. She was never the same.

"Oh, I'm afraid this disease is terminal," he said. "Daniel has Type 2 SMA. He will never walk. He will never be a regular boy. And you need to prepare yourself for the truth here: he could die at any moment. Even with proper, constant care, he is unlikely to live long enough to go to high school. You should appreciate every moment he has left. This is a terrible disease. I'm very sorry. It's going to kill him."

My mother pursed her lips and swallowed. Dr. Gallagher put his hand on my mother's shoulder, but she slapped it away. She didn't cry. She didn't pound the table again. She didn't scream. She just pointed a thick, meaty finger at Asshead Ned and said, "You can go to your fucking meeting in Champaign now. I never want to see your goddamned face again. And I can tell you one thing: Danny's going to outlive your pasty white ass. I can guarantee you that."

She then grabbed my car seat, sprinted out of the office, and cursed at him so loudly on the way out that patients came out of their rooms to see what the matter was. She stormed out of the hospital so fast that she crashed into the automatic doors.

"Then I put Daniel in the car, got in, sat down, and cried for a week," she says, capping off the story the same way every time. "Then I stopped. And haven't cried since."

4.

One of the many annoying things about being disabled is the obligation I always feel to make you feel better about your reactions to me.

I'm used to your reactions. You're the one with the problem here. While it's exhausting to have to privilege your reactions, it's even more exhausting, for me anyway, to constantly fight. So it's just something I have to take on myself. It shouldn't be asking too much for you to change, but apparently it is. So I try as much as I can. It's not enough that I have to deal with this every day. Now I have to make *you* feel better about it.

Anyway. It is not an accident that it has taken me this long to tell you about my SMA—one of the many reasons I prefer communicating with people through computers is that it allows me to stave off This Particular Conversation as long as possible—but don't confuse that with the idea that I don't enjoy answering questions about it. When you're disabled, whether you have SMA or are a quadriplegic or just a dude or lady who uses a wheelchair, the reason you are disabled is, I have found, absolutely the last thing anyone wants to ask you about. They'll ask you about the weather, or the local sports franchise, or today's tempestuous political climate, but they never, ever ask you about *that*. You could be screaming, "Hey, if you press this button right here, this chair turns into a Corvette, please press the button, all you have to do is PRESS THIS BUTTON!" right in their face, and they would try to change the subject to a viral video they saw of a cat playing checkers.

Take it from someone using the chair: people who do not use chairs do not like to talk about the chair. They are so worried about saying the wrong thing that they either don't say anything at all or, more likely . . . they say the wrong thing. But that's OK too! I like talking about the chair! I like it when people ask me how I'm feeling. I like it when people remember there's a person in here.

I get it. I know it's strange for some of you to see someone in a wheelchair, someone who can't move any of his extremities, someone who doesn't seem to have control of any element of his body, right there in front of you. You're not used to it, and you don't know what to do. It takes a second just to take in what you're looking at, to comprehend what a human body can be put through, and then it takes another second to process all the emotions you're feeling, the sadness, the sympathy, oh, that sympathy, *you poor thing*, what kind of world do we live in when this could happen to a child, an innocent child, *oh the inhumanity of it all, why is there suffering anyway?* One learns pretty quick—when one's whole life has been spent watching people try not to stare and still stare and then feel guilty about staring and then look away and act like it's totally cool—how to catch those flashes of human emotion flickering across a new person's face. It happens to every one of you, and, seriously, it's OK. Well, it's not OK, but I am used to it by now and have learned not to judge you. You don't even realize you've done it until you've already done it. I get it: I can be a lot to process.

You just want to walk down the street, maybe grab a beer and catch the end of the Falcons game, and then wham, you're contemplating how unbearably cruel life on this planet can be and wondering how any sort of kind and caring God could possibly allow a person to suffer so profoundly. As I said: I get it.

The point is that if we're going to keep moving forward, if I'm going to get to keep talking to you like this—and I'd like to—we should probably deal with the SMA thing right now, head-on. I could give you a full dossier of the disease, what it is, how you get it, what it's like, but I'm never going to be able to guess every question that you will have. So let's just dispense with it right now. Ask me. Ask me whatever you want. Let's get this over with. I am at your beck and call.

Really?

Really.

Wait, you mean like this?

Just like that. You're getting the hang of this already. How are you enjoying sentience?

It's . . . strange. I hadn't been expecting to be afforded this chance at life. I feel like Forky from Toy Story 4.

Don't get used to it. It's a temporary condition. It's just so you can ask some questions in a different font.

OK. I mean, are you sure? I don't want to upset you. Please let me know if I ask anything that offends you.

Christ.

All right. OK. So: You're in a wheelchair? Have you always been in a wheelchair?

Well, I didn't come out of the womb in one. Once it became clear that I was never going to walk, I had to get around somehow. (Also, I'm not *in* a wheelchair. I *use* a wheelchair. It might not seem like a big difference to you, but it is to me.) My model is an Airride P801E KSP Italia. It can go really freaking fast: I had mine up to twenty miles per hour once. Scared the shit out of Mom, but it felt fantastic. Oh, here's a tip, by the way: never tell someone using a wheelchair to slow down. We know what we're doing. We use these things all day. You're the one who should slow down. None of you people know how to drive.

So that's it? You can't walk? SMA makes you unable to walk?

SMA makes you unable to do a lot of things. Let's start from the beginning. SMA is not like quadriplegia, like I snapped my neck or something. We have some similarities with those guys— our spines are screwed up, taking a crap is a massive ordeal— but theirs is usually a result of some sort of injury, where ours is a genetic disorder. Something happened to them to make them unable to move. We were just born this way.

The key thing to remember about SMA is that it is *progressive*. It's not something that happens to you and then just doesn't heal. It's something you have that will always get worse. If you broke your neck diving into a shallow pool, that's terrible, but the challenge is accepting what has happened to you—what you can do moving forward, and what you can't.

That's not what SMA is. Here's the shorthand I use for what SMA is, to someone who has never heard of it. You know the Ice Bucket Challenge? Celebrities dumping water on their heads to raise money? Pretty great, right? That helped out a lot of people. That was for ALS, Lou Gehrig's disease, which attacks an adult's body from the inside, eventually devouring that body. Perfectly strong people, football players, firefighters, whatever, nerve cells in their brains stop sending nourishment to their muscles, and they stop being able to control their muscles. You know all about how terrible it is. You poured the ice on your head and shared it to Facebook. I'm not going to make fun of you for it. It really did help. ALS is the pits.

Well, SMA is, for the purposes of this brisk conversation, ALS, except it happens to babies. It's not *exactly* the same thing. ALS progresses a lot faster, for one. But the thing to remember about SMA is that it's always getting worse. From the minute that my mom realized that my legs couldn't hold my weight, my SMA has gotten worse. There are things that I could do last year that I can't do now. I was stronger when I was eleven than I am now. Every day this thing eats a little bit more of me.

That's a lot worse than I thought it was. So can you not move anything?

SMA goes after you from the core and then spreads out. It's like Evil CrossFit. The closer something is to my chest, my core, the more it's affected. Parts of my body that are farther away from my core work a lot better than the rest of me. My left hand, for example, works pretty well: I can move around a keyboard, I can hold a spoon, I can make shadow puppets on the wall. But the closer you get to my middle, the less it works.

I drive my chair using that left hand. One of the things I've noticed in the last few years is that if I don't do something for a while, my body forgets how to do it, and that's it, it's over. Because my power chair controller is on the left side, my left hand is constantly busy, so it still works mostly fine. But my right hand, now that I don't use it as much, is mostly done. This is one of the most annoying things about SMA. One day you wake up and are like, "Shit, I guess I can't do that anymore."

And you already said you can't talk. Why can't you talk? Can you talk?

Yeah, that's another problem. I used to be able to speak real words and have real conversations. But a couple of weeks before I turned twenty-one, I fell out of bed and twisted my jaw. It wasn't broken or anything, but it never felt right again, and I just never got the hang of it back. I can still talk, a little. But not well, and not comfortably enough that I want to put in the effort to say everything three times so people can maybe understand me. Travis and Marjani and my mom can make out what I'm trying to say, but few others can. I have a voice generator box on the iPad I attached to my chair, like Stephen Hawking. That is the only way I get to talk to strangers anymore. Well, along with getting yelled at for their planes being late.

So you can only move your left hand and your mouth?

My toes are wild. My toes are just going nuts right now.

And you live by yourself?

Yes. It's not hard. For what it's worth, from what I understand most dudes my age spend their entire days and nights doing exactly what I do anyway: staring at a computer, and sleeping. One might argue that history has bent itself over backward to meet me at this precise moment.

Sure, I need some help. Marjani comes by in the mornings and at night, and there's a series of overnight guys who are all super friendly and who are paid (underpaid, actually) by a Medicaid waiver program to come in and turn me over at night, because if I roll myself over the wrong way, I can't get myself back. (They also have to make sure I'm still breathing.) It's oddly intimate, some guy, either Charles or the other guy, Larry, Barry, maybe, whose only interaction is coming in my house, flipping me over like a pancake, and then leaving. Travis comes by for lunch a few times a week, and we hang out on weekends, but he's my friend, not my caregiver.

But life isn't that complicated. I've lived by myself since I left Illinois. Medicaid, a bit of private insurance, and a GoFundMe Travis set up for me after an accident a few years ago pay for most of my caregivers and equipment. The airline job allows me to split the rent with my mom—college towns are nice and cheap. A lot of SMA kids, particularly boys, are babied by mothers who never leave their side. But my mom pushed me to be my own person, not to sit around obsessing over stuff I can't do.

As soon as I graduated from college I told her I wanted to move to Athens. Travis was here, but while it is great to have a close friend, he wasn't the reason I did it. The weather's beautiful, I'm a short jaunt from Atlanta, which has the best hospitals in the world, there's college sports (and college girls) here, and there's even good music. Plus, it's a town where you can get away with not having a car if you don't want one. A lot of people with SMA actually have cars, but who wants that headache? This is a town of sidewalks and walking students.

I didn't want to live with Mom forever, and even though I know she'd never admit it, she's a lot happier not having to watch me 24/7 either. She visits every couple of months or so. She is proud of me. And I am proud of her. If I'm gonna live, I'm gonna live. Your assumption that living by myself is hard—that's your assumption, not mine. Not everybody can do it. But I can.

And it makes my mom happier. She put in her time. She loves me. I love her. But she wants me to live my life, and I want her to live hers. It's the best gift we could give each other.

That's very sweet. But doesn't she worry about you all the time?

We text nearly every day. She's my mom. But I want her to live her life. She has earned that right. She has always taken great care not to helicopter me, not to be one of those SMA moms who treat their kid like they're an infant a decade into adulthood. This was hard on her when I was younger. So many moms, when they learn their kids have this disease, hold their kids even tighter, attempt to control their lives even more, to protect them from as much as they can, because they realize that in the biggest way, they cannot protect them at all. But Mom never did that. She made me push my own chair back when I could. She made me always feed myself. "Everybody's life is hard," she would say. "Your problems are your problems the way everybody else's problems are their problems."

I'm a better person today because of it, and so is she. My disease didn't take my mother down with it. She's now enjoying the life she didn't get to while she was raising me. I'm proud of her.

How do you eat?

Right now, I can move my head down low enough to my hand to feed myself, though only if I'm propped up at the right angle. It's a lot easier to have Marjani or Travis help me out a little. Eventually, though, I'm probably going to need a tube. That's going to suck.

Um . . . how do you go to the bathroom?

I'm afraid that requires a condom catheter most of the day, though that's another example of something I won't turn down help for. A condom catheter works the way you think it would. They even make Magnum sizes.

But your brain is OK otherwise?

You tell me. Does my brain seem OK to you? How would you feel about being asked about how your brain is?

So, you can only move your left hand, your toes, and part of your mouth. Is that it? Is that all SMA does?

If only. Remember: This is a *progressive* disease. The place it really goes after is your lungs. It makes sense, right? This is a disease that attacks your core muscles, and there aren't more valuable core muscles than your lungs. My lung muscles are weak, and they're never going to recover. This messes up my coughing reflex too, which means I'm in constant danger of choking on my own phlegm, which, I gotta say, is not how I hope it goes down. I have to breathe into a cough assist machine if I have any sort of breathing issue whatsoever, which is often. I've got it set up now so that I can just wheel myself over to it and stick my face in it. It's sort of fun: it's like a car wash.

But the thing is, there's a clock. You try to forget about the clock. But it is hard to forget about the clock.

There are four types of SMA. There's Type 1, which is the worst kind: that's the one infants have, the one that almost always kills them by the time they're two. SMA is the leading cause of death in infants, but I already got that one licked. Suck it, Type 1.

Type 3 can be diagnosed later, but it affects your lungs less and can require you to use a wheelchair or walk with braces when you get older. Type 4 is adult-onset, and it messes with your arms and legs, to the point that you might end up using a wheelchair. But frankly, I've seen a lot of you people: half of you are one medical misstep away from a wheelchair anyway. It always feels like I'm behind you in line at Walmart a lot more often than you're behind me in line at Walmart, I'll put it that way.

I've got Type 2, which is the most common kind. That's the one you notice when you're about a year old, the one that changes everything. Every little piece of gunk in your throat could kill you. You could fall over and never be able to get back up. Your body could just someday say it's had enough. That happened to a buddy of mine a couple of years back. He was nineteen, and really into online gaming, fairly common for people with SMA. He used to message me with all these shady "coupons" to join some sort of gamer pyramid scheme, but he was a nice kid. His mom hovered over him too much, but it happens: not everyone's as lucky as me in that regard. But then one day he went to bed, and he never woke up. He had all the newest medicine, he and his mom took care of him the best they could, but one day, his body just cried "Uncle" and sent him home to wherever.

He was sort of rare. Most SMA Type 2s make it into their twenties, and some into our thirties. I know a guy who reached his fifties. But there are no guarantees. The clock is always there. I'm twenty-six years old. Is that too old? Am I average? Am I on borrowed time?

Your guess is as good as mine. I'm not gonna wait around for it to happen, though.

I'm sorry. This part just made me sad.

Don't kid yourself. You ain't around here forever either. In fact: it's probably time for you to go. Sentience over, Forky. I have to get back to work. These planes aren't going to delay themselves.

5.

Why would she have just gotten in some guy's car? (If that's her?)

And why would this guy just take her? (What kind of human is even capable of that?)

Two students last year got stabbed in the middle of the day outside the Showtime Bowling Center off Macon Highway. There was a man yammering nonsense in the parking lot, and he accosted them as they were walking into the bowling alley. One of them tried to just brush past him, but the man drove a pocketknife right into the small of his back. The other student was too slow to react, and the man pulled the knife out of his friend, pounced on top of him, and stabbed him twenty-two times in the chest, neck, and face. One of those twenty-two caught him in the jugular; the kid bled out in a matter of minutes. Cops showed up, quickly but not quickly enough, and they took the guy down. Two strangers just suddenly dead in a random parking lot of a random bowling alley on a random April afternoon, for nothing, out of nowhere. The world is a terrifying place these days. We're all operating right there on the edge of tilt, all the time. This shit can just happen. There are monsters around every corner. Pianos fall from the sky.

It makes you sometimes not want to leave the house. But you have to leave the house. I don't need to tell you how important it is to get out of the house, how much you appreciate the outside world when you're incapable of leaving. If I'm not careful, I could fall out of bed in the wrong way at the wrong time. I'm aware, every day, that such a future could be around the corner. So I get out. I get out as often as I can.

There's a bus stop right outside my house that has years of experience (and patience) with picking me up and taking me wherever I need to go. I type my destination into the iPad, which vocalizes it to Gus, who drives the bus and is very used to me by now, and he stops and lets me out when I'm there. You think I want to stay cooped up in that duplex all day? Have you been to Athens? When I first moved here from Illinois, I used to worry that anytime I wasn't outside when it was sunny, I was somehow "wasting" a nice day. It took me about a month to realize that they were all nice days here. Other than July and August, when this place turns into the surface of the sun, Athens is as lovely a place to stroll as any on this earth.

On Tuesdays, I have a lunch date with Todd. Well, neither *lunch* nor *date* is the right word, because neither of us eats nor talks during our lunch date. I'm quite sure Todd doesn't know my name. Tuesday is Azul Day at the Rook & Pawn. The Rook & Pawn is a bar/luncheonette in downtown Athens that revolves around board games. They sell cocktails and sandwiches, fancy hipster ones, drinks with cucumbers and weird herbs, and you play board games there. You show up, you pay five bucks for a table, and you play board games. There are whole subsocieties dedicated to the most complicated of these board games, your Settlers of Catan–type stuff. Some people come into that place at 11:00 a.m., sidle up to a booth, and stay there playing some sort of dragon castle game until the place closes at midnight. But you don't have to do that. You can also come in and play Connect Four with your five-year-old. I've seen some Georgia football players come in and play Uno, but with shots. (The Draw 4 is particularly painful.) It's an awesome place to go and pretend you're fifteen years old again.

Todd comes in at noon, every day, orders the same sandwich, a grilled cheese on wheat with bacon, and a glass of Aviation American Gin on the rocks with a lime. He eats the sandwich and then plays Azul against all comers.

Azul is a simple game for people who play board games all the time, which is to say it's nearly incomprehensible to the average human being. But it involves ornate tiles and patterns and points and there are squares and triangles and . . . all right, I've already lost you. . . . But trust me: it's a cool game, and a big deal for people who love board games.

They have a big Azul tournament here every Thursday night, and Todd is famous for always winning it. During the rest of the week, he just sits at the back of the bar and plays. He is legend there, even though he rarely speaks. He has his gin—the bartender just stops by and fills it every time it's getting low—and he has his game and that's what he does all day. He keeps a copy of the *New York Times* next to him, which he picks up and reads until someone challenges him to a game of Azul and he sets it aside. When the game is over, he picks up the paper again. He does this every Tuesday. No one knows where he lives, where he works, how he gets his money for his gin and his sandwiches. He just plays and reads and drinks. That is his life. Why would he do this? you ask. Why does anybody do anything?

So on Tuesdays I head to the Rook & Pawn for lunch and Todd. Because I love this game, and someday I'm gonna beat the sumbitch. It hasn't happened yet. Every time I have a terrific plan and a pattern to win, Todd is silently setting us both up to thwart it. He's constantly thinking three or four steps ahead of me. And I am not thinking about him at all. So I lose.

I've always found the slight grunt he gives after he defeats me—an utterly demoralizing grunt, a that-barely-even-counted-as-a-game grunt that reminds me of how lousy I am at Azul–dismissive in the most profound, who-gives-a-shit way. I sort of love it. Todd is patient with how long it takes me to play, how I have to tap commands for him to move the pieces for me, but he doesn't make a whole production out of it, and it certainly doesn't tempt him to have any sympathy for me. Todd gets dozens of players challenging him every day, and even though my games take twice as long as any of his others, he treats me the same as the rest of the losers. I appreciate it.

By 1:30 p.m. my early shift at Spectrum is over, and most of the lunch crowd is gone, so Todd is usually by himself. They always set me up with a table with a tray near my head so I can drink water through a straw. (I love my autonomy, but eating out at a restaurant by myself is pretty much impossible; I always eat before I show up.)

Todd, like he does with everybody, barely raises his head, just enough to acknowledge with a slight nod that, yes, you've got a game, and then we are off.

I'm fascinated by Todd. This is a man who can engage with the world in any way he sees fit. He can walk with people, and talk with people, and curse people out, and try to persuade them to have sex with him, and run down the middle of the street naked. He can get married, he can get a divorce, he can play video games, he can cover himself in peanut butter, he can go to Spain, he can smoke a bunch of opium, he can start his own religion, he can juggle Diet Coke bottles, he can start firing at people from the rooftops. He can do anything and everything he wants, at any time. But this is what he chooses. He chooses to sit here and drink and play Azul and scowl and not say a goddamned word to anyone.

He grabs his first tiles. I grab mine. I see a series of blue tiles that will get me points in the middle row, which is going to set up some red tiles below, and if I can just hang on to those green tiles I can maybe finish up that column pattern, and then . . . and fourteen minutes later I have lost.

I've just given him a gentle *hisssss* that I hope sounds like *Good game, thanks* but probably doesn't, when something unusual happens. Todd stands up, walks around the table, kneels next to my chair, and puts his lips to my ear. He smells like nicotine and cat urine. What in the world is this about?

"You are too nice," he says. He sounds like the villain in a Pixar movie. But there is a quiet warmth to his voice. He is trying to help me. "Everyone is trying to screw you. But do not stop being so kind."

He turns his head to face me.

"Stay kind, kid. No one will see it coming."

He then lightly taps my left cheek, smiles a mouthful of yellow, knotty teeth, and goes back to his seat and his gin.

I stare at him for a second. He's back reading his newspaper. I'm no longer there.

Two years of playing with Todd, and not a word. And then this. I keep looking at him, trying to understand, but he's ready for his next game. A kid behind me gives me a quiet "Sir," and it's time for me to let Todd play his next game. I wheel my chair back and accidentally knock over the glass of water onto the floor, where it shatters. I let out a little yelp, and an employee scampers over to clean up the mess. I quickly type SORRY into my iPad, and the employee says it's no problem. Todd hasn't looked up once.

No one will see it coming.

My shift at Spectrum is back on at three. I'm realizing my scheduling for this weekly trip actually allows for the fact that Todd will beat me quickly—a defeatist attitude, to say the least. I wheel back through the front doors of the Rook & Pawn to wait on the corner for the next bus when I ram right into someone. It's difficult to ram into someone with your chair. People typically go leaping out of your way the minute they see you; one guy jumped into traffic once. I don't even usually worry about it. But man, I plowed right into this lady. I was going fast, too, faster than usual. But she took it like a linebacker. She didn't give an inch.

She looks confused for a second, then turns around and walks right past me to the front door of the Rook & Pawn. I realize that she has three friends with her, all Asian women like her, and there's a pang of recognition in the back of my neck. They all look exhausted and defeated but resolute somehow. Two of the women are carrying boxes full of individual sheets of paper. The other is holding a roll of masking tape and a black Magic Marker.

The woman I plowed into, paper still in her hand, grabs the masking tape and heads right back to the front door. I am baffled as to what she is up to. And then I realize. She is putting up a sign.

I stare at it. It takes me a second. It shouldn't take me a second. I'm usually good at this. When it takes this much effort to talk to people, they don't typically talk to you, which frees you from that distraction and lets you study everything else about them. One of the advantages of this is that you can stare at people for an incredibly long period of time without anyone even noticing. It helps you burn their faces into your memory, whether you want it to or not.

It takes me a minute to know for sure it's her. First off, it's not 7:22 in the morning in the picture. It's night. She's standing on the edge of a cliff somewhere, carrying the blue backpack, with clipped black hair that bobs just below her ears. She's wearing eyeglasses, big eyeglasses, too big: they look like the sort of glasses a dad would wear in an '80s movie. She has her hands in the air, like she's signaling a touchdown, or she just won a race. She is smiling. She is smiling so wide. She is smiling like she is the happiest person in the world. She is smiling . . . like she smiled at me.

The woman I saw get into the car was Ai-Chin Liao.

6.

I feel like I'm about to spontaneously combust in my chair. I feel like I'm engulfed in flames. I look behind me for the poor girl with the posters I knocked over. She's her friend! She needs to know! But she's gone. Where did she go?

When I spin my chair around, a small crowd is staring at me. This makes sense. I just smashed into a lady, then spun my chair around and stared at the front door of a board game café for an eternity while making grunting sounds. I would be staring at me too.

I try to make eye contact with one particular person looking at me, mouth agape. He's tall and lanky and older than all the college kids surrounding me. He's wearing a Rook & Pawn hat. He works here! He's an authority figure! I start grunting and spitting a bit, trying to get his attention and make sure he knows that I'm trying to tell him something. He leans over. I begin typing furiously into my iPad, finish, and hit the Speak button.

"Girl."

"Posters."

"Where?"

People are always surprised my speaker doesn't sound like Stephen Hawking. It's a pleasant, vaguely British man's voice. A little like a mechanical, stilted Colin Firth. They give you a few options, and I like the aura of sophistication the English lilt gives me.

The Rook & Pawn guy gawps at me blankly. I repeat in my vaguely British computer voice.

"Girl."

"Posters."

"Where?"

He at last understands what I'm trying to say. "Oh, sorry," he says, fumbling with a cup of coffee in one hand and some loose papers in another. "I think she went over to the 40 Watt." I try to nod at him and then spin back around. I have to catch her.

The 40 Watt Club is a famous Athens music club just across the street from the Rook & Pawn. It's one of the most influential rock clubs on the planet—R.E.M. essentially was invented there, and Nirvana played there right before they exploded, in October 1991—but during the day it just looks like an abandoned storefront. There's no crosswalk between the Rook & Pawn and the 40 Watt, so I have to speed over to the street corner and wait for the light. Even then I have to make extra sure some crazy idiot college kid staring at his phone doesn't run the red and scatter parts of me and my chair all across the Creature Comforts brewery. I wait and wait and wait and wait and finally *zoom zoom zoom*.

I nearly flip my chair over making the hard left to the 40 Watt. Some guy yelps as I fly by and even gives me the "Slow down there!" line that I hate so much. I floor it to the 40 Watt. The posters are visible, on the wall there and at the diner next door. The Asian woman and her friends are not. I spin back around, left, then right, and don't see any of them, anywhere. I must look ridiculous, this drooling grunting kid in his chair doing 360s on the Broad Street sidewalk. They probably think my chair is broken. I wonder how long I could do this before someone ran up to try and help me. A while, I'll bet. I make a note to do this sometime. I should have my own prank show.

She's gone. Her friends are gone. I have no idea where any of them are. I need to tell them. They need to know that I saw her. *Girl. Posters. Where.*

I'm not going to find them this way. I motor to the corner to wait for the bus home.

7.

Back home. Gus said I looked "like your dog's a ghost" when I got on the bus. I don't know what that means. It's probably not good.

It's an easy rest of the workday. Tuesday is usually a pretty sedate day on Spectrum Air Twitter. The real action will come Friday, when the entire South treks to various college football stadiums sprinkled throughout the Spectrum Air coverage area. There is a specific level of rage that only a college football fan stuck in an airport rather than tailgating can reach, and I see it on every Friday night and Saturday morning in the fall.

(Oh, I just realized you might be wondering how I type. It's so simple you'll feel silly that you even wondered. I've got a little ball that moves the mouse over a special keyboard, which allows me to click letters. It's just a mouse. It works just like yours. I'm crazy fast with it now—I could kick your ass in *Space Invaders*.)

After dinner, Marjani comes over. She can tell something is wrong. She doesn't say anything, but everything takes her a second or two longer than it usually would, like she's lingering on something, like she's waiting on me. She brushes my hair a little more thoroughly, looks at me a little bit longer when feeding me dinner, raises an eyebrow when I fail to return her eye contact. She knows me well. And she knows when I am ready to talk. But I am not ready to talk to her about this yet. I am very, very tired.

She wordlessly cleans up the kitchen, wheels me to the bathroom, and begins undressing me. We washed my hair last night, so it's quick tonight, and she slips some San Francisco 49ers pajamas on me. I have no idea why I have 49ers pajamas. I have never even been to California. Marjani is so efficient at this process that it only takes about fifteen minutes. Tonight it takes twenty.

I can't stop thinking about that poster. Marjani, sighing expectantly, tells me I have fifteen minutes before bed. I am proud of my independence, and I am a twenty-six-year-old grown man, so even though I totally understand why this has to be the case—I cannot get to bed by myself—it is a uniquely demoralizing moment every night when I realize that another person, even one with only my well-being in mind, can set a specific bedtime for me, and I have to listen to them.

As usual, I choose to spend my last fifteen minutes sitting at the computer. I open up the increasingly active Reddit page about Ai-Chin. I stare at it for a very long time.

I was supposed to remind Travis to call the tip line. I am sure he forgot. Forgetting to follow basic instructions is a signature Travis personality trait. I could pester him about it now. But I only have fifteen minutes. And you know what? I can handle this myself, thank you.

For the first time ever, I open up a window to post.

I type this:

i live in five points and i might be wrong but i'm pretty sure i saw
ai-chin walking my block every day. and i think i saw her the day she

disappeared. i think it was her. i'm not certain. but i know she lives nearby and apparently she had class that morning, and i think i saw her. i think I saw her get into a tan camaro. does that make sense to anybody?

i also might be crazy and might just be making everything more confused.

but i just felt like i needed to say what i saw, so now i am saying it.

I float my cursor above the Post Now button for five minutes until Marjani tells me it is time for bed. I then click it, shut down my computer, and try to sleep. I had to say something. Right?

WEDNESDAY

8.

Marjani's main job is to watch people die. This is not her only job, but as she told me once, "It's my only important one." Marjani cleans, Marjani cooks, Marjani mops, Marjani dresses, Marjani bathes, Marjani sweats away for the benefit of richer, whiter people who see her every single day but never notice her. Marjani knows that "to be with someone as they die is the only thing in the world that matters."

Marjani told me that one time in an idle, stray aside, when we barely knew each other at all. She was in fact bathing me, a few years ago, back when I could talk a little better, back when I insisted on washing my stomach and penis and balls myself, back when I still had some pride about those sorts of things, back before that sort of shit stopped mattering entirely. This was far enough ago that talking about death felt like a theoretical discussion, the way you can talk about death with someone who isn't currently dying. It is easier to bring up death when it's not in the same area code as you are, and it wasn't back then. It is probably worth noting that nobody has mentioned it to me in the last couple of years.

Marjani was a little younger then, a little thinner, a little looser with a laugh. She spoke openly, happily, about her son, who was twelve then and is probably about to graduate from high school now, though I'm only guessing: she hasn't mentioned him in years, and I only know he's not dead now because I assume even Marjani would take a day off if her son died, and she hasn't missed a day since she started working with me. She has hardened slightly in the years since, taking a cue from my own silence, our series of grunts and nods and shakes our own private, efficient language. We can look each other in the eye and talk, just like I can with Travis. She has been poking and prodding and lifting and scrubbing and twisting and carrying and rubbing me for the majority of my adult life. We read and react to each other like a dance team, understanding every flinch and quiver, what they mean, what they say to do next. No one will ever know me as well as Marjani does, even though I am still never quite sure if she even likes me. Well, she likes me, or at least she doesn't *dis*like me. She is kind, gentle. But she is also doing a job, performing a function for yet another white boy that is either unable or unwilling to do it for himself. She cares for me, and makes me comfortable, and helps me every time I need help, perhaps above and beyond what is required of her as a condition of her employment.

But if my Medicaid quit paying Marjani, she'd stop, and I would likely never see her again. She would go on to something else, and I would die in this house, filthy and full of lice and alone. I know that, and more importantly, she does too. She has been doing this long enough to know that you must separate yourself somewhat, no matter how much you might care, or even no matter how much you might not. She has taken care of people who have died before, and she will do so again. How do you do that without checking your emotions at the door?

But three, four years ago, Marjani wasn't so good at this just

54

yet. She was still curious, and still a little more unguarded than you're supposed to be with me. She was just making conversation. This is a common occurrence around me: People *love* to talk when they're with me. Next time you're in a room with someone else, just one other person, try this experiment: Don't talk for fifteen minutes. By minute three, the person you are in the room with will be jabbering away about anything, *anything* to fill the emptiness with some sort of sound. So with me, people just talk and talk and talk and talk. They're talking for two. The air must be filled.

She hadn't gotten accustomed to my silence yet back then, or at least not accustomed to me not saying much more than "Ow" and "Yum" and "More," so she talked. She told me about where she was from (Pakistan), whether she was married (she was), and whether she had any thoughts on living in Athens for the last two years (it's too hilly for her to ride her bike). I am not sure any of these topics came up again in the next four years, or at least not anytime recently. This was her onetime information dump. People will just talk and talk and talk.

But then she told me what she did for a living. About half of her life is odd jobs, taking every opportunity she can to be a part of the gig economy. She helps out a cleaning crew, she works with the university to pick up trash after sporting events, she even picks up a couple of shifts at Jason's Deli downtown when school is in session. She does that to remain busy. Now that her son is in school all day, she told me, she tries to pick up every bit of cash she can; her husband works (worked?) at a restaurant downtown.

Her main job, though, is taking care of dying people. She is not a nurse, she explained, though she can do basic medical care if she has to. The job isn't about that sort of comfort.

"It's about being there with them when they are . . . true?"

she told me, washing my back in the tub. "That's the word. People are the real people they are when they are dying. Do you know?"

I grunted "Yeahhh," less out of agreement than out of an obligation to hear this stranger out. Sometimes people just need a reminder that you're there.

"To see them at the end, how they really are, it is very lucky," she said, and I wondered if she was like this with everyone, or just the ones who can't talk back. "It is a gift. So it is my job. My gift is my job. I am very lucky." She then started coughing for a second, left the room, returned, and put me to bed.

She never talked to me about helping the dying again. She shut it down, right there. I wonder if someone had died earlier that day, and she hadn't gotten it out of her mind yet. And then it hit her that it was my turn. It was my turn to make her lucky.

I still think about that conversation, such as it was, every day.

She comes in, does her job, smiles, is kind, says goodbye, and leaves. There is goodness in her gestures and clear pleasure in her work. But it's just work. I appreciate it. I love her. I need her. I think she needs me. It feels like there should be more. I think maybe it is my fault there is not more.

She is still here. She is closer to me than anyone has ever been. But does she know me better than I know her? Does she shed me like a jacket when she goes home? This is her job. This is what she has done, and what she has given me. Marjani is the center of my life. And yet I pray she doesn't miss me when I'm gone.

9

I am awake. Marjani is here, as always in the mornings. "You have a note, Daniel," she says, propping me up, unbuttoning my pajamas, wiping down my face. "It is from Charles, you should read it."

Charles is the only orderly from the service that comes by every night to turn me in bed whose name I actually remember. He'll clean me up and make sure that I'm still breathing. I like Charles a lot. Charles is in fact third cousins with Stacey Abrams, who ran for governor of Georgia last year and almost won. I had an Abrams bumper sticker on the back of my chair, and Charles wouldn't stop talking about it. He'd only met her a couple of times, and he said she was very nice. He actually came over early election night 2018 to watch the returns—"You've got cable," he said—and he kept me up most of the night yelling at the television. I eventually watched the final returns with him; he cried when Abrams lost. Charles is cool.

Charles has Tuesdays, Wednesdays, Thursdays, Fridays, and Saturdays, and the other guy—a skinny white guy whose name I can never remember. Harry? Frank? Maybe it's Frank? It might be Harry—has Sunday and Monday. They share a key: they unlock when they come in, and lock up when they leave—at least I hope they do. I only know of these men as shadows in the middle of the night, heavy-breathing phantasms who lift me and clean me up in silence. They are gentle, efficient, and always apologetic: If I wake up, it means they're having a bad night on the job. They always tiptoe in the back door around 2:00 a.m., check on me, and then tiptoe back out. They exist only to keep me alive in the night, and I might not recognize either of them by sight in the daylight. I do not know how much they get paid, but it is not enough.

As Marjani washes her hands for breakfast, she reads me the note.

> *Daniel you left your computer on last night. I shut it off*
> *so you could sleep but I promise I did not look at anything.*
> *You should be more careful I could have stolen all your credit*
> *card information and be halfway to the Bahamas by now.* ☺
> —*Charles*

"He is a very funny man," Marjani says, somehow scrambling eggs, sweeping the floor, and flipping on the television at the same time. "I worked with him at the hospital a few years ago. He is kind. Has four beautiful children and a wife who worries about him being out all night." She straps me into my chair and wheels me over to the table. "I am sorry, I think I am the person who forgot to turn your computer off last night. But he's right, you need to be more careful about your computer. It is bad for your eyes."

Marjani is always concerned about my health in useless ways. She is taking care of a man whose body is in a constant state of atrophy, yet an amusingly high percentage of our conversations is about little well-being tidbits far more applicable to someone who wouldn't find such alleged maladies as trifling as I do. Sure, Marjani, let's really get worked up about flossing. Last week I had a hole in one of my socks, and she lectured me for five minutes about frostbite. In October. In Georgia.

I give her a little nod and a raise of my eyebrow—Travis calls this move "the Groucho"—and she laughs, and it strikes me that Marjani is in an oddly cheerful mood this morning. It makes me happy.

I check the computer first thing. Marjani has me up and cleaned and brushed and clothed and then I'm grunting and bobbing toward the computer, there, there, *there there there.*

"You are like an addict with that," she says, and situates me in my seat. "You have ten minutes before breakfast. Try not to ruin your brain."

I've spent half the night thinking about what I'd posted. What if one of Ai-Chin's friends sees it and thinks I know more than I do? What if I've given them too much hope? Is that cruel? What if it wasn't her?

When you're alone all the time like me, you can't help but lose it a little at night, when there are no people to distract you and keep your mind occupied. All the lazy, thoughtless, instinctive things we do every day, we never consider their ramifications until we finally have some peace and quiet to ourselves, which is probably why we spend so much time avoiding peace and quiet. But I have all the peace and quiet I want.

The police can do their jobs. I will ask Travis to help me call them. Maybe this sort of internet rumormongering does no one any good. It gives hope, it takes away hope, and it accomplishes nothing. It feels real. But it isn't.

Maybe I should delete it before it sends someone down a rabbit hole.

The page is still open. My post is just sitting there, staring at me, flipping me off. Eff you, post. You are from a weaker me. I will be stronger today.

I take a deep breath before clicking Refresh. This leads to a light gasping fit, and Marjani has to come in and settle me down, and by the time I'm settled down, she's wheeling me in for breakfast. My eyes dart around the room as she feeds me grapefruit. At one point, distracted, I jerk my head left and knock the fork out of her hand as the juice runs down my chin.

"Daniel!" She jumps back like I tried to bite her. "What is wrong with you today?" I jerk my head back toward the computer. Her shoulders slump. She frowns. She looks at me as if I've called her something terrible.

"You are being a pill, Daniel. That thing is turning you into a mean robot."

I jerk my head again.

"A mean, mean robot," she says, wheeling me back to my room. She looks at me.

I look her in the eye so we can talk. This is basically like with Travis, maybe not quite as advanced, but she's picked it up in the past two years.

What?
I am coming back at lunch today, Daniel, and if you are still sitting there, I might throw you out the window.
Did you just make a joke?
I did. Did you like it?
I did. Now please leave me to my computer already.

I smile, and she smiles back, and all is fine again as long as she gets the hell out of this room so I can get rid of the goddamned post.

I finally click Refresh.

The post sits there . . . ignored. No one has responded, and, even better, it's being voted down by all the Redditors as irrelevant and pointless and "poop emoji." Hopefully you get outside more than I do and therefore have no idea how Reddit works, but basically, when someone votes down a post, it gets pushed down the page so fewer people see it. Redditors are particularly suspicious of anyone who creates an account just to post something one time, assuming they are a spammer, a bot, or just a jerk trying to promote something to the community without Respecting the Community. I've been monitoring Reddit for years, but I've never actually posted anything. I think of Reddit, and Twitter, and all the places we gather to yell at each other as fishbowls, aquariums: they are far too entertaining as self-contained ecosystems to be disturbed by my awkward, oafish hand. The fish are different if you try to be part of them; they change who they are simply because you are there; I wouldn't want to be a part of any club that would have me as a member; they're nice places to visit, but I wouldn't want to live there; you get it.

But I broke my rule. I stuck my finger in the fish tank. Now the fish are all downvoting me.

They are doing me a favor. They are making sure as few people as possible see my mistake. I feel better immediately after I delete the post. Let's call the police. Let's let them do their job. When Travis gets here, we're going to have ourselves an afternoon activity.

10.

'm lucky to have an online job. Yes, people call me a zombie cocksucker all day, but being on the internet all day is my dream job. My internet experience is different than yours. I think of the internet like my disguise. It's the only place where people don't treat me like I'm either a monster or a charity case to be pitied. People can't see me, so they can't treat me any differently: I'm just another internet asshole like everybody else.

On the internet—and especially on Twitter, a program that is specifically constructed for people to be abrupt and blunt with each other—no one knows they're supposed to be nice to me or politely ignore me. So they're not, and they don't. I can tweet something like "I don't think I like the new Childish Gambino album" and immediately people just start pummeling me, I'm an idiot, I'm a racist, millennials are all lazy know-nothings, I suck. And it is so awesome! This is the reason my profile picture on Twitter is just a close-up of my face, a smiling one where I look just like every other dumbass kid. If I had a picture of me in my chair, they'd be wary of slapping me, or they'd just make a bunch of "handicapped" jokes. But they have no idea I have

SMA, or that there's anything different about me at all. I'm just another anonymous punk to be taken down.

I'd much rather someone hate me than feel bad for me. Wouldn't you? Wouldn't anyone?

I know I said I'd let the cops handle it. But a little online sleuthing never hurt anybody.

And the more I read about Ai-Chin, the more I need to know.

She left a thin online profile. She had an Instagram account that she only used twice: in August, she posted an out-of-focus picture of an ugly cat, and two weeks ago she posted a picture of a bird sitting on the fence in front of a house just down the street from mine. You can tell she was working hard on her English: she posted a comment in English below the picture that said, "This is my pretty bird who is my morning friend." There are many comments below it in Chinese, and thirty-four likes.

She wasn't on Facebook, as far as I could tell, and no Twitter, though, to be fair, Liao is a near impossible name to narrow down on Twitter. All I could find out about her came from her student profile and news reports, which is a very 1990s way to learn about someone.

The morning routine continues. Marjani props me up and starts washing my head, neck, and shoulders. She hates that I like to sleep shirtless—she says it just forces her to wash the sheets more often—but it does save her the trouble of peeling a sweaty shirt off me every morning. In the last couple of years this odd film, a thin, white, almost mildewy substance, has started to form around my neck when I sleep. I don't know what it is, and to be honest, I'm afraid to find out. Marjani, bless her heart, has never once brought it up, even though she's wiping it off me every day.

She puts a shirt on me and apologizes when I groan, though she doesn't have to. My arms move so rarely that the act of someone raising them above my head first thing in the morning feels like being drawn and quartered, but that's not her fault. You can't roam the world shirtless every day, not even in Georgia.

She plops me in my chair and rolls me into the kitchen. She's being a little clumsy with me this morning, like she's in a hurry. I give her a couple of curious looks, but she doesn't seem to notice them. She just shovels Cheerios into my mouth and wipes down the table. The nighttime check-in guy appears to have left a beer can on the counter, and Marjani's gonna make him pay for that one.

I think about what I know about Ai-Chin from all the articles I've found.

- She's nineteen years old.

- She was born and grew up in China.

- She just got to campus two months ago.

- She is studying to be a veterinarian here at the University of Georgia. We have an excellent vet school.

- She didn't know anyone when she moved here but Melissa Lei. Melissa only met her because their families knew each other in China.

- She didn't know anything about Georgia, or the campus, or America. It is possible that one of her closest friends here in Athens was the disabled man who saw her every day without her knowing. She did wave to him once.

- She speaks halting, sporadic English.

- She was walking down my street just two days ago.

- She got into an old tan Camaro while walking down my street.

- No one has seen her since.

"Rrrrrghhhhawwwwwww." That was me. Marjani just brushed my hair a little too firmly, and I yowled. "Sorry."

"When is Travis coming by?" she says. But before she has a chance to say something disapproving about him, he bounds through the door.

"'Sup Mar," he says, taking a banana out of Marjani's hand and popping it in his mouth. Marjani *hates* being called Mar, and Travis knows this, which is why he does it. I suspect she secretly likes it. Marjani is a person who has learned how to be invisible in every room and has grown comfortable with it. Travis instinctively understands this and thus refuses to ever let her be invisible, which drives her crazy and also makes her smile more than I've ever seen her smile any other time.

"How's my baby girl?" he says, sitting at the kitchen table. He has book bags and iPhones and iPads and headphones and Lord knows whatever else strewn everywhere. How was he carrying this stuff around everywhere? Modern life turns us all into pack mules.

"I am running late, Travis, and you are making a mess," she says, gathering the spread of Travis Junk into a neat pile and gently placing it on the couch. "I have much work to do

65

outside of this house today." Marjani talks like this to everyone, but Travis is the only person for whom there's a little lilt in her voice. I realized a while back that Marjani never wants an emotional response out of anyone. She is too busy, and too efficient, to ask for anything more than just the facts. Travis is the exception. She likes that he goofs on her, because no one else ever does.

"Well, we don't want to keep you from your other job as a professional assassin," he says. "That's what you do when I'm not here, right? Silently kill people for hire?"

I giggle, and Marjani whacks him on his arm with the rag she's wiping the countertop off with. "Besides, we got all morning, don't we, see?" Usually on Wednesdays, Travis comes by in the morning and we walk around the neighborhood for a few hours before lunch, me just motoring alongside him while he talks and talks and talks. He calls himself my trainer and these my "sessions," though they're mostly just him walking for two hours and me stopping every few minutes so he can stretch my legs out. They're the highlights of my week.

But today's special. It's Game Week, which means the Redcoat Band practices at the intramural fields, which means we have to set up our picnic blankets and hear them play as kids throw footballs around and try to tackle each other. Travis always gets stoned before we leave, and when we arrive, we just sit and take it all in. He usually falls asleep, unless he sees a girl. It's the best.

So today's visit is short. But I have a job for Travis.

Marjani gathers her belongings and leaves—though not before Travis blocks her path to the door and makes her high-five him before she can head to her car—and I nod my head toward the computer in my room. He sits across from me.

I posted that I knew something.

You don't know anything. You're a moron, we know this. I tell you this all the time, dude.

No, I mean about Ai-Chin. I posted about her on Reddit.

Ha. Never mind, you aren't a moron. You're an idiot. I love it. Let's dig in.

11

So, after combing through all this, I have persuaded Travis to call the police for me. We've never called the police before. It's harder than you'd think!

The quickest way to get a police officer is to call 911, of course, but that hardly seems the approach here. My kitchen isn't on fire, no one's trying to break in, and Travis isn't currently pummeling me, though that might change if I don't stop passing gas in the middle of our brainstorming session.

So. Google "Athens police"? The first search item that appears is a phone number for the Athens-Clarke County Police Department East Precinct. I saw Ai-Chin just east of campus, which is maybe the same thing?

Try it.
Sweet, this'll be fun.

Travis used to make prank phone calls in high school while we hid in a back closet as his mom slept upstairs. He loves talking on the phone and is sad that it's becoming a lost art: "I wasn't made for these times, man," he likes to say. He dials the old rotary phone in my kitchen my mom put up to make the place look "homey."

"Yeah, my name's Travis, see, and I'm calling about that disappearance . . . yeah, that girl . . . the Chinese girl? . . . I think my friend saw her. . . . No, see, *I* didn't see her, he did. . . . Where? Just off campus, near Five Points. . . . Oh, OK, sorry, your number just showed up first. Can you transfer me? . . . All right, then, can you give me their number? . . . You can't? You don't have it nearby? . . . Fine, fine. It's a good thing this isn't an actual emergency. . . . Yes, I know, I'm supposed to call nine-one-one if there's an emergency. . . . I appreciate your lack of help, it has confirmed all my suspicions about public services in Athens-Clarke County, and America in general. . . . You have a nice day."

So: not East Precinct. We try Baxter Street Precinct. The conversation is friendlier, but they say it's not their jurisdiction either and transfer us to a number that hangs up on us. Then Downtown: we leave a message. West Precinct? They tell us to try the campus police. I don't think they even give campus police guns, but whatever. We call the campus police, but their line is busy, and honestly, I had no idea busy signals were even a thing anymore.

Travis shrugs and bends back down to me.

"Maybe they're getting too many calls?"

They don't sound like they're getting too many calls.

"Should we call again later?"

I remember something I probably should have already remembered.

Wait. I think there was a tip line.

Travis flips through his phone and finds Matthew Adair's *Athens Banner-Herald* story.

He reads it aloud: "Police ask you call the Ai-Chin Liao tip line at 706-234-4022 if you have any information. I wish you had remembered that one in the first place."

Travis dials one more time, and it rings for a minute or so. He raises his eyebrows at me, mouths *voice mail*, and takes an unusually deep, tired breath. "Yes, my name is Travis, see, and I've got a friend here, and he thinks he saw Ai-Chin the day she disappeared. We've been trying to get a hold of somebody, and we figured this line would be too busy, and I guess we were right, but we figured we'd call anyway, so here we are, see. Anyway, I'm Travis. My friend lives at 764 Agriculture in Five Points and wants to help out. Give him a call at 706-258-8463. Again, name is Travis. Uh . . . have a good day?"

He shrugs at me.

I think you forgot to tell them my name.
No one's ever going to listen to that message, man. Let's try campus police again tonight.
This is harder than I would have thought.

"Gotta go, man," he says, putting on a jacket that's three sizes too large for him. He looks like when a bunch of Muppets stand on each other's shoulders to try to pretend they're a real person. "See you tonight for the band practice, see. And if you run into the dude with the Camaro again, run his ass over for me."

12

I got to meet Ron Turner once.

You probably don't know who Ron Turner is, I'm realizing.

When I was seven years old, the University of Illinois invited me, my mother, and a gaggle of other disabled kids to come onto the field of Memorial Stadium in Champaign to say hello to the coaching staff of the Illinois football team. Local sports teams always think they're doing something wonderful when they roll out the wheelchair kids on the field before games, like they're all making our dying wishes come true, as if the only dream I've ever had in my life was to go meet the head coach of a middling Big Ten team. Coach Turner was a nice man, but he had better things to do than shake the hand of a seven-year-old, and so did I. He gave a grim smile and then jogged off to go chart a play, or block a kick, or run the wishbone, or whatever it is that football coaches do.

I've always found these awkward meet-and-greets excruciating. Ostensibly they're supposed to "raise awareness," a way to get us out in the community and get people to "be cognizant of the issue," whatever that issue might be. In practice, I find this little bit of public relations—and that is exactly what it is—more a pain than anything else. You can roll me out to every football stadium and pose for a photo with every person wearing an Illini jersey in sight, and the number of people who at the end of the day can tell you what SMA even is, let alone do anything to fight it, is precisely zero. We are not carted out there to raise awareness. We are carted out there so a bunch of healthy people who just want to drink beer and get away from their problems and scream for three hours—none of which I have any complaint with whatsoever—can overcome any lingering guilt they might have about the fact that they deeply love a cruel, brutish sport involving hundreds of unpaid, often disadvantaged kids crashing their skulls into each other solely for our amusement. They see us out there pregame, they say *Awwwww, good for them*, and they have their one flicker of human emotion for the day that they can then happily ignore, guilt-free, for the rest of their afternoon. These visits are not for us. These visits are for them, so they can feel better when they know they should feel so much worse. We're their props. And there isn't much I hate more than being used as a prop.

This is not necessarily to say I don't enjoy football. Football is a welcome distraction from how terrible the world can be sometimes, and it's impossible not to appreciate the raw physicality of the game: you never quite understand how truly violent it is until they've wheeled you within fifty feet of where massive people are sprinting at other massive people at terrifying speed. At one point during one of those old Illini games, a wide receiver came screaming down the sidelines right as a defensive back was bearing down on him. They collided at maximum velocity, and the receiver went sprawling out of bounds, flipping over a table of Gatorade cups and landing right at the feet of my chair. Everyone on the sideline came scrambling toward me, like they were afraid *I* was going to get hurt, but I looked down at that poor kid staring up at me, his eyes bulging out of his head, the look of someone who'd just been involved in multiple car crashes. I'm not sure how you recover from a hit like that. Yet there he went, up and in the huddle for the next play. The whole thing is impossible and thrilling and terrible. I am not above its dark pleasures.

As it turns out, I moved to the exact right town for football. Football was a mild curiosity in central Illinois, but here, it's the reason the whole place exists. I mean that pretty much literally. Sanford Stadium, home of the Georgia Bulldogs, is smack-dab in the middle of campus, and they've built the whole campus around it. It's basically a huge sunken pit that a major American university had to construct itself to conform to, even though it's only used eight days a year. There isn't a building on campus that doesn't have a view of Sanford. It's Athens's sun, and it is worshipped accordingly.

The game itself always takes a back seat to Game Week. This week's a Game Week in Athens, and in my five years here, I've never missed a Game Week. The whole town lights up, whether the opposing team is good or bad, whether the game is important or not. You get the first rush of campers coming in on Thursday, with their disturbingly detailed Bulldogs logos and paintings on their trucks. You can hear the Redcoat Band practicing on the intramural fields early in the morning and deep into the night. The alumni parties ratchet up on Thursdays too, which is why Marjani is always a little bit late during Game Week: there are cocktails to be served and spilled alcohol to be mopped up everywhere. The students, in a tradition I'll confess to adoring, even dress up in suits and ties and dresses, with all their sorority and fraternity formals scheduled around the games. On most days college kids dress like they just grabbed the first T-shirt they saw when they rolled out of bed, but Game

Weeks have them all in tuxedos and ball gowns. It classes the place up. I like it.

But to me, the best part is just the mood. Game Weeks inspire the citizens of Athens to come out and hang. There's always some sort of street party thrown by all the parents in Five Points on Thursday night, usually with a cameo appearance from a couple of the players, who are bowed to and fawned upon. Wednesday brings the official Redcoat Band public practice, which brings hundreds of people to the intramural fields to picnic and loll around and just socialize. There are no politics, and no disagreements, and no discord or anger. It's just a bunch of nice people lying around in a field, listening to college students play the tuba and march around in big hats. It's incredibly difficult for me to get over there—it requires scooting down College Station, a busy on-ramp to the freeway in which people drive insanely fast, and there is no sidewalk—but I never miss it. Travis brings a lawn blanket and some sandwiches, we listen to the band, we watch the kids run around, and it's almost like it isn't 2019, like everybody likes being around each other again.

That's what's in store for me tonight. It will be 75 degrees, the streets will be humming and people will be smiling when they pass by each other. The football isn't the point, but if it gets me this, it's all well worth it.

log in to the @spectrumair account and start filtering through the replies. Someone in Nashville is angry his in-flight WiFi doesn't work. A guy with a green frog smoking a cigarette as his avatar says his stewardess was rude to him. Some lady with "RESIST" in her bio wants to know how much we charge to check a pair of skis, and I can't even begin to guess where in the South she's flying with skis. Also someone calls me a cuntbag.

> @spectrumair your gate agent here at LIT is a mongoloid
> @spectrumair i think it is nice that you are giving retards a job and everything but its not getting me home any fucking faster
> @spectrumair you suck you suck you suck you suck you suck you suck #yousuck

Just another fun day online.

One of the bummer parts of my job is that nobody really cares how good I am at it. Spectrum doesn't care. If they cared, they wouldn't let some anonymous kid they don't even know has SMA answer all their social media complaints for them. All they want to do is avoid a blowup. They just want to say they have a guy. The customers don't care. They don't want me to actually solve their problem or to give them any information. They just want someone to yell at. I could be the absolute best at my field, the greatest freelance regional airline social media manager the world has ever seen, and the result of my work would be roughly the same as if I just responded to all complaints with a sneezing cat GIF. Now that I'm thinking about it, if I simply responded to all complaints with a sneezing cat GIF, that might actually *make* me the greatest freelance regional airline social media manager the world has ever seen.

The one upside is that on days where I'm just not into it, on days when I'm tired, or the wireless in my place is acting up, or I get a cold and thus things start getting dicey around here, I can basically just ignore it and no one really notices. One weekend when I was on duty, a slow February where nothing was going on, I suddenly could not stop gagging. You should know that gagging is incredibly painful—it feels like someone is taking my ribs and scrunching them into a wad of paper—and when a jag comes on, it's a serious situation. I have an emergency app on my iPad that I can text Marjani with, a sudden, jolting **BLEEP BLEEP BLEEP BLEEP** that takes over her phone and lets her know that she or someone else needs to get over here immediately. I just have to open up the iMedAlert app on my iPad and click it. It is just a big red alarm. I'm pretty sure my iPad starts shaking when I hit it. It is the Break Glass button.

I've only used it twice in the years I've known Marjani. One time was when I first moved in, when I didn't know her well and hadn't figured out this house yet, I accidentally fell off the porch and into the shrubs below. I ended up with cuts all across my back and shoulders, and I was urinating blood for a month. That was a bad day. The second time was this gagging fit last February, which, gotta say, was a lot scarier than the fall off the porch. That was just a onetime trip. The fit felt more like being thrown into the bushes, then being picked up and thrown back in again, then again, then again, and then someone cutting a hole in my rib cage, jamming the bushes inside, setting them on fire, and then picking me up again and throwing me back where the bushes used to be, then stabbing me in the stomach with a shovel and pouring sulfuric acid on the wound. That was a very bad day.

Anyway, I was off work for two days after. No one at Spectrum even noticed I was gone. When I logged back on to Twitter, none of the other "managers" had even filled in for me. Some poor schmuck had been yelling at me for three days, before his flight was delayed, while he was in the air, and then for two days afterward. I felt for him.

Nobody has been yelling at me nearly that long today, but I'm deep into explaining to a Tennessee Volunteers fan that we can probably reroute him through Nashville if he uses the Spectrum Air app, downloadable from the App Store, when there is a doorbell ring. This is the time of year when all the earnest young college students are going door-to-door for their political candidates, so I ignore the bell, as I always do. But this person keeps ringing and ringing, and then there is a pound at the door.

I pull back from the computer and wheel toward the door. Looking through the window, I see it's not a college student, or a FedEx guy, or Travis forgetting his key. It's a cop.

14.

He is big. All cops are big—cops are big even when they are not big; they must train them to loom larger than they actually are, like a blowfish—but this cop is unusually large. After I unlocked and opened the door for him on my phone, he had to duck slightly to fit under the doorframe, and he had to bend over at about a 30-degree angle just to notice who had opened the door for him. He has a thick Fu Manchu goatee, a thin, wispy hairline, and Oakley sunglasses with a camera built into them. The first thing I notice about him is his gun, because that's the first thing I notice about every cop. Isn't that the first thing everyone notices about cops? The gun? He is by himself and unusually sweaty, and that's all I can really tell about him because he has sunglasses on and he isn't talking. He's just looking around my apartment, trying to figure out who else lives here, because there's no way it can just be me. The tag on his uniform reads ANDERSON.

He remains awkwardly standing, shifting a little from one foot to the other, as he scans the room, and it occurs to me just how young he is. He is in his mid-twenties, tops—is it possible he's younger than me?—and once you get used to him and his uniform being in your house, and you adjust for his size, he stops becoming all that physically imposing. He's just a kid. (With a gun.) A kid who thought he was walking into one kind of situation and has found himself in another one and isn't exactly sure what to do with himself right now.

He takes off his sunglasses, and his eyes are darting—even a bit scared. I am used to this look.

"Uh, yeah, is Travis home?" he says, looking down, toward me but not at me.

I type into my speaker.

"No. Travis does not live here. I live here."

He looks down at his notepad. "Oh, uh, I got a call from a Travis at 764 Agriculture about a tip about, uh, a missing person. Do you know a Travis?"

I nod at him, but it takes him a while to register that I'm saying yes rather than having some sort of spasm. He is extremely young.

"He is my friend. Would you like to sit down?"

I see him scan the front room, into the kitchen, to my bedroom, through the back door off the side porch. He shifts his weight to his left side again and bumps into my cough assist machine, which is beeping slightly. It's doing that because it's charging, but to him it must sound like a bomb about to go off. "Oh, excuse me," he says, and then, realizing he's just apologized to a robot, mumbles something to himself. He clicks his tongue to the roof of his mouth, like a nervous boy on a first date that is not going well.

He is not going to be in this house for long.

"Well, um, could you tell Travis that I came by?" he says, and I realize that I may have only a few seconds to tell him what I know.

"Yes. But i can yellow he wandered."

He looks at me, confused and still scared. Godforsaken autocorrect. It's hard enough to type without that.

He starts to turn his head toward the door. "All right, um, look, I'm gonna leave my card, I'm Officer Wynn Anderson, when Travis gets here, why don't you have him call me?"

He turns around, grabs the doorknob, and begins to turn it. I have so much to tell him. And he is on his way out the door.

"*Waaaaaaaaaaaaaait,*" I yell with all my energy. He turns around, startled, and looks at me. I know what I just said to him was a word. But he doesn't know that. He only knows it as air, coming from the mangled man in the chair beneath him, and that he has seven other tips to follow up on before dinnertime, and that none of them involve this current situation, whatever this current situation is.

"Daniel," my iPad speaker says, meekly.

He looks at me sadly and frowns. Catching himself, he instead gives me a smile that is probably intended to be sympathetic. "Thank you for your time, Daniel." He points to the business card with the Athens Police Department logo on it that he's placed on the kitchen counter. "Have Travis call me if he wants to, uh, talk, you know, any further."

He pauses. "And, um . . . you take care of yourself, OK?" And then he walks out the front door, and that is what happens when the police come by my house, and no one is home but me.

15

Wednesday is the slowest day for our airline, during the day shift anyway. The poor guy who has the night shift, who I'm pretty sure is in prison somewhere in California, gets hit hard later: we've got a Nashville-to-Charlotte flight that gets canceled half the time. Otherwise, it's a good time for me to sneak in a few video games. A bunch of guys I know from the old disabled camp I went to as a kid like to get online and shoot zombies and monsters and (increasingly) Nazis all day, and they always invite me to join them, but those games aren't really my bag. My fingers and hands aren't strong enough to keep up with all the button mashing you have to do. I'm more of an old-school Nintendo player, the left-right, left-right, up-down, up-down, B-A-select-start Contra type of business. You can even play those straight out of your browser window rather than have to fire up a PS4 or an Xbox. Sure, you have to deal with flashing ads telling you how to expand your penis size in your peripheral vision, but if you're focused enough, you can still knock out Mike Tyson or save the princess without breaking much of a sweat.

But not today. I'm in Ai-Chin land. I've been refreshing the

Reddit about her disappearance all day, and new bits of information keep popping up. Her family just landed in America;
they're apparently quite wealthy. One poster said she thinks she
had a class with Ai-Chin, but she was quiet and never talked
and *you know how they can be.* (That's a quote: "You know how
they can be.") Another said Ai-Chin stopped going to class the
week before the disappearance, but a response to that said she
never missed a class, and then there was a response that called
that response fake news, and then someone called someone a
fascist, and then I stopped checking that thread.

One thread, though, catches my eye.

VIGIL TONIGHT AT REDCOAT BAND PRACTICE

Hey, Melissa Lei, Ai-Chin's friend here. We're going to have a vigil
tonight at the Intramural Fields. People will be out there for the
Redcoat Band practice, so we'll set up a circle of people to spread the
word, to see if anyone knows her. I'm going to make a press release
and send it to the Banner-Herald and all the TV stations to get them to
come. We need more people looking for her. I'm trying to get a hold
of her family so they can show up too. Anyway, we're going to be
there around 5:30 and will be there all night. Tell everyone.

"Are we stopping by this?" Marjani has let herself in, sneaked
up behind me, and is reading over my shoulder again. This
happens far too often to be an accident.

She wipes down the back of my neck. "I have noticed these
late nights of you playing around on these sites," she says. "You
need to get outside. You need some sun."

I nod to her and move my head in the language she is always
sure to understand.

She stands up and begins folding a dish towel. "Yes, yes, Travis already told me about this. You two really got yourselves worked up this morning, didn't you?" She's flitting about the kitchen, barely paying attention to me. Travis left soon after lunch to do whatever it is he does all day, but he should be back any minute: this is our Wednesday-night activity, after all, and he doesn't even know about the vigil yet.

"I suppose it is important for boys to have hobbies," Marjani says, and I notice that she is packing picnic baskets, big ostentatious wicker almost cartoonishly Picnic Basket picnic baskets, along with two blankets she's stashing under my chair. The oven beeps, and she pulls out the Dinner Porridge, which is actually just macaroni and cheese, but Travis called it Dinner Porridge one time, and the name stuck. She puts the bib around my neck, and as she feeds me, I look her in the eye.

Are you coming with us tonight? Why are you packing all the food and blankets?

She comes this close to blushing, though I have no idea why.

"I thought I might go with you and Travis, just to get the, how does it go, the cobwebs out of my hair?" She smiles. I have a feeling this has something to do with football. It never fails to amuse me how much Marjani loves football. Just seeing the band makes her excited. "Also I am curious what you boys are up to. You have the look of mischief."

As if on cue, Travis comes barreling through the door. "Sorry I'm late," he says, even though there was no set time for him to be here, and we have no particular deadline we have to hit. I think he says this out of habit, always assuming he's late to something, somewhere, somehow. I nod to him, beckoning him to the computer, to tell him about the rally, the vigil, our first real chance to be right there in the middle of all of this.

Travis looks at my screen and actually jumps. "Shit, dude, we gotta go to that. We have to tell somebody there what you know."

A cop came by.
What?
Yeah. He came here looking for you. He was confused that I wasn't you. I told you you should have said my name.
What did he say?
He was all freaked out by me. Anderson was his name. His card is on the kitchen table. I don't think he's much help. You should call him anyway. I think we might need a different cop.
Well, I bet there will be a cop there. It's a vigil! There are always cops at vigils.
I do not think you understand what a vigil is, Travis.

Travis pockets Officer Wynn Anderson's card, giving it a frown first.

"Let's just check it out," he says. "This is the most exciting thing that's happened around here in years."

"I am glad you are having so much fun with this family's misery," Marjani says, but not harshly. "Now let's go before someone takes our picnic spot."

"Look at you, see," Travis says. "Feisty minx."

16.

You know how when you go somewhere with a little kid, you spend most of the trek there exhorting him to hurry up and then, right when you're about to arrive, he takes off ahead of you, like a puppy jumping from place to place, sniffing everybody's butts, peeing on anything he sees? That's Travis anytime we go anywhere. He stares at his phone the whole walk, head down, occasionally whistling or chuckling at some dumb video of a baby, and then as soon as he sees people who *aren't* Marjani and me—specifically people who are girls—*whoosh*, he's gone.

It must have rained a little bit last night, because the intramural fields are damp and slightly muddy. I have to spin my wheels to gain traction, and at one point I spray some puddle water on Marjani's scrubs. I nod to apologize to her and notice that she's got a spatter of blood on the scrubs, near her left shin. What was she doing before she came over today? Marjani has so many jobs and wears so many hats that it's impossible to keep track of all of them. It also warrants mentioning that the blood could be mine. Every couple of weeks I'll wake up and either my sheet or my pillow is speckled with blood spots. I have no idea where they came from or why they are there. I used to find this unnerving, but eventually you stop. What can you do, you know?

Marjani finds a spot she likes and lays down our blanket, an old St. Louis Cardinals giveaway my mom got free at a baseball game twenty years ago that has somehow followed me to Athens and smells thickly of beer, cigarette ash, and peanuts. I do not like this blanket, but I keep it. It reminds me of Illinois, and Mom, and all kinds of tall adults. Marjani waves to Travis, who's already a football field away, talking to someone he's never met before like they grew up together. He nods, motions to the random lady he's talking to to hold on a second, and then sprints toward us like we're on fire.

"Hey, hey, hey, lemme pop open that wine."

For reasons I do not understand, my mother, when she comes to visit, stacks my kitchen with bottles of wine, even though I've never drunk wine in my life and it's against Marjani's religion. (Though boy, it would do her some good sometimes.) Travis is the only one who drinks it, and he's always coming over to grab bottles and take them home with him, or just stay and drink while hanging out with me, and I think I just figured out why my mom is always stacking my kitchen with wine.

"Dude, check it out," he says, pointing off into the distance. All I see is that Redcoat Band, carrying their instruments and wheezing. What a strange instrument a tuba is. I wonder how many different shapes they twisted that metal into until they realized that a tuba's shape was the exact one they needed to make that exact sound.

I shake my head at him. "No, no, *next* to the band," Travis says. And there, I realize, is the vigil.

This might have been the worst possible place to have a vigil. First off, *there are tubas*. It is difficult to conjure up the precise level of moroseness and quiet tragedy that a vigil requires when there are college students wearing big red hats blowing into brass instruments while stoners loll around drinking wine and children run around screaming. I mean, you are having a vigil next to a freaking marching band. You might as well hold it at a six-year-old's birthday party.

But if they wanted attention, they got it. The woman from the Rook & Pawn, the woman I almost ran over twice and then couldn't find as I terrified poor downtown Athens passersby, is sitting at a folding table with a huge stack of papers, many of which threaten to blow away. Next to her is a massive photo of Ai-Chin, the same one I've now seen thousands of times online, with a phone number to call with any information you might have about her disappearance. (Travis will soon call this number, get a busy signal, and roll his eyes at me.) There are three people sitting at the table with the Rook & Pawn woman, two Chinese and one an older white woman who instantly looks like every professor I've ever seen. (They must all buy their glasses at the same store.) They are handing out flyers and, it appears, trying to get everyone popping by to sign some sort of petition.

And next to them, I see Ai-Chin's parents.

They must be her parents. They look exhausted, first off, the sort of look you might have if you'd been up all night flying and then landed in a strange country you'd never been to with everyone speaking a language you don't understand. They are both wearing far too many clothes for a warm October evening in northeast Georgia, and thick sunglasses even though it's dusk. They are talking to no one.

Seeing them makes me feel ill. I am sorry that they are here. I am sorry any of this is happening.

"Let's goooooooooooo!!!" Travis says, and he bounds off toward the vigil, beckoning me to follow. I look at Marjani. She waves me on.

What's he doing?
Why else are you here, Daniel, if not to go over there?

Marjani always understands a lot more than she lets on.

"What is wrong with him?"

It is a relief to have someone asking me this about Travis for once, rather than the other way around. For some reason, all this sadness and tragedy has registered with Travis's malfunctioning empathy synapses not as "morose" but as "unspeakably thrilling." He will *not* stop asking everybody in the vicinity of the vigil about Ai-Chin.

What was she like? When did you last see her? Was she a good student? Did she ever hang around by the graduate student housing in Five Points? Was she impulsive? Was she shy? Did she, say, like to get stoned?

Travis has sense enough to avoid the parents, but everyone else near the vigil, and this is a growing crowd of people, is getting an earful of questions.

The young woman in front of me is less bemused by Travis than everyone else is, and she's asking me, of all people, if he's OK. It is incredibly rare that someone seeks my opinion, let alone looks to me as a character witness, so I like her already.

I wag my eyebrows up and down in a way that I hope says *Give me a second, I have a speaker box* and not *I'm currently having a seizure*, and she understands enough to wait it out.

"He's okay. He just likes to talk."

She doesn't seem terrified by all this. Another advantage of not using the Stephen Hawking voice.

"That's cool," she says, and I like her instantly, for no clear reason other than I just know it. "I'm Jennifer." She instinctively holds out her hand, then pulls it back, and I nod, *Happens all the time, don't worry.*

"Daniel."

"It's really terrible, isn't it?" she says. She's wearing a T-shirt that's about three sizes too big for her and has her hair pulled back, so she's obviously a college student. Only college students, new moms, and disabled people go out that haphazardly dressed to an event where there will be hundreds of people. I nod.

She looks me up and down.

"Do you have SMA?" she says. This is the first time I can remember a person asking me this in the wild. I've been asked this at charity events, 5Ks, benefits, all the galas we're paraded out for so everyone will feel guilty about how good they have it and write big checks that I never seem to see any of the money from, now that you mention it. But no one has got it cold like that.

I must have just shown this entire interior monologue on my face, because she jumps a little, like she just guessed which hat the ball was under on the video board at a baseball game. "I knew it! I used to work with some kids with my Young Life group who had SMA. That's some bullshit, right?" She grimaces, but only slightly. "Your chair kicks ass, though."

Without even quite realizing I'm doing it, I give my chair a little spin, a full 360, my little catwalk, and I do an exaggerated head bow when I'm back facing her. She squeals, delighted. A sound comes out of me that isn't close to the sound that she just made, but it is intended to and she gets it and thus our transaction is successful. We all squeal in delight differently, but we all squeal in delight the same.

At this point, Travis sees the hullabaloo and bounds over, because Travis is gravitationally drawn to hullabaloo. "Looks like you two are having too much fun over here," he says, and makes a mock grave expression. "This is far too serious a situation for tomfoolery."

This seems to click something with Jennifer, and she straightens herself and turns to Travis. She looks at him like she's mad—at him, at someone. Then her face falls, and she bursts into tears. For the first time since we got here, Travis seems to understand the enormity of what's going on around him, and he puts his arm around her as she sobs into his shoulder. The two of them have never met. He holds her for a full minute.

It turns out Jennifer lives down the hall from Ai-Chin at the graduate student housing complex. She didn't know her well, but nobody did. They had class at the same time in the morning and walked there together the first couple of days of the semester, until Jennifer added a second class later in the day that required her to start driving in to campus. Ai-Chin struggled with English, Jennifer said, but was trying her best and improving. She was very confused by the wide streets of Five Points; no matter how many times she walked to her classes, she'd always get turned around. Ai-Chin listened to Chinese-to-English tapes on her walks to school because she wanted to understand her new town better and because "Nobody here will want to hear me tell them their dog is dying in Chinese." (Jennifer laughed a little at that one, shooting out a snot bubble that landed near my leg.) All Jennifer really knew about Ai-Chin was that she was nervous about being in America, that she wanted to make her parents happy, that they weren't excited about her coming here but trusted her to do well, and that she deeply loved animals.

Jennifer hadn't thought much about any of that before Ai-Chin vanished. "I should have been nicer," she says. She seems about as nice as humans get, to me. I suppose she's still probably right.

"I just want someone to find her," she says. "I want her to get to give me another chance."

Travis puts his arm around her. "You know . . . we've actually been looking into this a little bit ourselves," he says. She looks at me, and I give her the Groucho, and she smiles and then she and Travis sort of walk off to the side, out of earshot. Our circle of sort-of, would-be, kinda knowledge has expanded to an attractive woman Travis is talking to, which is probably where it was always going to expand first, all told.

I look over at Ai-Chin's parents. They are surrounded by dozens and dozens of people. We have attracted quite a crowd. But I'm not sure her parents have moved an inch since we got here. They are just standing, looking at the ground, as if they might find her there, as if that place makes as much sense as anything else here.

I sit and stare at them longer than I should. Marjani comes up behind me. "It is so, so sad."

Ai-Chin's mother looks up, and she wipes her eyes and flicks something off the shoulder of her husband's jacket. She takes out a handkerchief and hands it to him. He blows his nose without lifting his head. He hands it back to her. She puts it back in her pocket and turns to her left.

She sees me, still staring at her. She gives me a little smile and raises her right hand. *Hello.* She lowers it and goes back to looking at the ground. Her daughter said hi to me the exact same way.

17

Back at home. It started pouring down rain shortly after I saw Ai-Chin's parents, one of those Georgia rainstorms that come out of nowhere from a clear blue sky, dump buckets on everyone for ten minutes, and then vanish as quickly as they arrived. The vigil scattered. The tubas would leak for days.

Travis called Officer Anderson's voice mail on the drive home, and Marjani put his card in her purse and said she'd follow up herself tomorrow morning.

I can't stop thinking about Ai-Chin's parents. They left shortly after I saw them. They looked tired, and a bit bewildered as to what they were doing there, or what any of this was at all. What would I have said to them anyway?

I aimlessly scroll through Reddit posts and let my mind wander.

It was right after the WIZometer said it was gorgeous outside. She was walking up the sidewalk. She was probably headed for the bus stop. It was always weird that she didn't have headphones in. Everybody always has headphones in.

The only thing noteworthy is that there weren't many people around. Usually it's not just her.

And she waved at me.

Marjani's sweeping up before putting me to bed, and I'm sleepy, and worn down, and I'm not supposed to push it when I'm this exhausted, but I click on my email anyway. Waiting for me there is this:

From: Southview Drive <wellbegyourpardon@hotmail.com>
To: flagpolesitta1993@yahoo.com
Subject: Hello Friend.

Well. Well. Well well well. What have we here?

I must say, it was quite a surprise to come across this little shitpost:

> >>> *i live in five points and i might be wrong but i'm pretty sure i saw ai-chin walking my block every day. and i think i saw her the day she disappeared. i think it was her. i'm not certain. but i know she lives nearby and apparently she had class that morning, and i think i saw her. i think I saw her get into a tan camaro. does that make sense to anybody?*

This was certainly a remarkable post to come across. I didn't see anybody out there, and trust me, pal, I looked: I cruised down that street for 20 minutes and did not come upon a soul until she walked by. I have no idea how I missed you. I mean, you saw my car. How did I not see yours?

So. It appears you are a sly one. Because you obviously were there, because you know my car, because you sure have a lot of details correct for someone posting horseshit theories on Reddit. How did I not see you? Where were you hiding, my friend?

I do not know the answers to these questions. But I will find them. Because it appears we are going to get to know one another.

So hello. Turns out the internet keeps finding ways to connect people. I love it. Yeah: We're about to become real close. I hope you are ready.

Best,

Your New Reddit Fan

"It's time for sleep for you," Marjani says.

THURSDAY

18

How much can you know about yourself if you've never been in a fight?

Travis was almost dangerously obsessed with *Fight Club* when we were in high school. It makes sense. That movie is a satire of toxic male masculinity, a nightmarish version of a fractured mind coming apart, but teenagers, they are not so good about satire, particularly when it's as compulsively entertaining as that movie is. Travis left that movie wanting to punch people in the face, and get punched in the face, and set fire to the whole goddamned world, and when you feel like that, but you're not sure you actually should do all of those things, you show the movie to someone else to see if they feel the same way as you, to make sure you're not alone, to make sure you're not losing your mind.

The weird thing about this, which Travis quickly realized, was that he was showing this movie to someone who was physically incapable of punching someone and who, had he been punched in the face by Brad Pitt or Edward Norton (or Meat Loaf, or Helena Bonham Carter, or even Jared Leto, though I'm pretty sure I could take a Jared Leto punch if I absolutely had to), it would almost certainly collapse his lungs and kill him within the hour. It is a lot easier to romanticize being punched so that you can feel alive when you can be certain you will, in fact, be alive after the punch.

I could still lift my arms a bit back then, and during one of the actual *Fight Club* scenes, I grunted and gestured to Travis. "Lemmmeee go," I said, balling my gnarled right hand into a fist.

"That's the spirit, man!" he said. "Fuck it up! Let's fuck shit up!"

With all my might, I slingshotted my wrist toward his face, where my fist landed with a limp splat, a sound more akin to a slab of raw pork being dropped on a counter than the THWACK you'd see in a *Batman* comic. Travis, love him, careened backward like he'd been thrown off the back of a truck. I snorted a laugh, but then gave him a serious look.

Please don't hit me.

Travis chuckled and gave me a faux slug to the jaw.

But I got it. I might have decreased levels of testosterone, but I am still a man, and, more to the point, I was once a confused, messed-up teenage boy. Something about that movie made you want to just wreck shit. It speaks to that person all boys, all men, really, have inside them: no matter how stable we may seem, no matter how much we're all trying to keep it together, there is something primal inside of us that just wants to watch the world burn. We don't want to do it, not really, and part of getting older is having that destructive impulse fade, letting go of all that irrational built-up anger. There's a reason there aren't any fifty-five-year-old terrorists, or at least there weren't until they all started watching Fox News. Destroying things is for the young. And, strapped to a chair or not, I was still young. I am still young. And my blood can boil.

And I can get my hair up just like everybody else.

Of all the disadvantages this disease gives me, the one that drives me the craziest is that everyone thinks I'm nice all the time. Suffering from a disease automatically makes people empathetic toward you, which sounds like something you'd want but absolutely is not.

I learned at a young age that there were all sorts of activities that other kids were capable of that I never would be. This makes me like every other human who has ever existed. I am still inside here, with my own thoughts, and my own worries, and my own obsessions, and my own rage. I don't feel any differently from you. Or rather, I don't know how you feel. I am just me. I feel like a normal person because this is normal to me.

But not when you look at me like that. When you look at me with that you-poor-thing mist, that little pit in your stomach that shows me you're working something out, that you're feeling less stressed out and upset about not getting that promotion because you've got to appreciate what you have. You look at me like I have something to be sad about. My existence makes you grateful you are not me. I was fine . . . until you looked at me like that. I was fucking fine. Now apparently there's something wrong.

It makes me angry. It makes me want to get in a fight.

The instinct in a moment like this, they say, is fight or flight: stand your ground or to get the hell out of Dodge.

I find myself strangely relieved to learn this about myself: I want to fight.

We're about to become real close. I hope you are ready.

Am I? I do suppose we are about to find out.

19

The sumbitch emailed me. Just like that.

I hadn't deleted that damn Reddit post fast enough.

My email address, which (luckily) is not connected to my actual name, is linked in my Reddit profile. The internet is supposed to make the world bigger. But it always ends up feeling smaller.

Marjani wheels me to my computer after wiping me down. She's not ready to hear this yet. I reread the email while she makes breakfast. The first thing I notice? He's lonely. Maybe someone who doesn't have a lot of people who talk to him enough to tell him what they really think about him. Someone who spends a lot of time alone. I can relate.

He didn't see me. Of course he didn't. I just blend into the porch, particularly when you're on the lookout for people of normal height and width, not shut-ins in a wheelchair getting a little bit of air before heading back in to be screamed at by aggrieved travelers. He didn't have any idea anyone had seen him. He was casual and relaxed and as normal as anyone driving down the street on a morning. He said something—what was it? Something that made her get in the car. Did she know him?

Did she think he was someone else? I'm just guessing. All that matters is that she got in. She just got in. He drove off. And that was that. No one saw him.

Except me. I saw him. I saw her. I know that now. I am not making it up. I am not imagining things. I really did see that Thrashers hat and those boots. It really did happen.

I would be lying to you if I said I was not experiencing a considerable amount of relief.

And now he knows. He knows I saw him. He doesn't know who I am, I don't think, or where I saw him, or what I've done, or what I'm going to do with this information. He just knows that he thought he got away with it, and now he's not sure. He's startled. He's angry. But more than anything else: he's scared.

He's afraid. And hey: he's not alone in that.

Sometimes it's nice not to feel so alone.

So. What do I write back?

Wait. *Do* I write back? What do you say to a guy you've never met before that's so immediately threatening? As someone who runs social media for a regional airline, I should probably have a more immediate answer at hand for that particular problem than I do. I have more experience being threatened than 99.9 percent of the planet.

The arguments in favor of ignoring the email altogether are strong. Writing him back not only confirms there was a witness—which the tan-car ID essentially does anyway—it also further connects that witness with . . . well, me. If I don't write him back, all he has is an email address and a deleted Reddit post. Every response brings him closer to me. Of course, as far as I know, this guy could be some teenager in Idaho who read about the case online and decided to hop on Reddit and start messing with people. (It is my theory that at least half of Reddit's posts come from teenagers from Idaho messing with people.) If I write him back, it starts a game that I might not be particularly skilled at playing.

If I don't respond at all, he'll probably think he scared me away—a reasonable assumption!—or that I was just full of shit in the first place. He'll be able to go back to doing what he has been doing all this time: thinking he's getting away with it. Giving him any sort of response confirms that somebody saw this. And that will only intensify his desire to find out who that somebody is. But it'll also get his heart racing.

I think I want to get his heart racing.

He's also just trying to get a reaction out of me so I'll give something away. He wants to instill the same fear in me, now that he *knows* that someone saw him. He wants me jumpy and jittery. He wants me to get back to him so he can further get under my skin.

Writing him back is a bad idea. It's what he wants. It'll put me in peril. It might even make it more difficult to catch him. It's a terrible idea with hardly any positive outcome.

But he still has her.

First things first: I forward the email to Travis. He won't be up for a few hours, but I need him to see it. He can at least confirm that it exists, that I did not imagine it. My forwarded note to Travis reads:

> holy shit dude look at this psycho. you still got that cops card? send this to him. holy shit.

And then I stare at it some more. A half hour passes. Another half hour. My email needs to be completed before Marjani comes back in here from making breakfast, because she cares for me and thus absolutely will not let me send it. Yet I sit here, blinking along with the cursor on the empty email draft.

> YNRF—
>
> i am happy to hear from you. i was afraid i imagined you, and ai-chin, and your stupid car. my life was rather dull and empty and pointless until you came along. youve got my heart beating again. you have given me something to do. you have given me a purpose. thank you.

Best not send that one. He'll think he has met his sociopath soul mate. (Has he?)

DELETE DELETE DELETE

What do you say to someone who could kill you? This guy could be the sort of person who kills people, no?

> YNRF—
>
> i dont know what youre talking about. you are freaking me out. i dont want any trouble. i didnt see anything. i was just making a joke. im just some kid from idaho. have you been to idaho? we have, uh, potatoes here i think. point is i made it all up. please go about your day and lets pretend this never happened.

DELETE DELETE DELETE

What do you say to someone who doesn't know?

> YNRF—
>
> do your worst shithead

DELETE DELETE DELETE

I sigh deeply, which makes me start breathing hard, taking me entirely out of commission for a few minutes. Once I avoid the worst of it, I look back at the blank cursor.

Maybe I'll *Fight Club* it.

YNRF—

i saw what you did. i didnt know for sure until you sent me this email but now i do. i saw you. she got in your car. where is she? is she still alive? if you tell me or tell the police maybe they wont give you the chair.

you made a mistake sending this email. im gonna get your ass. look out behind you motherfucker. im gonna end you.

That felt good. It was like yelling at an airline.

But for some reason, I think of Todd. That's a man who knows how to deal with an opponent. *Stay kind, kid. No one will see it coming.*

This person doesn't have anyone to talk to. He's reaching out to be seen. I really can understand that. Maybe to help her, I have to help him too.

YNRF—

its true. you got me. i saw you.

im just trying to help man. you can talk to me. is she ok? if shes ok its not too late.

but im here. i saw you. i know. so let her go. or just tell me your name. lets do this together.

The door starts to swing open. Breakfast is here. Travis will not awaken for several hours.

The mouse hovers over Send.

I click it.

Whoosh. It's gone. And here we go.

20

M arjani has a bounce to her step, like she needs to tell me something.

She does. "Have you seen this? This is today. This is tonight."

She hands me a pamphlet. It's another event, another rally to raise awareness of Ai-Chin's disappearance. But this is not a hand-drawn, hastily scribbled sheet to be taped on the wall of the Rook & Pawn. This is official. This is on university letterhead and thick, laminated paper stock. This is . . . bigger. This is *serious*.

RALLY FOR AI-CHIN LIAO
Hosted by the University of Georgia Chinese American Society

Come to the Chapel Bell tonight 6 p.m. for a vigil for Ai-Chin Liao, a graduate student who disappeared from campus this week. Have you seen this woman?

In attendance will be U.S. senator David Perdue, university president Jere Morehead, and head football coach Kirby Smart, along with

All-American kicker Thomas Jongin Craggs. The Georgia community rallies around our own. **WE WILL FIND AI-CHIN.**

Marjani looks at me. "This girl, she is everywhere."

Once Marjani heard that Kirby Smart was going to be there, she would have dragged me there behind her car if she had to. Marjani is a quiet, peaceful woman who, once you turn the television to a sporting event in which unpaid college students try to turn each other's brains into pudding, transforms into a barbarian at the gate, one of the spectators at the Colosseum screaming for blood. I am not certain when a mild-mannered middle-aged Pakistani woman became a face-painting lunatic Georgia Bulldogs football fan who once screamed "You are the devil Spurrier I spit at you!" at the television, but it is definitive proof of what Athens can do to you if you are not careful.

After finishing up with @sabanmaga27, who doesn't seem to understand how standby works—highlight: "fuk you I'll stand by your corpse"—I get an email from Travis.

> Holy shit dude. What the fuck? WHAT THE FUCK. Forwarded it to the cop, though I don't think cops check email. Maybe they do? Anyway: WHAT THE SHIT.
> I'll see you at the rally thing tonight. Remember that Jennifer girl from last night? we've been hanging out! She's coming too. We'll see you there, bitches.
> WHAT THE SHIT.

Out of habit, at this point, I check the UGA Reddit page and the posts about Ai-Chin. In the wake of the publicity of the last twenty-four hours, the page, once a sleepy outpost for halfhearted true crime wannabes, has turned into a hothouse of craven conspiracy theories, all of them far more outlandish than Travis's Ai-Chin-is-a-stoner hypothesis. She has run away because she hates school and doesn't want to disappoint her parents. There's a secret sex slave society out in Watkinsville. She discovered an experiment the vet school was doing on lab rats and was murdered to silence her before she went public. Some guy has somehow tied this to Hillary Clinton. By far the most popular theory is that she was trying to defect from China, and someone decided to disappear her to make sure the Chinese government was not embarrassed publicly. When people don't have a story, they will make one up.

I flip back to the email and read it again. It seems insane. Yet . . . there is something I understand in it. I wonder what people are thinking about me all the time too. How can you not? Are there people who don't?

I hear a gasp behind me.

"Daniel! What is this?" I have told her so many times how rude it is to look over my shoulder when I'm on my computer but . . . yeah, here we are.

Marjani has, reasonably, decided to call the police again. I've downloaded what little information I have to her, about as much as Travis has now, but she barely registers any of that, she's so freaked out about the email.

She acts like she's the first person to come up with this idea of calling the cops, like Travis and I haven't been trying and failing for two days now, like there wasn't a cop in this house just yesterday. But one constant is that Marjani always wants to call the police. She has a first-generation immigrant's faith in the police, in the idea that, in America, unlike the country where she was born, there is an impartial, fair-minded, sober group of people whose job it is to sort through the chaos and find order in the madness. I don't have the heart to tell her the truth.

I have to admit that she has a point this time. I am not just some idiot in a chair: *I am evidence.* There is a whole town looking for Ai-Chin. Her friends are weeping in the streets. It was rather disorienting, I gotta say, to see the 11Alive crew talk about something that happened in my front yard, before throwing it to Chesley McNeil with the weather, looking like a 10 on the WIZometer today, perfect football weather out there for you folks.

This is more than a kid with a laser pointer. We need to call the police. Again.

While pulling up the sheets and wiping down a scary stain on my pillow that I've never seen before and can't come up with much of an origin for, Marjani straps me into my chair.

I am going to call them right now. I will call the man who left his card.
Yeah, good luck with him. What are you going to say?
I have to tell them that you saw something. That you saw the man. And the girl. And now this threat.
This is what I've been trying to do.

She begins dialing the phone. I'm proud of my home's landline, just hanging on the wall there, waiting for some lady wearing an apron to pick it up and hand it to a guy wearing a black suit and a fedora. It makes me feel like I live in a '50s sitcom. It is worth noting that every person who comes into this house assumes it doesn't work and is just there for show.

Marjani calls Officer Anderson, frowns, and mouths *Voice*

mail. She leaves her name and number. She then dials the university police again.

"Hello, yes, this is Marjani. . . . Yes, yes, I know you have heard from me before. . . . Uh-uh. . . . Well, yes, I know that you are very busy, that is why I am calling. . . . No, no, I know that, I am saying that . . . no, I see that, I am not trying to bother you, I am trying to help you. . . . Well, excuse me, I—hey!"

Clearly, Marjani got the person who usually answers the phone when Marjani calls about a fraternity party going on too late, or a stray cat howling in a yard down the street, and this person had no patience for her today. Not the day after the national news has picked up the story of a missing Chinese national on the campus of a major American university, one that, not incidentally, is hosting a Very Important Football Game this weekend, let's go to Kirk and Corso for their picks. Marjani slams the phone down and says a phrase in Urdu that I suspect is banned from Pakistani broadcast television.

Marjani dials again, hangs up, dials again, hangs up, dials again. Busy. Busy. That sound, a goose honking in your ear, over and over, mocking. She sits and stews for a moment, then wipes her brow and straightens her shirt.

"I have to go. We will have to do this later, Daniel," she says. "Unless you want me to drive you down to the station and drop you off."

I do not want this.

I do not want this.

"Fine," she says, harrumphing. "We will try again tonight if they have not caught this man by then. Do you agree?"

Yes.

She wipes my head again, looks at me, and frowns.

I will see you this evening for the rally. You will be OK between now and then?
I will. It will be fine.

She is so worried. That she is so worried starts to make me worried, so I smile the best I can at her.

It'll be fine. We're getting too worked up. Go do what you have to do.

She stares at me a beat too long, then grabs her jacket off the chair. It's gorgeous out, so she knows to open the front door and steer me out to the front porch. She pats me on the knee. "You be careful, Daniel," she says on the way out to her car. "This is a lot. This is quite a lot."

As she reaches the porch, she stops and turns around. But she doesn't say anything more.

21

You will hopefully forgive me if you are a patron of Spectrum Air expecting a certain level of service today, but you see, I'm corresponding with a guy who may have murdered a young woman, and I am waiting for him to write me back. Forgive me if I have little patience for the fact that your seat does not recline.

But it's busy, because a game-day weekend awaits. Even our sleepy hamlet's tiny airport is busy on football weekends. Here is one of my favorite factoids about this beautifully weird city I live in: on Georgia home football weekends, all open container laws are suspended. It's actually in the city charter: the tourism bureau happily advertises it. Any other day, the county fills its coffers, its entire budget, on the underage and illegal drinking of college students and other miscreants. Travis's grandmother got carded at a restaurant here, and she's eighty-four and looks like she died around 1983. (She was using a walker! Still carded!) Illicit drinking is the lifeblood of this town, as it goes, the source of and solution to all of civic life's fiscal problems. But when Georgia football plays a home game, well, all rules are forgotten—this slightly Puritan college town turns into New Orleans.

This ends up being less sloppy than you might think. Athens doesn't have the fake regality on football weekends that, say, Oxford, Mississippi, has—that place looks like the party from *Get Out* on football Saturdays; everybody's got bow ties and straw hats—but we don't set fire to the world just to watch it burn like the lunatics at LSU either. It's just a special weekend holiday that we have seven times a year in which everyone involved, pretty much everybody but the players themselves, just drinks for about thirty-six hours straight. The goal is not obliteration. It is to achieve a steady, warm glaze for the whole weekend, enough to make you forget the otherwise omnipresent collapse of civilization . . . but not so much that you pass out before the game starts. And this is everyone, mind you. This is not just a select group of asshat backward-hat frat dudes. They come from the whole state, the more genteel North Georgia folks, the younger recent grads from Atlanta and the Atlanta suburbs, the young black professionals from Atlanta proper, the farmers from South Georgia, the shaky, sorta scary folks from the Georgia-Florida border.

Athens is a progressive city in just about every possible way, thanks to its status as a college town. (Our mayor is an avowed democratic socialist!) But on football weekends, this place is simply the home of everything Georgia, the place where old hippies and drawling white-haired southern judges and soccer moms and rappers and preachers and cokeheads and music nerds and accountants and schoolteachers and physics professors and chicken farmers all come together to turn their bodies into 65 percent bourbon and scream for the Dawgs.

The football stadium at the literal center of Athens is the light that beckons us all. It's the only thing that matters in this whole state for seven weekends out of the year, and I have to tell you, it is beautiful to behold. We can't agree on anything in this world, we can't even sit with each other long enough to decide whether we *want* to agree on anything, but of all things, it's football, this awful game that destroys the brains of college students without even paying them a dime for the privilege, this last refuge of the helplessly meat-headed, it's football that brings us together, goddammit, and we can assemble and wear red and bark at each other and push all the awful shit down to a place it won't return until Tuesday at the latest, and we do it seven times a year and that's seven times a year when we don't have to live with the rest of it and I gotta tell you, that ain't nothing.

Another great thing about football weekends is that they are rare Georgia weekends in which the car is discouraged, or at least discouraged by the nonfoolish. People who live here park their car on Friday and don't even think about it until Sunday afternoon. It's a foot-travel Valhalla, these football weekends, and that's of course right in my strike zone: when there are more people walking, drivers notice them more and are less likely to take blind right turns directly into your friendly neighborhood motorized SMA traveler.

I've been hit twice already in the six years I've lived here, both times by people who forget that the world exists outside their immediate windshield. One was just a tap, a big old redneck who was idling through a stop sign and slammed on his brakes right when he saw me. He leaped out of his truck and sprinted over to me. I was fine, he really only chipped the paint on my chair. I could still talk a little back then, and I said, "Fine, I'm fine, it's OK," and he looked at me and just broke down crying right then and there. It was quite a sight, this three-hundred-pound bearded dude with a Don't Tread On Me bumper sticker bawling, snot coming out his nose, wailing, "I'm so sorry, I'm so sorry." He came out much worse for the wear than I did on that one. The other was a college girl in a Ford Escort, about eighteen months ago. She was on her phone, of course, and let her foot off the brake while scrolling at a red light as I was zooming in front of her in the crosswalk. This one took a little bit more out of me, bouncing me about three feet forward, nearly into the passing traffic, and kicking me out of my chair, where I landed on my right wrist, shattering it on impact. She didn't even notice until people started honking. She got out of the car, dazed, and saw me writhing around on the ground like I'd been tased, or like I was a soccer player flopping around so I could draw a penalty. It must have been quite something—I personally wasn't awake for it. I woke up a couple of hours later in the hospital with Marjani and Travis sitting next to me. They'd had to use the cough assist machine on me to control my breathing, but all told, the wrist, along with some nasty scratches on the left side of my face, was somehow the worst of it. It wasn't even my chair-controlling hand. It could have been, and absolutely should have been, so much worse. I remember hearing Travis cry a lot, but mostly I slept through it all. We didn't press any charges against the girl, but her insurance is going to put her in the poorhouse for the next twenty years now, I have no doubt. Welcome to my world, lady.

But everyone remembers to look both ways on football weekends. Georgia is playing Middle Tennessee State this weekend, a nothing school with a nobody football team. It's the perfect opportunity for me to people-watch. I can just scoot on over to campus and just sit there for hours, looking at people. The stoned college kids tossing a Frisbee around. The frat bros sitting on their Milledge porches, looking for something, someone, to crush. The young girls, foals really, dressed up for sorority formals in their classic gowns. The football diehards, with their DirecTV setups so they don't miss a play of any game all weekend, always crouched in the corner drawing up reasons the Dawgs can never win the big one—are we cursed, are we doomed, goddamned Kirby gotta get us over the hump. The old alums, coming in from all over, their weekly pilgrimage to Athens, back home, back to the place where they once ruled, a place where they can remember who they used to be and pretend they can be them again. The children running everywhere, aware that they have a little more freedom this weekend than they usually do but not entirely certain as to why.

Thursday is always a heavy workday in the fall down south for those of us in the travel industry, if that's what you want to call what I do. They encourage us to know the college football situation of our travelers on weekends like this, so I sneak in a couple "Big weekend for the 'Noles!" responses to those delayed on Spectrum Flight 227 to Tallahassee. They initially respond with "I know THAT'S WHY I'M TRYING TO GET THERE," but eventually they appreciate that you understand the stakes of their travel. People spend so much time yelling at brands on the internet that they're always a little surprised to realize that the brands live in the same world that they do, and that they know what time the game starts. Brands are people too, you know.

I'm in the middle of talking some dude from Chattanooga out of sending a pipe bomb to my mother's house when I hear that familiar Gmail ding.

I switch windows, catch my breath back, and start reading.

Flagpole—

I'm sorry. I was taken aback by your post. Who wouldn't be? I was unnecessarily confrontational with you. This has been a bit of a whirlwind week, as you might suspect, and it was disorienting to learn that somebody saw when Ai-Chin and I first met. It had been a private moment for Ai-Chin and me, one that I thought just belonged to the two of us. It was just a surprise to learn that someone was watching us. She was surprised to hear it too when I told her.

So let's start over. I'm going to guess that we have more in common than we might think, and if we're going to have this correspondence, let's try to do it like men. That's what we are, after all. We are men. You are a man. I can tell you are a man. Men are kinder than women, by nature. We are more forthcoming. You just came out and said what you were thinking and what you wanted. A woman would never do that. This is one of the reasons Ai-Chin and I get along so well. She tells me what she wants. That's rare in a woman.

We share a secret, you and I. Only three people in the world share this secret. You know she got in my car, I know she got in my car, and she knows she got in my car. Have you seen the television? Everyone's trying to find her. I suppose I should have seen that coming. Everybody freaks out when a girl goes missing. I could die in this office and be rotting out for weeks before anyone would even think to look for me. But one little Asian girl goes missing for a couple of days and it's an international incident. That's the world we live in.

The only people who know are the three of us. I don't know how you know. But clearly you do. So let's be friends.

Can we be friends? Tell me about yourself. If it helps, I will tell you a little about myself.

My name is Jonathan. Look. Look at that. I just told you my name. That's more than you have done. I showed you mine. Now show me yours.

Best,

Jonathan

That was it for work for the day.

116

22.

He is reaching out. I shall reach out back. I vow to finish before Marjani runs us out to the Chapel Bell rally.

jon—

gonna call you jon. jon takes fewer letters. hope your cool with that.

i have to ask. is ai-chin ok? she seemed very nice to me. id seen her around a few times. her parents came all the way from china for her. i saw her mom yesterday. you should tell her her mom is here and looking for her. she might want to know that. my mom would be so scared if i disappeared like that. would yours? i bet she would.

you want to know more about me. i spend too much time on reddit like you it looks like hahahaha. im just a regular dude. at home on the computer all the time. you do have a cool car though. does it help you with girls like ai-chin? i bet it does. i have trouble with girls. i dont know really what to say to them. maybe thats why im on reddit all the time hahahahaah

so im a little confused. is ai-chin with you? does she just hang out with you at your house? do you speak chinese? are you guys friends?

does it feel good to talk about this? it does for me. i hope it does for you too.

also my name is tom. but you can call me tom hahaha

tom

SENT. SENT. I sent it. SENT. I shut my computer off, violently, disposing of evidence.

Marjani enters shortly thereafter in a rush. "We are late, we must go, there is Kirby, Kirby will be there."

Also I need to tell them what I know.
Oh yes that too.

I'm eager for us to get there too. The internet has me thinking the indoors world is the worst of all possible worlds. We're in such a hurry, in fact, that we get halfway down Agriculture Drive before we realize we forgot to lock the front door and have to back up and bolt the damn thing up. Upon our return, Marjani stops.

"Daniel, was Travis here late last night?"

No. Why?

"This front porch has mud everywhere," she says. "What a mess." I wheel out to the front door, and she's right. Someone has stomped mud all over our front porch. It's on the steps, it's in front of both windows, there's even mud at the feet of the rocking chair my mom bought when she visited last year. It is a sloppy, sludgy mess. By the front screen door, I see what looks like a boot print.

Why are there footprints on the porch?
It's strange. I don't know.

Marjani sighs. There's no time for this. This is just more shit that has to be cleaned up.

"Probably some drunken undergrad who got lost," she says.

Travis was not here last night. Or at least I didn't hear him. He would have come in, yes? Maybe it was one of the orderlies. But they are, by job definition, meticulous and tidy. Stomping mud all over my porch would be very much out of character.

But there is no time. Marjani sweeps the dried mud off the porch, pushes me down the ramp, and off to campus we go.

23.

A thens is already buzzing. Most professors cancel any class later than 2:00 p.m. on a football Thursday and ignore Friday classes altogether, lest the students openly revolt. Even on such a lovely afternoon, getting from Five Points to downtown is a long trek, and Marjani, who has to keep up with the guy who hates being told he's going too fast, is matted with sweat by the time we arrive. As Marjani and I approach North Campus, we can already hear the chants, a full hour before the big rally for Ai-Chin is supposed to begin.

"Justice! For Ai-Chin! Justice! For Ai-Chin!"

The whole area surrounding the Chapel Bell, from Broad Street all the way down to the UGA Fountain, is swarming with people, and unlike last night's event, this is not a sedate gathering. The crowd feels more like a political rally, or even a protest. Last night was about sadness, about those poor parents and their suffering. But today's rally has an undeniable tinge of anger. There's a woman, probably in her late twenties, standing on the edge of the fountain with a megaphone as a few student volunteers work on constructing the dais, presumably where the university president and the senator and Kirby Smart will be standing later. She is wearing a shirt with a picture of Ai-Chin and the legend WE WILL NOT BE SILENCED. For a shirt that was only conceived and manufactured in the past few days, it's pretty nice.

This woman does not seem like a featured speaker, but she seems to have plenty to say. "The University of Georgia has long attempted to marginalize its Asian students," she yells, "and the foot-dragging on finding out what happened to Ai-Chin Liao is yet another example of it. Do you think it would take two days to start looking for a little white sorority girl who went missing? It is only our voices that are getting them out here to stand for Ai-Chin. Stand up for Ai-Chin!"

The crowd of fifty or so people scream in response: "Stand up for Ai-Chin!"

I'm so fascinated by this woman and this protest that I zoom ahead of Marjani and, frankly, forget she's with me altogether. (I'm soon reminded as she catches up with me and flicks my ear for taking off without her.) The woman speaks for a few more minutes, then hands the bullhorn to someone else. By the time she steps down off the dais, she almost steps on my chair, which was exactly what I was trying to get her to do.

"Oh, I'm sorry, excuse me," she says, and her face softens immediately. She is sweating and her hair is all ruffled and it looks like the speech took a ton out of her. I grunt slightly, *It's OK*, and nod toward Marjani, who, not for the first time, must be my mouthpiece. The woman gives Marjani a quizzical look.

"I am sorry," Marjani says. "My name is Marjani, and I work with Daniel here."

"HELL. LO," I say through my speaker, and try to grin sheepishly.

"Based on the fact that he dragged me over here," Marjani

says, "I think Daniel wants to know more about your organization. I will admit I am curious myself."

The woman smiles again and waves us over, away from the crowd. "Of course," she says. She touches my chair like it's my arm, and I feel suddenly quite warm. She tells us her name is Rebecca Lee, and she grew up in Gwinnett County, about sixty miles away, toward Atlanta. Her parents are both first-generation Chinese immigrants and professors at Emory University. She went to school here at Georgia and stayed on as a graduate student in philosophy and is now getting her doctorate. She'd like to teach someday. I have noticed that she looks at me when she talks, not Marjani. That's always appreciated.

Rebecca has always been involved with Asian American organizations on campus and believes quite strongly that Ai-Chin's disappearance, and the amount of time it took for the university to do anything about it, is indicative of a larger culture of discrimination, not only within the university but in the American scene at large. "People either ignore us or think that we are taking over," she tells us. "We just want to be a part of this school, and this state, and this country, like everyone else."

Marjani interjects: "It does seem like they were searching for Ai-Chin pretty quickly, no?"

Rebecca frowns. "Not quickly enough," she says. "The first twenty-four hours are so important. Now it has been several days, and there are still no leads. It's fairly typical, I'm sad to say."

She then turns back to me. "I'm very glad you came to this," she says. "We need all the help we can get." She hands me a card. "This is my email address," she says. "Contact me anytime. We need more curious minds."

Oh, I have something that will make your mind curious. This woman is absolutely worth expanding the circle for.

I'm just finishing typing "I. Saw. Her" into my speaker box when I see Marjani making the strangest face at me. She is moved by Rebecca? By this rally? No, it's more than that. Her face is stricken in a way that's beyond grief or sadness or empathy. She looks scared. No, more than that: she looks *alarmed*. She looks like there's a bear behind me.

She makes an "Oh!" sound loud enough that Rebecca's soon making the same face.

I have no idea what's going on until I realize, Oh, I get it, I see what they're so worked up about: I can't breathe right now. That's what's causing all the fuss.

I can't breathe. They appear to have noticed before I did.

I have now noticed.

24.

I can swallow, by the way, in case that's something you were idly wondering. This simple statement probably sounds obvious, and maybe a little gross to you, but it's something I'm pretty proud of. Not everybody who has SMA can swallow, and if I lose the ability to do so, I'll never get it back. If you put a straw between my lips—and you're gonna have to do that—I can suck water out of the straw into my mouth, back to my throat, and down my esophagus. It's something that some friends of mine with SMA can't do, and some have never been able to do, but I can. I can swallow. Boom.

I cannot, however, cough. Coughing is not something that most people have much emotional investment in. You do not cough for fun. Coughing is just a thing that happens. It is the scratching of an itch, the blinking of an eye, the clicking of a tongue. I try not to think about what people who don't have SMA take for granted on an everyday basis, because down that path lies madness, and besides, everybody has something they can do that someone else can't: I don't walk around all the time thinking, Man, it's freaking awesome that I can see, I'm so lucky, even though there are blind people all over the planet. I don't expect the able-bodied, if that's how you want to put it, to walk around all day being appreciative of all the things that they've always been able to do and never thought about. Do your thing, dude.

But coughing is something everyone takes for granted. You take it so for granted that you don't even imagine what life would be like if you couldn't do it. You probably didn't even know that some people couldn't do it.

But I can't do it. I've never been able to. SMA is a disease that attacks and degrades the muscles—it's right there in the acronym—and among the most important of these are the intercostal muscles. They are located between your ribs, and basically, they are how you breathe. But when you have SMA, your intercostal muscles are weak, essentially from birth, and muscles that are weak when you have SMA don't get better as you get older. The muscle that allows us to do all of our breathing is the diaphragm. But it needs assistance from those intercostal muscles, and if you have SMA, well, the intercostal muscles aren't much help. Thus our lungs are weaker, we don't produce as much carbon dioxide as the rest of you, and—here's the rough part—our muscles are not strong enough to cough. It is easy to understand SMA if you only think of your legs. Your legs have muscles, SMA is bad for muscles, and thus you can't walk. But coughing requires muscles just like walking does. If you can't walk, that sucks, but it won't kill you. Not being able to cough will kill you.

When your esophagus, or your trachea, or your lungs have something inside them that's not supposed to be there, you cough to get it out. That's literally what coughing is. If you can't get it out, you die. Maybe you choke. Maybe whatever's there gets infected and spreads everywhere. (This is why for many people with SMA, pneumonia is a death sentence.) Maybe

125

it blocks your airway, and you can't dislodge it, and, well, that's it right then and there. You wanna know how people with SMA often die? This is how they often die. Something gets in the way of your mouth and your lungs, and it won't get out, and all it takes is a couple of minutes, and *whoosh* it's over. One minute you're watching a stupid game show and wondering if the host has a hairpiece, and the next minute you can't breathe, and 120 seconds later, you get the grand question answered. There is no warning.

This has happened to me hundreds of times, but it's usually not a big deal. If it happens when I'm sleeping, I don't even notice, because I'm wearing a mask when I sleep. That mask is connected to a cough assist machine, so when I inhale, it gives me some air to expand my lungs, and when I exhale, it provides a sucking force to take in anything that might be blocked in there. As long as whatever is blocking my airway isn't *completely* blocking it, there's enough back and forth in there to dislodge it so I don't have to. You know how you're sometimes scared when you go to sleep because it's dark and you feel helpless? I'm actually safer in the night. I'd be just as safe if I constantly went around the world while awake with that mask on, and people do that, but I'd rather not, myself. I'm not a Stormtrooper.

So anytime I'm out with anyone, we have a cough assist machine with us. It's not massive: it's just a little tank that fits under this Humvee of a wheelchair, along with a whirring battery-powered contraption that provides the sucking motion. You just put it on my face, and within forty-five seconds or so, everything gets back to normal. I just motion to Marjani, or Travis, or whoever happens to be with me, and they know to flip the switch on the machine, take out the tank, and attach the mask to my face. It's not unusual and it's not weird and it's not scary. It is just another of the billion annoying little things that you don't even think about when you have SMA. If I stop breathing for a second, you grab the mask, you put it on, you assume that'll do the trick, you move on with your day.

Except.

Marjani's face is a wall of panic. It takes me a second, but it begins to dawn on me. We were in an unusual rush to get out of the house. Marjani wanted to see Kirby. I wanted to get away from this Jonathan bullshit. I was distracted by the police visit. There was mud on the porch. There's so much activity downtown. It's a beautiful day. There is little in this world lovelier than Athens on a fall day, with people of every stripe and class and demeanor, the stoners and the jocks, the rednecks and the Normaltown hippies, the parents and the grandparents and the children, all in a big green field in the middle of a big green campus, all together, all away from their screens and their troubles and their fears and everything that keeps them awake at night, I believe we went over this. They're here for Kirby, they're here for Ai-Chin, they're here just because it's sunny outside. They're all here, and it's exciting, and life isn't that exciting sometimes, and sometimes when it is, when something special is happening, you get in a hurry to get out and see it, to be a part of it, and you forget that every once in a while some little piece of mucus will appear out of nowhere and lodge itself in your trachea, and when that happens you need a machine to get it out, except that you were in such a rush that you left the fucking machine in the kitchen, right by the blender.

And you realize that you have no idea where your next breath is coming from, or if it is coming at all.

And then you are out.

26

In the movies, when you wake up after some sort of accident, you open your eyes and see the face of a loved one hovering above you, calling out your name, an incantation of love and worry and devotion. You look for the light. They bring you back from the brink.

As someone who has woken up in this situation dozens of times, I regret to inform you that it is not like that at all. First off, you never wake up lying on your back, looking directly up at the ceiling, and thank god for that: that's how dead people lie down. Being alive, and staying alive, requires far more contortion. They've gotta poke you with things and turn you over and upside down and turn your leg this way and your arm that way. You're inevitably twisted up. The first thing you see when you wake up is never someone's face. It's usually your own armpit, or your own ass, or the tile of the floor, or, one memorable time, a friend's cat, looking at you, bewildered, wondering what the hell you're doing down here.

The strangest thing about passing out and then waking up an indeterminate amount of time later is the displacement. It takes a few minutes to answer questions that are rather basic and vital to one's well-being and manner; again, the sort of questions you don't think to ask in the normal day to day. Where am I? How did I get here? How long have I been lying here? Who are these people around me? What happened? Who the hell is that cat?

This time, I wake up to my left foot about six inches from my face. I'm wearing only underwear, a Batman novelty pair I'm suddenly self-conscious about, considering I have no idea who is in the room with me right now. I make a mental note: *No more Batman underwear.* Disabled people have a hard enough time with people thinking we all have the mental capacity of children without them seeing me in Batman underwear. Leave me alone.

There is some sort of beeping sound. The room has ugly fluorescent overhead lighting, bright white everywhere that makes it impossible to figure out any of the questions I have about where I am or who's in here with me. I hear mumblings, and then a very sharp pain in my lower back, like I've been stuck with something. It feels like a needle, but a big one, like someone weaponized a garden hose and jabbed me in the spine with it. There's the whirr of an air conditioner in the corner and a ceiling fan flapping above me, but it still feels about 110 degrees in here. My hair is matted with sweat, and I can feel beads dripping down my neck onto my back. There's a little bit of blood on my right hand. It's probably mine. (I hope it's mine?)

Someone has their hand over my mouth. They're closing it and opening it, rhythmically, in regular intervals; every couple of seconds, they grasp, then release, and grasp, then release. Why are they doing this? Who is this person? And why is their hand so cold? Then I figure it out: I've got a mask on. This is good! A mask is good! Not having a mask was the problem! Someone found a cough assist machine, wherever I am. This means someone is helping me. This means I'm probably in a hospital, or else I'm in the most well-equipped dorm room that has ever existed at the University of Georgia.

Anyway, I'm not dead. This is good!

I pass back out. It takes a lot out of you to nearly die but then not actually die.

I wake up god knows how long later, with my foot no longer in my face. There's no cat in sight. I'm propped over on my side, with my mask still on, but I'm not sure I need it. Nothing seems blocked in my throat or in my lungs, I'm breathing easily and freely, and all told, I feel wholly fantastic, like I've just slept for about three days. I lean my head over to the right and all sorts of joints crack, my neck yelling at me for disturbing its slumber. I open my eyes. The room is less white now. It's just a normal hospital room like all the others.

I'm able to take better stock of the world around me. The television is turned to ESPN with the sound off, though even with the television on mute, I still can faintly hear two middle-aged men screaming at each other. The window shades are closed, but I can tell it's dark outside. How long have I been here? The beeping has not stopped, which means my heart is still going, I guess. The bedsheets are clean and crisp, which means something horrible must have happened on this bed earlier that they had to hide. There's a chart on a clipboard at the end of the bed. Two visitor chairs with folded copies of *Flagpole*, the alternative weekly here in Athens, sit empty against the wall. (I took my online screen name from *Flagpole*, combining it with the old Harvey Danger song "Flagpole Sitta." You know, because I sit all the time. I'm very clever.) There is a picture of former Georgia football coach Vince Dooley mounted in the corner, with his wide signature: "Thanks, Athens Regional, Go Dawgs!" My wheelchair isn't in the room. Maybe they want to make sure I don't make a run for it. Traffic honks and squeaks in the distance. It might be starting to rain. I can hear a faint moan down the hall. My knee hurts.

I finally have my bearings. And I'm still alive.

The door opens. Marjani. Her makeup is running. Marjani has been wearing makeup all this time. I have no idea what women have to do every day. Her hair is poking out from under her headscarf in a way that would upset her if she had any chance of noticing it.

"Oh, Daniel," she says, and throws herself on top of me, emotional in a way I'm not sure I enjoy. I grunt a little, and she lets up and brushes a strand of hair out of her face. "I'm sorry, I was so scared."

Thank you. Am I OK?
Yes. We got you here in time.
Are you OK?
[A silent, sad nod. She wipes her eyes.]
How did I get here?

"There was a police officer," she says. "She saw me panicking because I couldn't get you unblocked, and you were starting to turn blue, and she ran over to you and started giving you mouth to mouth." I chuckle. Everyone always wants to do this. It doesn't help, but it does make them look heroic.

"After I got her off you, a man picked you up and carried you out of the park," Marjani says. "That nice woman Rebecca had her car nearby, and we drove here immediately. Someone called nine-one-one, but we did not have time to wait. We got you in the building and they put the mask on you immediately.

132

But we were very frightened. It looked like you had barely been breathing for a considerable amount of time."

I look down at my body. It is cut and scraped and bloodied, from my ankle all the way up to my thigh, on both legs. I raise a Groucho to Marjani.

She begins to cry. "The man did drop you at first," she says, and she puts her head in her hands. She feels terrible about this, but she shouldn't: the idea of a Good Samaritan attempting to help what he sees as this poor cripple who can't breathe but then bouncing me off the pavement the minute he picked me up is objectively hilarious. Did everybody gasp? Did they think he was *trying* to body-slam me? It's like an absurdist sketch. *I'm here to help! To the rescue! But first: We must dribble him like a basketball!* My chest starts heaving up and down, and Marjani leaps to attention before she realizes I am laughing. She smiles, and I suspect it's the first time she's smiled in several hours.

I don't know if I've ever seen Marjani so worried.

The door opens again. Kramer comes bounding into the room, studio audience applause, look, everybody, it's our wacky friend Travis from across the hall. He has a policeman with him. It's our old friend Officer Wynn Anderson.

"Dude, what the hell," Travis says. "No wonder I couldn't find you at that rally, see." He looks me over. "Did you pick a fight with a wolverine?" He lays his hand on my head gently and puts the straw in a glass of water in my mouth. He whistles lightly. "This shit never freaks me out any less."

I look at Detective Anderson. Our eyes meet in recognition. He is trying to keep his composure, and failing. I give him a wink.

I notice there's a woman behind him. She doesn't seem to mind that the rest of the room has completely forgotten she is there. "Hi, I'm Jennifer," she says. "We met at the rally." I remember. She was nice. "Wow, are you OK?"

Unlike nearly every other person who sees me in this state, she's not talking to me as if I am a three-year-old, or staring past me like a tree stump. She's looking right in my eyes. I like this girl already, and I feel like everything is going to be just fine.

Detective Anderson speaks up. "Listen, Daniel, I just wanted to make sure you were all right, but Travis has been telling me some rather pertinent information that I was, uh, unable to procure during our visit yesterday." He is still a massive man, but when he is unsure of himself, he is back to being a boy wearing a police officer's costume that is too big for him. "When you are, um, better, well, adjusted, I will come by and we can file a report."

When I nod at him, he looks away. I notice an Atlanta Falcons tattoo on his left biceps. He is eleven years old.

I look at Marjani.

Can I get out of here?

"There's a doctor coming to check on you, but yes, I think they're going to let you go. They got the mucus out of your throat, and everything else is checked out. They even did a . . . Oh my, what happened here?" She rolls me over, and we realize that there is a small pool of blood in the bed, right where my lower back just was.

"Oh, shit," Travis says. "Check this out. It's a nail." It is a nail. There is a tiny nail in the bed. That would be the garden hose I felt earlier. How the hell did that get there? Why is there a nail in my bed?

Jennifer chuckles. "Of all the possibilities, you're gonna die of lockjaw," she says. Like I said, I like this girl.

27

So the question you're asking yourself is: Why am I not dead? While the occurrence of something blocking my airway is a fairly common one, not having the tank and the suction mask there to clear it is not. If that mucus was in there, and I couldn't get it out, and it blocked my airway for longer than, say, two minutes, . . . why am I not dead?

In the back of Travis's truck, Marjani attempts to explain it to me.

Of all the reasons to love Travis, the fact that he has custom-fitted his F-150 truck so I can ride in the cargo bed is maybe the best one. A couple of weeks after I moved out here, he and his mom went out to a body shop and asked them if they could construct some sort of contraption for me to lock my chair into. The mechanic, an older, burly goateed man named Bryan who said he had a son with cystic fibrosis, accepted the challenge and built, somehow, a four-tiered system to let me ride along in the back of the truck. We call it the Woolly Mammoth. The tiers:

1. ELEVATION. You have to get me and my chair in the thing. Bryan built a mini conveyor that carries me to the front

of the bed of the truck and locks me into a seat, with my head facing away from Travis's back window out onto the street. I like to give a thumbs-up, when I can, to the people behind us in traffic. They go nuts.

2. ENCLOSURE. The chair clicks in and then has lock bars on each wheel that clang into place to make sure I don't go rolling off the back of the truck every time Travis accelerates.

3. BUCKLAGE. Bryan put in industrial-strength seat and chest belts that he procured from an Air Force friend who stripped them out of an old fighter jet. This absolutely fucking rules just as much as it sounds like it does. You can ride my tail anytime, Maverick.

4. COPILOT. There's another chair for my caregiver, right next to mine, with straps and belts and lock bars of its own.

When we ride in it, Marjani and I end up looking like the king and queen of the most redneck Fourth of July parade you've ever seen, just two goofs ridin' off the back of a truck. This contraption is entirely safe, but not entirely legal. The visual is so striking and people love it so much that every cop who has ever seen it just asks where we had it done, though. I wouldn't recommend taking me off-roading, and it's probably best to avoid freeways and interstates, but driving around downtown Athens, we cut quite a figure.

As for me, I get to have the wind whipping around my head at forty miles an hour with the sun on my face.

For what it's worth, Marjani hates the Mammoth, and she particularly hates trying to talk to me in the Mammoth, and she *particularly* hates trying to talk to me in the Mammoth when she has been crying because she feels guilty because she thinks she may have just almost killed me.

"You were not entirely blocked!" she yells, trying to be heard over the engine and the wind and all the rustle of a game-day Thursday night in Athens on Broad Street. I lean toward her, trying to make my eyebrows ask a follow-up question, but they're all tearstained and runny right now anyway. It is difficult to communicate with Marjani in the back of the Woolly Mammoth, but it's worth it because we're outside and it's nice out and the wind is making my hair stand up everywhere and I just almost died.

"It was just a small piece! It was blocking you for a second, and that's why you couldn't breathe, and that's why you passed out!" We're at a stoplight. She pauses to catch some air and wipe her eyes. Marjani has had a long day. "While you were out, and we were all running around, part of the plug must have dislodged and cleared out. That's what let you breathe again. Ooooomph!" Travis hit the gas a little too hard. He always accelerates faster than he needs to at a green light, mostly because he knows I like it and Marjani hates it. She really despises the Woolly Mammoth.

She pounds the window. "Travis! Stop that!" I can hear him laughing through the wind. Jennifer, still sitting next to him even though she just met him about two days ago and has spent most of that time commiserating about a missing girl and helping his disabled friend with the disease she surely still doesn't entirely understand, laughs along with him. What a second date.

Marjani composes herself and continues. "So you just were lucky. This is what I feel so terrible about, Daniel. The only reason we did not lose you today is because a chunk of that mucus broke off. That is pure luck."

I look at her.

Gimme a second, I have a joke.
This is not a laughing matter, Daniel.
Just hang on, will ya?

I furiously tap my phone to activate my voice box. I screw
up and have to start over. She taps her foot.

I do not feel like laughing right now, and I do not understand
why you would want to, either.
Dammit, Marjani, just hang on a second.
I have no idea why that piece fell off.

Got it. My speaker booms.
"It. Fell. Off. Because. That. Guy. Dropped. Me."
Marjani smiles, wanly, so exhausted, not ready to be chuckling about this but relieved that I am. "I am just glad you are
OK. But my mistake is unacceptable." She stops. "Unacceptable. I could have killed you, Daniel. I was in a hurry, and I
am doing too much, and there is so much activity, and I ran off
without your tank. I cannot believe that I did that. It is unacceptable."
I meet her eyes again.

Stop. It happens. I forgot too.
It is my job to protect you.
*No. It is your job to be here for me. And you were. You are. You
are here right now.*

I look over to my left.

*And we are home. I am safe. You are safe. We are lucky. Let's go
home.*

138

The Woolly Mammoth rumbles to a stop, and Travis and Jennifer hop out of the truck and drop the cab door down. She jumps into the bed of the truck and unstraps me and unhooks the chair like an old pro. I look up at her quizzically. "Well you can't sit there all day," she says.

Marjani remains behind, still quiet, still looking down. I grunt toward her, trying to get her up, to get her going. This isn't her fault. I'm a guy with a disease that eventually kills everybody who has it, and eventually it's going to kill me. I am glad it wasn't today. I hope it's not for a long, long time. But let's not kid ourselves. It's going to happen, and when it happens, I don't want Marjani or Travis or my mom or this Jennifer person who is suddenly the matriarch of this weird little family to be kicking themselves up and down over it.

I can't have Marjani doing this. I can't have anyone doing this. Today was scary. But they're all scary. We can't fret around the planet waiting for something to kill us, or worried something's going to kill someone we love. I'm not going to stare off into the void waiting for it all to end. I sure as hell am not going to let her do that either. I demand better company than that.

Before I can grunt again, Jennifer, without warning, bonks Marjani on the nose with a rolled-up pamphlet, like a dog who peed on the rug again, with a cartoon "Boop." This woman. Has she even met Marjani?

"Out of the truck, lady," she says. "Colbert's on in twenty minutes."

Marjani, formidable, terrifying, weary, wonderful, looks at her, this strange woman who came out of nowhere and started acting like she owns the place. She stares at her for a beat, another beat, far too long. I see Jennifer's back tense up.

Then Marjani pulls her hand into her sleeve, raises her arm, and lightly taps Jennifer on the nose.

"Boop."

I try to laugh but can't. The moment of levity, and my slight gasp in response, appears to snap Marjani back into attention. As soon as we're in the front door, she commences cleaning the place, straightening up, returning to default mode. She's begun to sweep up the kitchen when she stops suddenly.

"What in the world?" she says. "There is mud *everywhere*."

There is. The entire kitchen floor is caked with wet, sloppy mud. Not dried mud, either, but fresh mud, with glops of rainwater dripping across the floor and a pungent, humid smell that feels . . . recent. Marjani turns to Travis to yell at him, but he took his shoes off when he walked in. Jennifer's shoes are right next to his. This mess is new. And it is not ours.

I look up at Marjani.

Was one of the orderlies here?
They are not usually here so early. And they are never so rude.
This is gross. What is this?
I do not know. Who has been in this room?
Marjani.
Yes?
I am very tired.

"Of course you are, of course you are, I am sorry," she says. She wheels me into my bedroom and has started to unbutton my shirt when my phone starts whirring and braying at me. FaceTime is ringing. A smiling, tanned face looks back at me. She had that picture taken in Barbados last year. She was with some guy. Frank? Carl?

Oh. Mom. There is so much happening.

140

28

Yes, yes, I can get him on the FaceTime. Hang on one moment, Angela."

We're back home, and I'm tired, and everybody's tired, and man, what a day, but once she heard about all that went down today, I can hardly blame Mom wanting to check in.

It occurs to me that I have no idea where my mother is right now. When I talk to Mom, I sit in my chair and look at the computer screen so she can see me through FaceTime and then talk with her through Gchat. I don't entirely understand why this is satisfying for her, considering all she's watching me do is move my joystick in response to whatever she is saying, but I guess she likes to see me, crammed into my chair and all dolled up in my pajamas like a six-year-old. (I hate these pajamas.) Plus, it's an hour earlier in Illinois, so maybe she's not as drained as the rest of us.

She's not at her house now, anyway. I feel like I see a pool behind her. A beach? There's a shadowy figure moving in and out of the background, a male figure, some sort of droning noise, maybe drying his hair or something, I can't really tell. Who is that guy? Where is she?

"You look awful."

(. . .)

(. . .)

(. . .)

Thank you. That's very nice, Mom.

"Marjani told me about all of it. Don't blame her for what happened. That used to happen to me too. I know it should be easy to remember that tank, but it just isn't. I tried to keep it in the chair all the time so I didn't have to think about it."

(. . .)

(. . .)

(. . .)

I do not blame her. Where are you?

"I'm in Jamaica! I'm at a resort here with a . . . friend of mine. From work! School hasn't gotten back from break yet, so I wanted to sneak in one last trip before all the students return."

I am curious who that "friend from work" in the background is, but again, it has been a long day. She can tell me later if she wants to.

(. . .)

(. . .)

(. . .)

I hope you are having a good day. I am very tired, Mom.

"I understand, I understand! I just wanted to check in on you. It has been a while since you had one of those."

She looks worried, but unflustered. I'm sure Marjani minimized the seriousness of what happened, and it's not like she can really tell much over FaceTime anyway. She seems . . . light and silly. I am happy for her. And I am not going to break her reverie.

She begins to giggle at something she sees just off-screen, and now I am no longer curious and do not want to know any more. "Stop, stop!" she says to whoever, some hulking dude probably dripping with coconut oil, in a Speedo, balancing some sort of fruit on his genitals, who knows, good for her, I guess. "Stop it! I'm talking to my son, sheesh!"

She brushes some hair out of her face, pulls it back in a ponytail, and puts on a hat. "Well, we're off to go play some tennis," she says, and suddenly I'm really confused about Jamaica's time zone. "Tell Marjani to keep me updated on anything that's happening over there. I'm just glad you are OK." She wags a finger at the screen. "Don't forget that tank."

(. . .)

(. . .)

(. . .)

I won't.

I pause.

(. . .)

I'm putting on a brave front here, and I want her to have a good time, but . . .

(. . .)

. . . I dunno, I guess I *am* a little shaken up by today? I can't get my heart to slow down tonight. I can't get myself straight.

(. . .)

Why, I wonder? Is it just that it has been a while since something this scary went down? Maybe it's just a matter of getting older. I'm in my mid-twenties, which is the prime of life for all of you but creaky old age for someone with SMA.

(...)

All those other kids I grew up with who had SMA? A large percentage of them are dead now. There's a friend back in Illinois who is hanging in, but he's bedridden full time, living on his parents' farm, never leaving the house, idling, whittling away the days until there aren't any left. There's a girl I met up with a couple of times in Atlanta who is in better shape than I am, and she even has a boyfriend. (She told me she once broke her hip while they were making out, though that was a few years ago.) But otherwise: Not a lot of us still kicking around. The kids growing up today with SMA, they're gonna be able to last longer. They'll have been on Spinraza since they were babies, working up their strength. If I had been born two decades later, I would have had a better chance to make it into my forties, my fifties, even my sixties.

(...)

But I'd be kidding myself if I didn't admit I *do* feel a little weaker every day. I recover more slowly. The little aches and pains linger more than they used to. Getting out of bed irritates me. I have always taken pride in my desire to meet the morning, to meet *life*, with vigor and enthusiasm and an appreciation of the world I'm so lucky to get to embrace. But I can feel myself getting more tired.

(...)

I want to tell you this, Mom. I just feel so fragile sometimes, you know? You raised me not to feel that way. I have never felt that way. I have worked to make sure I did not feel that way. But I do. I feel fragile. I feel weak. I feel *in danger*.

(. . .)

Also . . . there is this man. And this girl. And he knows I saw him take her. And he wears these boots. And there were boot prints on my porch. And what is going on in my kitchen? There is just so much happening, Mom.

(. . .)

Can I tell you this? Should I tell you this? I do not want to ruin your vacation. It looks beautiful there, and your friend from work looks ready for his tennis.

(. . .)

"Daniel? Daniel, you still there, buddy?"

(. . .)

(. . .)

(. . .)

Yes, Mom. I am just tired. Have a wonderful time. We will talk when you are back. I love you.

"I love you too, honey. Take good care of Travis. And yourself."

I'm gonna do my best, Mom. I always do.

29

Marjani seems to notice I'm a bit off, and understandably she credits it to today's near-death experience. Her assessment of the situation is correct, but only partially, in a way I still haven't entirely figured out myself. Either way: I need to get some sleep.

"You all good here?" Travis says. "Jennifer and I are gonna go hit the Manhattan bar downtown, maybe get a nightcap."

"You call a drink at ten p.m. a nightcap?" Jennifer says, tugging on the bottom lapel of his shirt. "You *are* old."

She walks over to me. I am in my pajamas, lying in bed, under an extra blanket tonight. It's not cold outside, but it sure feels cold. It feels cold everywhere. Jennifer is not fazed by my vulnerable appearance, or that we've just met, or that she almost saw me die tonight. She puts her hand on my chest. "You kick ass, dude," she says, and leans over and kisses my forehead. "We need more like you."

Marjani smiles and puts another pillow under my head after they leave.

"Are you OK?" she asks. She sits down next to me and starts lightly stroking my left leg. This question is much more for her than it is for me. And frankly, I'm more worried about her. I am certain following me around from campus to the hospital to here has forced her to call in to one of her other jobs. I cannot be her lone responsibility. She is going above and beyond here.

I am fine. Are you fine?
I am better. I was just so scared.
Me too. I still am. But not about this. Not exactly.

"I am going to stay here tonight, Daniel, if that is OK with you," she says. "I have to get to the tailgate early tomorrow morning, and it will be easier if I just sleep here."

I am relieved.

I am relieved. I want you here. I know you have other places to be. I am grateful.
What a day, Daniel.

I bet there is an email from him waiting for me. But I cannot deal with that right now. I must sleep. I must rest. Marjani shuts down my computer and grabs the remote to turn off the television. A high school football game has just ended, and the evening news, the same Atlanta NBC affiliate with all my morning friends, is beginning its opening segment.

"Students in Athens held a vigil tonight for a missing student," says the perky lady at the desk, "and the football team, on the eve of game day, is getting involved. Our own Jimmy Daulerio has the story."

A ten-year-old child holding a microphone wider than his torso comes on-screen. Television reporters are going to be infants in a decade, I tell you.

"Thanks, Marianne. On Friday, a Chinese national studying veterinary medicine here at the University of Georgia named Ai-Chin Liao was on her way to her morning classes when she disappeared, somewhere in the campus area. And now a student group is trying to find her."

We see footage of the rally, and then of the students gathering, and candles, and vigils. Then our friend Rebecca is on the screen, talking to ten-year-old Jimmy. She's identified as REBECCA LEE, CONCERNED ASIAN, which, uh, is maybe not the best chyron I've ever seen.

"Her parents are here, and we're just trying to make them feel comfortable and welcome," Rebecca says. "It's obviously a terrible situation."

Jimmy again. "I had the opportunity to talk to Georgia head football coach Kirby Smart, whose Bulldogs play Middle Tennessee State on Saturday at Sanford Stadium. He told me he's just trying to help out a community searching for answers."

Smart, like all football coaches a little too intense and a little too certain of himself, but otherwise essentially decent, says, "We just hope they find the girl. We have faith in local law enforcement and pray that girl can be found. I just wanted to be here to show the campus that we're behind them." I half expected him to go sprinting onto the field right then and there.

Then we get our montage of Concerned Students, and Worried Onlookers, and a brief interview with the Clarke County sheriff, who says they are "exploring all possible leads" and not much else. Then more montage, and more sad students, and then a long line of Asian students with their arms linked together in solidarity and then—

HOLY SHIT HOLY SHIT HOLY SHIT HOLY SHIT

I spasm so hard I almost fall out of bed. Marjani leaps over to me and grabs me like I'm going to jump out the window.

"Daniel, what is it, what is happening?" she says, real panic in her eyes.

I stare at the television.

"Mmmmph. Mmmmmph. Mmmmmmmphhhhhhhhhhh!!!!!"

In the long chain of mostly female Asian students locking arms to show their support for Ai-Chin, there is a man. The chain is filmed from a distance, so you cannot see anyone's face, but he's a white man. He is well-dressed, like a teaching assistant or a graduate student, and he is wearing a hat. They appear to all be singing a song, and he is singing along with them, part of the vigil, one of the devastated students of the University of Georgia trying to come to terms with this tragedy on this campus. He has his left arm around one young Chinese American student, and his right arm around another. He is part of the chain.

His hat is Thrashers blue. I have seen this man before.

HOLY SHIT HOLY SHIT HOLY SHIT.

I look, surely crazy-eyed, at Marjani, then back at the television, then back at her, then back again.

"Mmmmph. Mmmmmph. Mmmmmmmphhhhhhhhhhh!!!!!"

FRIDAY

30

Here is a story about Travis:

About ten years ago, when I was in high school, my mom picked me up from school in her old van, the one that didn't have the hydraulics in it yet, so that she always had to get one of the janitors and gym teachers to help carry me and my chair through the back door, like an old unwieldy couch or something. No matter what else she had going on, she always picked me up from school, and never a minute late. A lot of kids with SMA go to special schools, where there are no "regular" kids, but Mom wanted as normal a life as I could have. My SMA hadn't progressed as much in high school as it has now. You could just wheel me to the back of class and let me be as bored as everybody else.

Anyway, this day she was several minutes late. She showed up as frazzled as I'd seen her, with hair mussed and makeup running down her cheek and two buttons on her blouse in the wrong order. My mother is organized and structured and always, *always* composed, so my presumption was that she'd been in a car crash on the way over, or maybe attacked by a bear.

Halfway to the house, she turned off I-45 onto a sad, freezing stretch of country road and drove, silently, until you couldn't see a car for miles in any direction. She pulled over, shut the car off, and sat there, her head in her hands. Her shoulders heaved, and her breath blew heavy clouds through her hair. I had no idea what was going on. I tried to help. "Mom, are you going to kill and bury me out here, or do you just have to pee?" She snorted a half ton of snot through both nostrils in a laugh, and I realized she was sobbing.

"Shut up," she said, and then she unbuckled her safety belt and crawled through the bed of the van to sit next to me. She touched my hand. She always makes sure to touch me. Another deep breath, an exhale so deep that I briefly couldn't see her face. "Daniel," she said, and right then I knew—I had no idea how, I just knew. She didn't even need to tell me that she'd just gotten back from the doctor, and that the lump she'd told me not to worry about was cancer, and that she would lose her hair and her breast and God knows what else.

I knew, and she knew that I knew, so she stopped talking and just grabbed me and squeezed me like I was able-bodied, like I was strong. There I was, a lump of flesh and bones in a chair, in the back of a frigid van in the middle of nowhere Central Illinois, and I was keeping her upright. She squeezed me until finally I grunted, and she let go, wiped her nose, said sorry, and lightly clenched my face.

"We're a couple of pieces of work, aren't we?"

I smiled. "Let's go home, Mom."

The news devastated everyone who knew my mom, the way everyone is always devastated when they realize someone they had thought to be indestructible has turned out to be most definitely not. Nobody knows how to be around someone who is going through chemotherapy and fighting for their life, and they certainly don't know what to say to them when their death will mean their son will likely be shuttled off to a home where he'll surely die alone in the next fifteen years. (To be fair, neither Mom nor I was great about tackling that thorny little bean either.) I joked with Mom at the time that she now finally understood part of what it was like being me all the time; the oh-you-poor-dear look that I got all the time was now a part of her reality too.

The one person my mom relied on during this time, other than me, was Travis's mom. (Mom told me years later that she got an email from my dad three weeks into chemo that read, with no subject line, "You OK? I heard you were sick.—R," which is as close as anyone got to *actually* saying "Fuck off and die.") Travis's mom was over at our house essentially every night, making dinner and putting me to bed so Mom could rest, before heading back home to Travis and her own family. She never made a big deal about helping us, or about Mom being sick, or any of it. I never saw her cry, or show any pity, or ask me how I was feeling. She just came in, took care of what needed to get done, bugged me about my homework, and generally acted like everything was perfectly fine and nothing unusual was happening at all. It was the nicest thing anyone has ever done for either one of us.

The message filtered down to Travis, who never once asked me how my mom was doing, or if I were OK, or if I needed anything. He just did the same thing he always did: used every opportunity when his mom and my mom were away to go smoke weed behind our shed and then come inside and play video games with me. Teenage boys have their limitations, but they are uniquely skilled at dealing with pain. *Just get stoned and play video games.* It's really ingenious. People should have Comfort Teens during tragic periods in their lives to help them deal with grief, just sixteen-year-old pimply-faced slack-jawed morons who follow them around and shrug a lot. Travis was perfect because I didn't want to think about what was happening, let alone talk about it, and he gave me hours upon hours of not having to think or talk about it. He just never brought it up. He'd come by, knock on the side door, look around, make sure neither my mom nor his mom was home, smoke a joint, come inside, flip me a controller, and sit next to me while we played *Call of Duty* for hours. We wouldn't say a word other than "Look out for that dude!" and "Yeah, EAT THIS YOU NAZI FUCK!" and it was the entire world. It got me through that whole time.

One day a package arrived at our front door, delivered at night, late, way later than UPS usually came by. Mom and I had fallen asleep on the couch watching an old *Larry Sanders* rerun, and the doorbell woke her up. Groggy and weak, she opened the Amazon package. Inside was, simply, a button. It was like the beginning of a *Twilight Zone* episode. The button was just a big red plastic thing, like one of those Staples Easy Buttons. There was no packaging, no note, no clue as to what this was or where it had come from.

She laid it on the coffee table in front of the couch. We looked at it, puzzled. What was this button? Why had it been sent to us? What would happen if you pushed it?

Mom looked at me. She was fully bald then, wan, pale, empty. She had taken to calling herself "Skeletor." She glanced at the button, then back at me, then back at the button.

"Should I push it?"

"I don't know, Mom. I'm a little scared of it."

"Fuck it. I'm pushing it."

She took as deep a breath as she could, all raspy and rattling, and touched my upper arm. "Here goes."

The second she hit the button, a loud, wailing siren went off.

"WOOOOO . . . WOOOOOO . . . WOOOOOOOOOOOOOOO!" The button lit up and began flashing wildly. "WOOOOOO. . . . WOOOOOO. . . . WOOOOOOO!" Then:

"FART DETECTED! FART DETECTED! CLEAR THE AREA! A FART HAS BEEN DETECTED!"

Mom picked up the button and read the labeling on the bottom. It was, in fact, a fart detector. *When a fart is detected, hit the button to warn the village!* "FART DETECTED! FART DE-TECTED! CLEAR THE AREA!"

I swear, Mom just about coughed up every cell in her body, she was laughing so hard. I don't think either of us had smiled in weeks, and God, we laughed and laughed and laughed. At one point I actually fell out of my chair, and I fell on the floor, still heaving, and Mom looked at me and just laughed even harder. I rolled around, and then she got down there with me. We hit that button, over and over again, for an hour.

It sat on our coffee table for months. But in the week after we received it, we still had no idea where it had come from. Why was it delivered to our house? Was it a mistake? Did one of us order it while sleepwalking? Was it a message from God? Nearly ten days went by before the mystery was solved. Travis came by for one of his visits, and after several hours of *Call of Duty*, he stood up, every bone and joint cracking and popping, to grab another Mountain Dew out of the fridge. On the way to the kitchen, he saw the fart detector and, like everyone else who ever saw it in our house, began to chuckle.

He loped back into the study. "Aw, I see you got the package."

I looked over at him. "What?"

"Yeah, I totally forgot I ordered that, man," he said. "I was just home one night and thinking about how bummed out you and your mom looked, so I figured you all could use a laugh, see. So"—he paused dramatically here, as if about to reveal the solution to a particularly difficult algebra problem—"Fart detector!"

"Why . . . why didn't you bring it over yourself? Or let us know you were the one who sent it?"

"Huh, I dunno," he said. "I guess I just forgot, see. Well, I'm glad she liked it. You ready? Unpause the game, let's go."

That's Travis. That's a guy you weld yourself to.

31

There was an email the next morning, of course. This is that email:

Tom—

Thank you for the compliment about the car. I need to get it washed. It's just . . . been a little busy lately. You know how it goes.

I must say that the car has never helped much with girls. They are hard to talk to, no? These college girls are the worst. They'd rather stare at their phone than actually interact with the world. They're always complaining about guys, how mean they are, but there are nice guys everywhere around them, if they'd just look. They never look. Some of us are right here, standing right in front of them. If only they'd look.

One of the nice things about Ai-Chin is that she was friendly and smiling every time I saw her. I'd seen her walking down Southview for a couple of weeks too. (I really am surprised I've never seen you, by the way. I've never seen anybody out there. I am usually there quite early, to be fair.) It's a nice neighborhood you live in—isolated, but still connected to everything you'd need. Someone like her can just walk down the street there and not worry about getting run over by a drunk college student or raped by some guy from the projects. She can just be a happy smiling person. It's hard to find those places anymore, you know? That's why I always liked her when I'd pass her on my morning drive. She just walked along like nothing bad existed in the world. She was innocent. I didn't have to swipe right to find her, and she didn't have to swipe left to reject me. We could just meet like regular people, out in the world. No judgments.

It's the judging that's the hardest.

But she is fine. It is nice of you to ask. We are becoming closer. I think she is beginning to trust me. And I might someday be able to trust her.

Best,

Jonathan

32

There isn't much time to digest and recover from last night, because there is a large adult child wearing a police officer's uniform in my kitchen.

I really am feeling fine, by the way. Each one of these incidents takes a little bit out of you, no question. This is the thing about a progressive disease. You don't so much heal as much as you just adjust to your new reality. There's a tiny scratch, an irritating little *nick*, on the inside of my esophagus that wasn't there yesterday that I woke up with today, and it's going to be there the rest of my life. Is it from the phlegm that got stuck? Is it from when the guy dropped me? Is it just a general weakening of my lungs? Hey, maybe it's all three! It doesn't matter. It is just the way I am now. Every breath will now come with a small whistle in my chest, a pinprick of an *oomph* every time I draw air, until I die. That happened yesterday. Today is always different than yesterday.

It would be nice if I could communicate all this to the massive police officer sitting in my kitchen this morning, drinking out of a too-hot mug of cheap mass-produced coffee that was surely sitting in the cabinet for months. No one ever makes coffee in this house, and it took Marjani twenty minutes to find it. But apparently Officer Anderson needs his coffee, and he is doing his honest best right now to choke down a brew made from beans harvested sometime during the Carter administration.

"Thank you for the coffee, ma'am," he says, though I think his eyes are starting to run.

"You are very welcome," Marjani says. "Travis, would you like a cup?"

"You know I could probably use one, see," Travis says, and he's not kidding. I do not remember the last time I saw him before 11:00 a.m. He looks like the Crypt Keeper. "But I think I might be better off snorting rat poison, right?"

Officer Anderson turns his head slowly to him.

"Oh, I don't snort anything. I didn't mean to say that. I'm clean. Clean living. Just say no."

"I think it would be wise for you to stop talking, Travis," Marjani says.

"Totally agreed, Mar'," Travis mumbles, and stares intently at his suddenly quite fascinating left thumb. "Right there with you."

Officer Anderson clears his throat. It makes a huge rumble that echoes throughout the room. "OK, so I talked to Travis last night at the rally, before everything went down, and he told me you had some information for me that I was, uh, unable to procure on our last visit," he says. He's big, but seriously so young. I notice that his beard covers a not-inconsiderable amount of acne, and his face is round, almost roly-poly. I am definitely older than he is.

Marjani takes some bread out of the toaster, butters it, and puts it in front of Travis and the officer. He nods thank you but doesn't even glance at it. His eyes are darting all over the room. I can't be the first disabled person he's ever met, can I?

"So, what can you tell me, Daniel, about Ai-Chin?"

I look at Travis.

So how do we do this?

How about I just talk, and you nod if you agree and shake your head if you don't?

I am not sure we should introduce anything you say into official police evidence.

Laugh it up, shithead.

"All right, so here's the deal, see," Travis launches in, and it's sort of charming to watch him attempt to give this presentation, like he's a visiting lecturer with a slide projector or something. But only momentarily.

"Daniel's all outside, on the porch, see."

"This porch?"

"What?"

"The porch at this house."

"Yes. Yeah. This porch. This house."

"What day?"

"What?"

"What day?"

"The day she vanished?"

"So, Friday?"

"Friday! Wait, Friday, right? Is that the day she disappeared?" Travis looks at me. I nod. *Jesus, man.* "Yes, Friday."

"What time?"

"The morning."

"What time of morning?"

"Breakfast time."

Officer Anderson sighs heavily. "*What time?*"

"I don't know."

He looks at me. I activate my voice recorder: "Seven twenty-two."

"Is that an exact time?" he asks.

"Yaws."

"What's that?"

Shit. "Yes. Yes. Yes. Exact time."

"Thank you." He turns back to Travis. "OK. He's on the porch."

"And he sees her walking down the street."

"Was that the first time he saw her on the street?"

"Yes. No, wait, no. Wait. Shit, I don't actually know. Daniel, was the first time you saw her? Did you tell me? I might have forgotten. I've had a lot going on, see!"

I see Officer Anderson, exasperated with Travis already, look at me. I nod. Maybe we can just eliminate the middleman here.

"Look," Officer Anderson says, "maybe I'll talk directly to Daniel, and you can chime in when I need, um, clarification."

It's probably for the best that I take over here. You're gonna get arrested for something if you keep talking.

Shut up.

Don't tell him you have weed on you.

I don't have weed on me.

You always have weed on you.

Shut up.

"So, Daniel, can you tell me: Did you see Ai-Chin that Friday morning?"

"Yes."

"Do you see her every morning?"

"Most."

"Did she ever see you?"

I look at Travis.

Just that morning.

Just that morning?

Just that morning.

"Just that morning," Travis says, very proud of himself.

"OK," Officer Anderson says. "Are you sure it was her?"

Yes. Finally. "Yes."

"At seven twenty-two."

"Yes."

"And Travis says you then saw her get in a vehicle of some sort?"

"Yes."

"Did you see what kind of car?"

"Yes." I pause to type out *Camaro* a couple of times. My phone keeps wanting to make it Crayola for some reason. "A tan Camaro."

"Did you see the person driving it?"

"A little."

"What does that mean?"

"I saw a hat. And a chrome-tipped boot."

"But not his face."

"No."

But I have more information than even Travis knows I know.

Marjani cuts in. "Daniel believes he saw the man on the television last night," she says.

"What?" Travis says. "Does he have a show?"

Yeah, it's Jimmy Kimmel, dumbass.
Again: Shut up.

Officer Anderson has had enough of this slapstick. To me, Travis and I are communicating in the way we have since we were children, a system we have mastered, sort of our version of twin language. But yeah: to him it's just a confused stoner staring at a disabled man lightly bobbing his head left and right. He slaps his hand on the table a little harder than he meant to, snapping us all to attention.

"Wait, what?" he says, pushing his coffee mug to the side. "You saw him on *television*?"

I tap furiously into my speaker.

"News. Vigil. Boot. Hat."

Marjani coughs and starts to pour Officer Anderson more coffee before realizing his cup is still full. Apparently coffee beans do eventually spoil.

She clears her throat. Officer Anderson is scribbling furiously in his notebook.

"We were watching the news last night after Daniel's incident," she says, "and he says the man in the car was at the vigil and captured on video." I notice a hint of skepticism in her voice, which I don't like.

"Did you see his face in the video?"

"No. Far away. But him. Boots. Hat."

Officer Anderson folds up his notebook and puts it in his pocket. He has had enough of this. "Well, this is certainly more information than I got when I was over here the other day," he says. He starts to stand up. "I am very appreciative of all of this. We'll get a copy of that tape—maybe that'll tell us something."

He looks at me. "Um, you've really been very helpful. We

now know what time she disappeared. We wouldn't have had that information without you. So thank you."

But I'm not done giving information. He can't leave yet. "Wait. Wait. Wait."

I look at Officer Anderson. "Email. We email."

He frowns, sneaks a fleeting, perturbed look at Travis, and shifts in his chair. Travis coughs.

"Yeah, um, your friend told me about that. He forwarded me the emails. We know all about that guy."

I look at him, baffled. What?

"Yeah, that's a man named Jonathan Carpenter. He lives out in East Athens. We've dealt with him before."

I wheel my chair toward him, and he jumps back a bit. I think he forgot I can move.

"Jonathan. Carpenter."

"Yeah, this is, um, this is kind of what he does," Officer Anderson says. "He's known all around the department for trying to pretend he's involved in crimes. We've been dealing with him for a couple of years now. He claimed responsibility for two sorority break-ins last year. He also tried to convince the guy a few desks over from mine that he was going to rob a bank. None of it was true. He's just a disturbed individual who lives by himself and, I think, just wants police to pay attention to him. I actually went out with my old partner and visited him after he called a tip line claiming that his neighbor was abducting high school girls and hiding them in his shed. His neighbor didn't even *have* a shed. He just calls to feel important. I think he is lonely. He's a sick individual."

I think he is a lonely individual.

"Travis told us . . . you made some sort of post on the internet about this case?" he says, looking at me for the first time in a while. "For the record, it's always best to call the police if you know something rather than just blogging about it, or whatever it is you were doing. Anyway, he must have just seen your post and decided that if he couldn't convince us he was some criminal mastermind, maybe he'd try it with you."

So Chrome Boot Tip Man and Jonathan are not the same person? I was just duped by an internet stranger?

God.

I have never felt so stupid in my entire life.

"I wouldn't beat yourself up over it," he says, and immediately looks guilty, like that wasn't the right metaphor to offer me. "Cases like this bring out all the crazies. And as I said: every lead is important. We know more now than we did before we heard from you. Seriously. Thank you."

He at last stands up from the table and gives Marjani his card. "If Daniel thinks of anything else, please don't hesitate to call me," he says. "Maybe before he goes on the internet, OK?"

He walks to the door and looks back at me. "Thank you for your coffee and your hospitality, Daniel," he says. "You're a brave young man, I mean it."

I'm sure I'm older than he is. But I don't feel like it right now.

33

Marjani slept in my room last night. I feel terrible about it. She has so much to do on a football weekend, I should be the least of her worries. She has to get to Sanford Stadium first thing to start cleaning up and setting up the catering for all the rich alums who sit in the skyboxes, getting drunk and popping shrimp.

After that, she has to run over to the student center by Stegeman Coliseum to help them cater the big pregame meal for all the players, mostly washing all the slop from their trays and then hauling huge bags of trash into the dumpster and then driving them out to the landfill in Oconee County. Then she has to return to campus and get over to the ZBT fraternity house, where she passes out hors d'oeuvres to sloshed alumni and underage undergrads. This is all before 3:00 p.m., mind you, and the day before there is an actual game. Saturday will be even worse. Marjani has never had a sip of alcohol in her life, but she stinks of beer like a Supreme Court justice in college when she comes back to check on me Saturday nights. People always talk about college sports as an "economic driver" on game days, and I suppose this is what they mean: poor first-generation im-migrants like Marjani following behind an endless queue of trashed southerners, picking up all they thoughtlessly leave in their wake.

It's such a full weekend that she usually takes Thursday nights off and lets the orderlies or Travis put me down, and she rarely stays over here. But this Thursday, well, we were all in a bit of a state this particular Thursday. Such was my manner and mood after turning on the television last night that we all sort of forgot that I almost died a few hours earlier.

It was him.

I have no question about it. It was him, down cold. Same reedy neck. Same hat. Same boots. Same innocuous, sad sack shoulders, the sort of shoulders that made Ai-Chin think it was OK to get in his car.

The guy on the TV is the guy. The guy on the internet is just not the guy. They are two different people.

I feel relief being just a bystander again rather than an active participant. I saw her. And I saw him. And . . . jeez. What in the world was he doing at that vigil? If you had done something horrible to the exact person everyone is there to pray for—and it dawns on me, just saying this, that I in fact have no idea what he did to her, or where she is, or any of it—why in the world would you show up at her vigil? There are cameras everywhere. Everyone is crying. Her parents are there. *Her parents are there.*

What kind of sociopath does something like that?

The type of sociopath who would lure a college student with ill intent. Theoretically.

Look: I have done my part. They know when she got in the car. They know that because of me. I hope that helps catch him. And my work here is done.

Which means I've just been emailing back and forth with

170

another loner without much else going on who was just fascinated with this case. *Like I was.* I hear ya, pal.

His email sits in my mailbox, waiting for a response, waiting for someone else to listen to him. It's pretty messed up to pretend to be a guy who abducted a girl just to feel important. But I don't have any scorn for him. He seems sad. I don't want to indulge the fantasy. But I do want him to know someone is listening.

34.

jon—

youre right, this is a nice neighborhood. the students arent around here too much. only on game days. one dude a couple weekends ago barfed in the bushes outside my house. i just sat and watched him. he never noticed i was here. kinda like you hahahahaaha.

i agree, its hard to meet people on a college campus. everybody is so young and goodlooking and yeah theyre all looking at their phones all the time. but i dunno. everybody looks at their phones all the time. im not goodlooking enough to get them to look up i guess hahahahaaha. girls everywhere none talking to me nope.

so have you been watching the news? this thing is all over the place. even the football coach is talking about it. you gotta be a little nervous about that. im a little nervous about it and i didnt do anything. are you ok? scary. i havent been able to tell anybody about this. first i didnt really see you not really and second there aren't many people to tell anyway. this is probably my longest email chain in a year. guess i need to get out more hahaahahaaha. whole things crazy.

so what happens next? like whats your plan?

i just want you to know that you can always be honest with me. im

glad we have this and itll all turn out ok just know that we cool. well get
through it. it gets too much for me sometime too. its nice to have someone
to go through it with.

also my name isn't tom. i was just making sure you werent gonna
hurt me or anything. but i trust you now man. my name is really daniel.
nobody ever calls me dan. but you can if you want to.

—daniel

I am impossibly tired. The weight of all this does a number on
me a little more each time. Travis has gone and Marjani has
gone and Officer Wynn Anderson has gone and it's just me in
the house, staring at my computer, not working, not sleeping,
just blankly, mindlessly gaping at the screen.

This is probably how it will happen, when it happens. It
won't be dramatic or violent. My nightmare/dream scenario of
Jonathan being a psycho murderer who strangles me in my sleep
isn't how this is gonna go down, turns out, not that it was ever
going to. I won't die in the heat of passion. It probably won't
even be in public like last night. I'll be in this chair, scrolling through Twitter on a weekday afternoon, whittling away
hours, knowing I should be either sleeping or doing something
at least slightly productive but lightly snorting at TikTok videos
instead, when all of a sudden I stop breathing, and there's no
one here to help, and then that's it, it's over. No one will notice
me until Marjani comes in to put me to bed. She'll gasp, and
maybe cry a little, I'm not sure, and then she'll turn off my
computer, grumbling that Daniel is always spending too much
time on that thing.

There would be something fitting about dying in front of
the internet. My cousin Scottie died last year. I didn't know
him that well, but I liked what little I knew. Most of the time
when relatives came over to our house, they acted like they'd

just put something in the oven and needed to hurry back lest it burn. They would hug my mother a little too tight, they'd speak to me like I was a four-year-old child when I was well into my teens, and they'd shuffle out the door, their obligation fulfilled, checking in on Angela and Daniel so that they didn't feel like they were terrible people.

Scottie wasn't like that. Scottie always came over with his mom Julia, whom he lived with through his mid-thirties. Actually, Julia was not actually my aunt, which means Scottie wasn't actually my cousin, but she and my mom had worked together at some restaurant before I was born and didn't get to see each other that much, so they just called her my aunt to make sure that she knew Mom considered her important. Scottie had a tough job on these visits, because Mom would go off in the other room with Julia and drink margaritas and gossip and laugh and cry and just talk talk talk. Scottie's job was to sit with me. I can be a tough sit, but Scottie just went about his business. He just chilled. He was a little overweight, and he always wore this floppy old-man cap that made him look like he was dealing poker in some seedy speakeasy somewhere. One time, when we were watching some old Clint Eastwood Western, he even let me sip one of his beers. He put a finger over his lips and grinned. Even though that beer tasted terrible, I smiled as widely as I had in weeks.

Scottie wasn't married and never seemed to be too far from his mother, who fretted about him and constantly complained about his weight and how his hair was too long, but it was pretty clear that he was taking care of her more than she was taking care of him. Scottie wasn't living in his mother's house because he was a layabout. He was living there because she needed him. I never heard either of them say a word about this. It was just understood. One day he woke up and complained to Julia about having trouble catching his breath and a splitting headache. She gave him an aspirin and sat with him on the couch. He inhaled deeply, exhaled deeply, cracked his knuckles, stretched his neck out, took a drink of water, and said quietly, "Ma, I think something might be a little wrong." Five seconds later his eyes rolled back in his head and he fell onto the floor. Two minutes later he was dead. He'd had a massive heart attack, right then and there in the family room. He was thirty-seven years old.

Mom came down here and picked me up and drove me back to Illinois for the funeral. There were about a dozen people there, fewer than I would have thought. It was an open casket: he was wearing that dumb hat. Julia stood next to the casket, dressed in her finest blue dress, which my mother had bought her years before, and she didn't say a word the entire time. She didn't cry. She didn't speak. She just stood there the whole time until they closed the lid and buried him. Then she let out a wail that sent birds scurrying out of the trees.

When I got back to Athens, I looked up Scottie's obituary. It was the usual boilerplate obit that understands that it's so difficult to capture a person's soul in prose that it's a mistake to even try. He was a member of some church. He enjoyed playing cards. He is survived by his mother and his grandfather, of Des Moines.

At the bottom: *Online condolences may be expressed at,* etc. etc. I clicked on the link, and then the header that said "Obituaries." I scrolled down past some elderly people and found Scottie. I clicked there too.

There was a picture of Scottie, in that hat. Below his photo was a box that read "Share" with the logos of Facebook, Twitter, and Google Plus and an envelope representing email. There was a red button that read "Send Flowers," which sent the grieving to a national flower consortium, and a blue button that read "Share a Memory," which, strangely, sent you right back to Facebook. Next to Scottie's picture was the "Tribute Wall." Here you could type your thoughts about Scottie for . . . someone.

On this page there were four entries. One was from the American Cancer Fund, which said it was "sorry to hear of Scottie's passing. We have received a memorial donation in his name from his former employer Aldi's and our sincere condolences go out to his family." One was from someone who clearly thought they were posting on Facebook, which simply said "Sad to hear about Scottie he was in my homeroom in junior high nice guy ☹." The other two were virtual flowers that anonymous web users had cross-posted to Scottie's page from their own Facebook pages. One was called "Enchanted Cottage." One was "Sweet Tenderness." Each of them had GIFs of flowers waving left to right, slowly, mournfully, a mournful GIF, it was definitely a mournful GIF. The page is sponsored by the local grocery store, and there was a banner ad promoting a special on sliced ham.

And that was it. When I closed the window, a pop-up ad asked me if was sure I wanted to leave. I X'd out of the windows and turned my computer off.

Someday, maybe soon, I'll have a Tribute Wall page of my own, full of pop-up ads and spam. That'll be all that's left of me. Scottie's life was one fully lived, one lived for others more than himself, and his lasting monument is a grocery corporation making an empty gesture of charity, two dumbly blinking virtual flowers, and an idiot who doesn't know how to use Facebook. This is probably all of our legacies. That's what's coming next.

I need to get some sleep.

35.

Daniel—

Thank you for your honesty about your name. That will make all this easier. I had a sense that Tom wasn't your real name, Daniel. It didn't sound right. That's strange, isn't it? We know nothing about each other, we've never met, and still, somehow, the name "Tom" sounded wrong. Huh. Anyway, it's good to know the real you. Considering this thing that we now share, this thing that only you and I know, we should absolutely be honest with each other. If we cannot be honest with each other, there is no one we can be honest with. In a way, Daniel, you know me better than anyone ever has.

Here's the thing about girls: They watch all these movies, all the time, about how wonderful everything's going to turn out, how it's all a fairy tale where they just have to meet their perfect long-haired boyfriend who cares about them and listens to them. That love is the only thing that matters in the world, that everybody lives happily ever after. And then when they see some tall handsome guy they immediately just drop all of that and do whatever he tells them to do. They ignore all the terrible parts of his personality and excuse all the bad shit he does. Or they blame themselves for it. Or they just give up.

They act like they want this beautiful life. But they don't, not really.

And it's frustrating, because it's just getting harder. Look around, Daniel: I feel like every girl I see on the street keeps looking at me like I'm going to try to rape her or something. It almost doesn't matter if you're a nice guy because now women think all guys are assholes. I've spent my whole life being sweet and nice and trying to make these girls realize how great they'd have it if they were with me, and it turns out now they've just decided that you go in the trash just because you're a guy. If that's how this was all going to turn out, maybe I should have just been a shitheel in the first place.

Do you know how that feels? I bet that you do. You are nice. We are nice. And yet we are alone. There is something fundamentally wrong with that.

This is what's different about Ai-Chin, Daniel. You saw it. The way she looked walking down the street was so free of . . . anger. She wasn't walking around with some chip on her shoulder, blaming guys for all her problems. She's not upset with the world. She didn't want to burn it all down. She just walked down the street living her life, open to the world, open to meeting someone nice, open to being loved. You see how it is out there, Tom. Girls aren't like that anymore. But she was. I saw it. I saw it every day.

She's still a little bewildered by everything that's happened over the last few days, and if I'm being honest, I can't really blame her. It's been a lot! And her English is pretty rough. It's a wonder she even made it through vet class. Did you know she wants to be a vet? She'll be such an incredible vet. We're working on the English. She's starting to get it a little more. It won't be long until she understands what's going on. I am slowly getting her to understand. She will soon understand. And she won't be so scared then.

It feels strange to be typing to you about this. But can I say again that it feels good to talk to you about it? This whole thing has happened very quickly. I'm glad you're here to listen. It makes me feel a little less alone. Let us enjoy this fleeting time together.

Best,

Jonathan

Jonathan's fantasies are vivid and detailed, in a way that's disorienting and a little bit overwhelming. But when you allow for the Ai-Chin delusion—and boy, that is awfully detailed for a delusion—there are . . . things I understand about him? I understand how hard it can be to be alone. I understand how feeling like you are a part of what you are seeing on the news every night can make you feel important and needed. I understand needing someone to talk to. And I understand needing someone who's willing to listen.

I shut off my computer. Later, orderly Charles, not the other one (Larry, Jimmy maybe?), pulls the curtains tighter while doing his nightly checking in, slightly disturbed that I'm still awake. "Storms comin'," he says as he rolls me back over. I feel sad for Jonathan and where he is in his life. I am also grateful for him in a strange way. I sleep in fits and starts, deeply but abrupt. I see her wave in my dreams. I thought she was saying good morning. Maybe she was saying goodbye.

SATURDAY

36.

There was a girl once.

Don't look so surprised. I've used a wheelchair most of my life, but I wasn't always mute and drooly. I was a sixteen-year-old boy just like everybody else. I stared at boobs, I made out with my pillow, I started sweating when I thought about the college girls Mom worked with, I got boners. I didn't really start deteriorating physically, to the point that someone had to physically place me into my chair, until I was about to graduate from Eastern Illinois, which was one of the reasons I wanted to move to Athens, where Travis lived, as urgently as I did. I could feel myself starting to get a little weaker, to have more difficulty impersonating a regular person, and I knew if I didn't get out of there soon, I never would. If you're lucky enough to have a window of independence with SMA, it's a small one, and I wanted to take advantage of it before it was too late. Had I stayed, Mom would have seen me start to slow down, and she would have put her life aside to help me in the exact way I didn't want her to. There would be no tennis or whatever that was in Jamaica for her if I had stayed. I had some strength left. That strength got me to Athens. I'd rather be weakening here than there.

So. The girl. The girl's name was Kim. She was from Sullivan, about a half hour drive northwest of Mattoon, another of those Central Illinois towns slowly dying, no industry, no jobs, no future, a downtown that once served as the social hub, with diners and drugstores and doctors and clothing shops, now boarded up and abandoned, left in the dust by Walmart and freeways and all the factory jobs being done by robots.

Kim was a counselor at Camp New Hope, which is a summer camp for the developmentally disabled in Neoga. Every summer, kids from all across Central Illinois, kids with Down syndrome, mostly, come to Camp New Hope to have an experience that's specifically catered to them and their caregivers. There's a playground, a mini golf course, a cute little train track that circles the place, and, most important, little cabins for the kids to stay and sleep in that are theirs and theirs alone. Kids with Down syndrome spend their entire lives having someone holding their hand to do anything, and the best thing about Camp New Hope is that it gives them a place that is *theirs*. It is a place just for them.

When you grow up disabled like me, you end up spending a lot of time with kids with Down syndrome. The public schools in Illinois have limited funding, and the teachers are overworked as is. As much as my mom wanted me to have a normal kid's life, there is no time or energy to make sure a kid in a wheelchair who needs to be fed and could theoretically stop breathing at any second has a "normal life." You get thrown in there with the other "special needs" kids from a very early age. That they are *developmentally* disabled is, to your average rural school administrator, essentially indistinguishable from someone like me, who would be in the gifted program if he could use his arms and legs and lungs but instead is still trying to explain to his fifth-grade teacher that he doesn't need to watch the goddamned *Letter People* again . . . well, it's frustrating.

But god, those kids are the best. I don't know if it's because it's more difficult for them to grasp some of the more horrible aspects of being a human being—death, pain, white nationalism, lawyers—and therefore can't get bogged down in cynicism and despair. Maybe I'm bringing my own limitations and misconceptions to the table here. But I cannot deny that I wanted to be around them as much as I could.

I spent my summers at Camp New Hope. The people at the camp knew who I was and knew the kids loved me, so they always let me go out there and help the counselors during the day. It made me feel useful, but it wasn't just that. I enjoyed getting to be on the side of the assisting rather than the assisted. It was nice having the counselors see you as one of their own. It was nice to be needed.

Kim was a year younger than me, which is a lot more than a year when you are sixteen. She leaped out to me because she never stopped being a counselor. Most of the kids who come to Camp New Hope as counselors have a ceiling on their volunteerism. They do what they can, because they want to help, and because they want to put on their college applications that they spent their summers assisting kids with Down syndrome, but after about four hours with the kids, they're generally spent. The empathy meter nears zero. They wander away, they start fiddling with their phones, a few sneak away to smoke weed or make out. I don't blame them. They're teenagers. That they spend any time at all with those kids, even if they're just doing it to try to get into Northwestern, is a net positive for everyone involved, as far as I'm concerned. Expecting them all to be driven wholly by the spirit of volunteerism to cheer the souls of the developmentally disabled is to ask far too much. They're there, and while they're there, they're trying to help.

But Kim wanted to be there, because she had lived it. Her older brother Ryan had Down syndrome, and she had grown up with it, with everyone thinking she was the older sister, with her parents only having so much time for her, with responsibilities asked of her that no one else her age could have ever fathomed. She didn't treat the kids like they were disabled, or even like they were kids at all. She even dealt with the older boys with Down syndrome. I once saw a boy—no, a man—in his twenties grab her left breast and try to lick her, a dangerous, scary situation for a fifteen-year-old girl out at a camp in the woods. She moved swiftly and compassionately. She elbowed him in the stomach, tapped his left cheek, and barked "No, Thomas, NO," right in his face. "I am sorry, Kim," he said, and he hugged her and cried. Kim was patience and courage and strength.

We used to take walks together, back when I was in my older, cheaper chair, after the kids were in bed and all the other counselors had left for their parties. I don't remember the first time we spoke, but it was obvious immediately that she had spent enough time with the disabled to understand that while I used a wheelchair and occasionally had to have my lungs compressed, I was just as much of a confused and hopeful teenager as she was. My speech had just started to degrade a little then, but just a little, and we would walk and wheel and talk all around the campground. She wanted to join the Peace Corps, but she was scared she'd never leave Sullivan and she hated the boys at her school and she thought people are inherently good though she was starting to worry and she smelled like cinnamon and every time she smiled, I wanted to leap out of my chair and crawl in her lap.

She didn't talk to me like there was anything wrong with

me. The opposite—most of our conversations ended with me reassuring her that she was wonderful, that what she was doing was right, that there was no one like her. There really wasn't. There wasn't anyone like her. I told her how being at this camp made me feel like I was finally doing something for someone else after having people do things for me my entire life, like it was a chance to pay the world back, but she stopped me.

"You don't owe anyone anything. They help you because they love you. Why else does anyone help anyone? Letting someone help you is the nicest thing you can do for anyone."

I told her she was probably right, and she laughed and said, "I'm always right, Daniel, don't you know that by now?" She had dark brown hair to her shoulders and a tiny scar on her nose. I think she floated above the ground.

One night, toward the end of the summer, we stopped by the pond to watch the sun go down. There is nothing like a midwestern sunset. The land is so flat that you can see forever. She bent down on one knee so she'd be at my eye level, and she turned to me.

"I just wanted you to know that I think you are wonderful," she said. I'd had this said to me before. But not like this.

"I think you are too," I said.

"Can I come visit you at EIU sometime? Maybe we can walk around campus. My mom wants me to go to school there, and even though I don't really want to, it would be an excuse to come see you."

"I'd like that."

She looked out onto the water. "Do you sometimes wish things could be different, Daniel? Do you think things don't work out the way you want them to for a reason?"

I hoped she was talking about me, but I didn't know for sure. "Yes," I hedged. "But I like things how they are sometimes too."

She turned to me.

"You have to email me when you get home. I want us to always be friends."

Friends. "Yes. Please."

She took my wrist in her right hand and my face in her left. She looked at me for a long time, either three seconds or forty years, I can't be sure. She smiled, moved closer, and gave me the lightest kiss on the lips. She then gave me another one. Then: I will leave it there. That's all I'm going to give you. The rest belongs only to us.

Later, she stood up and took my left hand. We walked together back to the camp. She hugged me and went back to her cabin. She left a week later. Last time I checked on Facebook she was living in Philadelphia, working on some political campaign. She has a boyfriend and a dog and likes the Eagles. I am glad she is happy. She messaged me a couple of years ago, saying she heard I moved to Georgia and how awesome she thought that was. I told her thank you and that I was glad she was happy. I think about her every day, and I suspect I always will.

hear Travis bound through my front door. He pauses to do something it is extremely difficult to get men to do: he takes his shoes off and holds them in his hands before walking across the carpet.

"Dude, there is new shit *everywhere* on your porch again, see?" he says. "Did that cop stomp mud all over your front porch again yesterday? He must have stomped his boots when he came in, or came out, or something. It's a mess out there, see."

I wheel to the door, and Travis is right. There's stomped mud and boot prints and gunk up and down the steps, and next to the rocking chair my mom bought for decoration last year, and a whole pile of filth right under my living room window. Had it rained before Officer Anderson came in? I know it rained last night.

"Gross," Travis says, extracting chunks of dirt from the bottom of his shoe with one of Marjani's finest carving knives. "People are just so rude." He puts the shoe, which isn't much cleaner now than it was when he took it off, right in the middle of my kitchen floor.

"So . . . game day!!!!"

It is game day. Before Travis came in, I'd put the finishing touches on a response to Jonathan before our day commences. You've gotta be kind, after all. I think I can help Jonathan. Letting someone help you is the nicest thing you can do for anyone.

jon—

man your dark. it aint so bad man! people can be nice. people here are very different than where im from. in a good way. half these kids are from china or india or japan. i never met anybody like that where i grew up. just boring ass white people like me hahahahaha. its good to be in a place where there are different people. i just sit and watch them. they never notice me just like you didn't. you can learn a lot by watching.

you sound like you don't get out much either. i get it man. trust me i really really do. but you cant let it make you so mad. being by yourself aint so bad. it doesnt mean youre alone. it just means you get to do your own thing. i know what its like to be alone. but youre never really alone. we can work this out.

can we work this out? i'm here man.

Daniel

I decided not to push the Ai-Chin delusion. Officer Anderson was tough enough on him. He can talk to me.

But he can talk to me after the game.

38

Travis has me in my game-day costume. I am not sure how much dignity this costume affords me, but I cannot deny its inherent popularity. I am never more loved than I am on a Georgia football Saturday.

He came bounding up the steps on the front porch like nothing had happened at all over the last two days, like I didn't almost die, like we haven't been hanging out with cops all week, like this is just a perfectly normal morning. This is one of Travis's greatest gifts: the ability to make all unpleasantness and worry disappear simply by not paying attention. He's like a goldfish with a head injury.

He has his vape in his left hand, a backward St. Louis Cardinals hat on, dark sunglasses even though it's 9:00 a.m., and he smells of so much weed that we might as well be . . . well, I was going to say at Coachella, but honestly, these days, we'd just as likely be with all the moms in the carpool line. He's carrying the massive duffel bag he always shows up with on football Saturdays on his back, a massive red monster with the Georgia logo on the side and the words DANIEL'S LINEBACKER TRANSFORMER KIT written in deep black Magic Marker across the top. He makes a big theatrical moment out of unpacking it in front of me, like a guy trying to show someone how to fix a leaky sink on a YouTube video, *Here are all the tools you're going to need.*

The duffel bag's contents:

- Two cases of beer. Terrapin Golden Ale. Midwesterners hate hops. Travis never shuts up about how wrong southerners are about their fancy beers.

- A full handle of Maker's Mark.

- Three Frisbees.

- An extra pair of Travis's underwear. "Just in case, you know?"

- Then, my costume. First: a Georgia football jersey. It's red, with the circular G logo on the collar. In place of a name, the back says MOVE IT OR LOSE IT. The number is 69, as if you hadn't guessed that already.

- Shoulder pads. My shoulders increasingly look like the McDonald's logo these days so Travis has the smallest possible set of shoulder pads, size child's small.

- The Georgia helmet. It is not a regulation helmet. It's just an oversize plastic thing that makes my head look like the center of a pinwheel.

- I think there are a few more stray beers rolling around there as well.

Travis meticulously lays everything out on the porch, opens up a beer, and says, "Let's get to work. Oh, wait . . . you wanna hit?" I nod, smiling, and he puts a fake joint up to my lips, and I pretend to inhale. One real puff would kill me, but goddammit I love him so much for always asking.

And now I'm all costumed up.

Travis hauls me into the Woolly Mammoth and straps me in. He hops up into the bed of the truck, puts his face right in front of my helmet, and puts his vape between his teeth in imitation of Hunter S. Thompson. Travis loves him some Hunter S. Thompson, though it's all from that Johnny Depp movie; I'm sure he's never read a word he's written. "Faster, faster, faster, Danno," he says, his eyes cartoonishly darting all over the place behind his glasses. "Until the thrill of speed overcomes the fear of death. DEATH FROM ABOVE!!!!"

You're a dork.
You love it. It's a savage journey to the heart of the American Dream!
I don't know how much gas I have for today.
It has been a long week. Are you OK? Are you up for this?
I am. This is always the best day of the week. I am just tired. I am very tired.
We won't push it. You just gimme the signal. Or if I'm not around, holler at Jennifer.
She's coming?
Is that OK?
Yes. She is great.
Good. She rocks.
I am glad she will be there.
Me too, man. But you sure you're all right? That was some shit the other day.
I wouldn't miss this for the world.
Mammmmothhhhhhhhh!!!!!

193

This whole production is a lot of work for someone who didn't even go to Georgia and doesn't particularly like football. But one does not spend a football Saturday taking half measures.

After an unnecessary but scenic drive through campus that gets me cheered by every Athens tailgater—it is flabbergasting how many people are already out here at 9:30 in the morning for a 4 p.m. game—we arrive at our tailgate, by Stegeman Coliseum, where the Georgia basketball, volleyball, and gymnastics teams compete. I enjoy this spot because it's highly populated, so you can just sit and watch all these weirdos, and it's close enough to my house that I can leave anytime I want. There is a limit to how much of this I can take. Eventually, you realize these people just like football too damn much.

But it's an irresistible scene. The South has all sorts of problems—the Confederate flag, systematic voter suppression, not a single decent sushi place—but this is not one of them. Folks drink their bourbon and sit in their chairs and watch the cars go by, perfectly content just to get themselves lightly wasted, together, as one, as the day goes along. Eventually there's a game at the end, and the game is important, but it's more the nightcap than the main course. Most of the fans don't even go to the game. They just take these seven days a year to go sit with all their friends, the ones they've met and the ones they will, and enjoy a day of everyone casually pulling in the same direction.

I just sit and watch, like the rest of them. As always, I'm not totally a part of it. But for a while, in this ridiculous helmet, I also am a part of it.

• • •

Jennifer sidles right up next to me and puts her hand on my leg. She is very touchy, this girl. Her hands are always everywhere. I don't mind.

"Daniel, how you hanging in, dawg?" she says, in a way that's a little forced and clearly for the benefit of Travis, who's standing nearby pretending not to pay attention, but I don't mind that either. "You had quite a night the other night."

Jennifer hasn't figured out how to communicate with me without words like Marjani and Travis have, obviously, but she gets the general gist through my series of head shakes and bobs that I'm just fine, thank you, nothing to worry about.

"Oh great!" she says aloud. "Then let's get drunk!" She kisses me on the cheek and throws her hands in the air. "Shots! Shots! Who has some shots?" She and Travis strike me as compatible.

As usual, everyone goes along with their tailgates and forgets I'm there, so I just sit and listen to what's on everybody's mind. Tailgates are like my own little news feed, a way to tap into the hungry, yearning brain of your average Athens, Georgia, resident. The topics this week mostly skirt the bounds of the usual. *Sure am glad all that heat's over with, you can finally go outside now. Why doesn't Georgia just run the danged ball? Did you see what the president tweeted? There was the funniest video of a baby and a kitten, here, you gotta watch it, gimme a second, lemme find it on my phone. Did you hear about Debbie's sister? It's the saddest thing. Just the saddest thing.*

But it is clear that the lead story, as it surely had to be, is Ai-Chin. The rallies this week have everybody abuzz with theories. One of the college kids one tailgate over, after casually doing a keg stand, as if being upside down and chugging beer while two strangers hold your legs in the air is just like hanging around the watercooler, says she heard Ai-Chin had a fight with her boyfriend and "he's a really shady guy." One guy who works at the record store downtown informs Travis, loudly, that she's just scared she was going to fail out and disappoint her parents, so she's hiding somewhere, and she'll show up any minute now once she realizes the ruckus she has caused. A cop strolling by jokes to a lady waiting for the porta-potty that "everybody keeps calling us every time they see an Asian girl on a college campus, which is every second of the damn day." Out of the corner of my eye, I see Jennifer bristle.

There are posters on every light post and street sign now, and it's not just the ones from the Rook & Pawn anymore. This cause has been taken up by the entire campus. Three different groups of people, two of them for Asian students, one a campus women against sexual violence organization, have marched down Sanford Drive, chanting "Justice for Ai-Chin" and "We will not be silenced." Four different news trucks from Atlanta are interviewing anyone they can find about Ai-Chin, and I overhear one talking head (not Chesley McNeil, sadly) doing a live hit: "The euphoria of a college football weekend can't help but be dampened by the Ai-Chin tragedy, the missing girl a haunting fog that hovers over every Georgia Bulldogs fan."

Everybody's talking about it. But nobody knows a damn thing.

Not even me. Not anymore.

39

My iPad buzzes. An email from a guy at work, wondering why I didn't book any hours yesterday. Nate Silver has just released some new numbers that I will find very alarming if I click right here. Your Pie has a two-for-one special this weekend. The Supreme Court issued a ruling on something I do not understand.

And then there is Jonathan. I haven't looked at my phone for most of the afternoon, but he apparently returned my email mere minutes after he received it.

I move my chair to the side of the tailgate, away from a man loudly extolling the virtues of his current stock portfolio while wearing loud red pants with pictures of little bulldogs on them, sporting sunglasses that are attached to the top of his head by some sort of string and drinking a Bud Lime-A-Rita. I open the email.

Daniel—

See, now I'm not sure we're on the same wavelength. You know that neighbor of yours? The one from another country? You know he probably has a better job than you do, right? Or at least he will someday. I'm not a racist or anything like that at all. I hate racists. But let's not kid ourselves, Daniel. This is not a time for you and me.

Last week, one of the teachers at a high school here in Athens wrote an op-ed for the campus newspaper. It talked about how difficult it is for her to teach white boys. She specifically said that: "White boys." Why did she say it was so difficult? Get this, Daniel: "They barely try and expect to be rewarded." All teenage boys are little shits like that. But she calls us out. And then if one of those students were to happen to say, "Hey, you made me feel bad about being white," you know what would happen? They'd kick him out of school!

I'm no Nazi, Daniel. Fuck Nazis. Punch Nazis in the damn face. But think about this, Daniel. There are teachers who think it's less their job to teach than it is to tell dumbass teenagers that they're assholes just because they're white. The one time in a kid's life when he needs someone to put an arm around him and tell him he's gonna be great, he can be whatever he wants to be, and instead they're telling him he's personally responsible not only for all his problems but for the problems of everybody else as well. No wonder he's pissed off. Just by breathing the air and walking around the planet, we are suddenly assholes.

Why I gotta get kicked in the face every time I leave the house just because I'm a white guy? Do you personally feel like someone who has a ton of advantages over everyone else? I know I sure don't.

It just makes me angry sometimes. Not just sometimes. It makes me very fucking angry. A lot. I don't mean to get caught up in the race thing. It's not just that. It's everything. It's the way girls look at you, shit, the way everybody looks at you. Like they all know a joke that you don't. It's a sneer; they're sneering at us. They think they know better. But they don't. I KNOW BETTER. People smile like they're nice, but they're not nice. I've got something to offer this world, but they don't want to hear it. They don't care. They don't give a rat's ass. It makes me want to scream. Does it make you want to scream? You have to feel this way. I can tell that you feel this way. We share more than I suspect you think, Daniel.

This is another thing that Ai-Chin gets. She sees me in a way that no one else sees me. She listens. She listened right from the beginning. The whole place has felt different with her around. I finally have someone here who understands what I have to say. Who understands that I have a lot to say. I'm starting to think I might love her, Daniel. Wow. You're the first person I've said that to. It feels good to say it. She's gonna love me too. She might already. She might not know it yet. But she will.

It's different with her here. It makes me want to scream less. It makes everything . . . calmer. I don't know how I made it without her. I can't be without her. It's so much better now.

Oh! I think she remembers you. I asked her if she ever saw someone when she walked to school in the morning, and she said yes, yes she did. It took a while to get it out of her. But I got it out of her. So that was interesting.

Best,

Jonathan

40

It is probably time to stop these emails. I'm indulging something I shouldn't. Fake phone calls to the cops or not, something is clearly up with Jonathan, and it doesn't seem like a particularly good idea for me to be all that close to it. He's having a psychic break or . . . something.

Just to be safe, I forward Jonathan's email to Officer Anderson with a "this dudes too much" attached. Cops must have to deal with people like Jonathan all the time. It exhausts me just to think about it. Then again: I wonder what Officer Anderson thinks about people like me who keep emailing back and forth with those people like Jonathan.

The game is a blowout. They usually are. I don't know much about football, but you can tell how close the game is going to be by how many people leave the tailgate to actually enter the stadium, and today, that percentage is low.

Travis and Jennifer are happily skipping the game, instead casually throwing a Nerf football back and forth, doing shots every time Georgia scores, strolling by occasionally to make sure nobody has tipped me over and sneaking away when no one's looking and returning smelling like . . . well, like Travis usually smells.

By halftime, with Georgia winning 27–7 and the vast majority of tailgaters roaming the streets already unable to write their name in the ground with a stick, I'm tired and ready to go home. I've made Travis take off my ridiculous costume, which seriously diminishes any novelty value I might have left to contribute, and the blowout has thinned out the crowd. Three years ago, I would have happily just sat here and watched the ongoing Athens madness, maybe make secret bets with myself on which tailgater will pass out first, but I've seen it all before, and I just don't have the energy for it that I used to. The late-afternoon October chill, even in Georgia in an age of a global rise in temperatures, takes a bit more out of me than I'd like to admit. By 6:00 p.m. or so, I'll start to gasp a little when I inhale, and while it's anything but a matter of grave concern—it's just a little wisp, a tickle, a minor frog in the throat—it has a tendency to scare people when they see it. It's always best practice to head back home before drunk people start looking at you askance, like there's a small possibility that something terrible is going to happen to you and they're far too schnockered to be of any help when it does. When you're a twenty-six-year-old with SMA, it's smart to leave any party a half hour before you have to. Particularly when that tickle, that scratch, still quivers in your throat.

I wheel over to Travis.

I'm going to go home.
Need a lift?
I got it. It's a quick trip home. Nobody seems to be passed out on the sidewalk, so I should be all right.

Marjani's there around eight, yes?

Should be, smelling like stale craft beer as always.

All right. Jennifer and I are going to stay here.

She is great.

I know.

He then finishes the rest of his beer, pops open another one, fits it in a koozie, and then dances off into the night, not a care in the world, it's all gonna be just fine for Travis, it always is.

As I turn the corner away from Stegeman Coliseum and on the way back down Agriculture Drive to my home, the tailgates slowly wither. Tents are being taken down, RVs are already pulling out to beat the traffic, the college kids have already skipped to bars downtown. Even with the game still going, the activity abates, and the people exit, and the streets are messy with Dixie cups but increasingly thinning. The night feels colder now, and as I wheel toward my home, dusk approaches, and the streetlights flicker on and hum, and it is calm. I am acutely aware that, in the midst of a place that was electric just hours ago, I am suddenly very alone.

41

Home. Marjani is here, ready to put me to bed, stopping by before the next gig, an alumni mixer at a Milledge frat, distracted as always on a home game Saturday, a little rougher than usual, a little rushed.

"You need to take a day off, Daniel," she says while buttoning my pajama top and wiping some spittle off my cheek. "You look too tired. There has been too much activity. You maybe should stay on the couch tomorrow. Should you watch the Netflix? There is much to watch on Netflix."

I snort at her without realizing I'm doing it.

"Well, excuse me," she says, and brushes my hair with a little extra elbow grease. "Go wear yourself out then, if that's all you want. Don't listen to me, I'm just the one bathing you. What do I know?"

I lose a little air from my lungs and then let out a moan. She stops brushing my hair and touches my face.

"I'm sorry, Daniel," she says. "It has been quite the week."

It's OK.
I really am sorry. It's all just a bit too much sometimes.
It'll be better tomorrow. You are right. I do need to rest.
We all need to rest.

I slope my head toward my desk. I am tired, but I need to wind down, check in with work, get synced back up with my real life. I have been tailgating, and passing out right there in the middle of campus, and pretending I'm Columbo, or Batman, and I've ignored my regular world and responsibilities. I've only billed five hours with Spectrum in the last three days. Not even the prisoners they employ to do this job could get away with those few hours.

I scroll through my email as Marjani pulls down the shades, always the five-minute warning: it's her passive-aggressive *Wrap it up, pal.* There are no angry missives from my bosses at Spectrum, no emails from Mom in the tropics, not much of anything going on. We spend too much time, when we are away from our computers, worrying about what we are missing. The answer is almost always *Not much.*

Except Jonathan. There are four new emails from him. They are progressively shorter.

Marjani looks at herself in the mirror after laying me down in bed.

Please leave the iPad. I am not done reading.
I will see you tomorrow. Do not stay up too late. I have to go.
I am sorry.
Goodbye, Marjani. May I have my iPad now?

She leaves. I take a deep snort. The first email came at 3:30 p.m.

Daniel

Sorry about that. I just get frustrated sometimes. Doesn't it get frustrating for you? You try to be a good person, you try to do the right thing, and everyone thinks you're an asshole anyway. That's all I'm trying to say. It sticks in my craw. Does it stick in your craw?

This is one great thing about Ai-Chin: She's different. She doesn't think she's owed anything. She just accepts me for who I am. She didn't at first. But she is understanding me so much better. We are understanding each other so much better. She even called me by my name today. Her English is improving. I am happy to do that for her.

Regardless: I didn't mean to sound so angry. That's something you'll learn about me: Sometimes it just pours out like that. But then it goes away. Just as quickly.

Promise!

Best,

Jonathan

4:54 p.m.

Daniel—

Are you at the football game? I find this town's infatuation with football pathetic. Just a bunch of pituitary cases smashing each other in the face. And all the good ole boys down here, they think it's the only thing that matters in the world. They sit out there with their perfect wives and their perfect hair and their dumbass golf shirts, and they scream and yell at black boys they'd never associate themselves with otherwise. If they saw their favorite player on the street wearing regular clothes, they'd cross to the other sidewalk. It's embarrassing. I hope you're not at the football game. I hope you are better than that.

Best,

Jonathan

6:58 p.m.

Daniel—

Sorry, I know, too many emails. I sometimes talk too much. Everyone always says that. I don't feel like I talk too much. I think I'm totally normal. You know that movie *Punch-Drunk Love*? The weird one with Adam Sandler? He's at a dinner party, and everyone there thinks he's a weirdo, and somebody asks him, "Do you feel like there is something wrong with you?"

He says, "I don't know if there is anything wrong because I don't know how other people are." I don't think there's anything wrong with me. But I don't know how other people are.

This is why I'm happy we can talk, Daniel. I think you and I are not like other people.

I may go to bed. I'll keep an eye out for your email. Write back!

Best,

Jonathan

And then one more, at 10:01 p.m. This one arrived about five minutes ago. Unlike the others, it got caught by my spam filter. It doesn't take long to realize why.

It reads:

我叫爱钦 我被困在一个小屋里 我不知道我在哪里。 有一个叫约翰的人，违背了我的意愿，抱着我。 我需要帮助 你是谁？ 可唔可以　吓我呀？

With great effort, I turn my head behind me. There is no one there.

SUNDAY

42.

I wake up to sunshine, bright sunshine, noontime sunshine. Why am I still lying here? I hear a television in the other room playing a football game. Is there NFL on? Is it the afternoon? How long was I sleeping? I am confused. Why has no one gotten me out of bed?

I roll over, away from the wall on one side of my bed, and I blink my eyes to get them moving. I look up and there is a dog. He is a Doberman pinscher, one of those dogs with the lean, chiseled, angular face that looks like a bullet pointed at you. His mouth foams. He stares at me for several seconds, with curiosity at first, then menace. His eyes are venom and blood.

He leaps at my throat. I fall backward into the wall and smash my head, which wakes me up for real this time. I am covered in sweat and urine, gasping for air.

43.

I t is still the afternoon. There is still NFL on the television.
Marjani is cleaning me off in the bathtub.

"I came by this morning, first thing, but you were still sleeping," she says, throwing an armful of wet clothes in a plastic
trash bag. Ninety percent of her daily activities involve off-
handedly doing things that would make most people gag. "And
you were very deep sleeping. I was in fact worried at first! But
you were resting in the way that you needed. You needed to be
down. So I let you be down."

The light is shining too bright today. There must be so many
hungover people out there. If you saw what a college campus
looks like after a hundred thousand drunk people come into
town and tear the place apart for fifteen hours, and then realized the work that people have to do to clean it up, you'd feel
too guilty to ever attend a football game again. Marjani is already covered in soot and grime and beer and god knows what
else. She smells like she slept in a dumpster outside a Waffle
House, but she just spent the morning cleaning up tailgates. As
she sticks a washcloth so far into my right ear that I can hear it

with my left, I scrunch up my nose in disgust. Travis calls this my Tryin' to Be an Anus face. I am all puckered and tight.

She dries me off, pulls some pants and a shirt on me, and straps me back in my chair. "You now get to have breakfast for lunch," she says. "Though it's just eggs either way."

It is the afternoon. I am not sure I have ever slept so long and hard in my life.

Before Marjani takes me on our Sunday walk, I open up the email again.

我叫爱钦 我被困在一个小屋里 我不知道我在哪里。 有一个叫约翰的人，违背了我的意愿，抱着我。 我需要帮助 你是谁？ 可唔可以　吓我呀？

Is this maybe Jonathan taking the joke too far? Officer Anderson said he was desperate to be involved, and learning Chinese is certainly desperate. I didn't even know keyboards had a Chinese-language option. He must have a Mac.

I cut and paste the email into Google Translate, which of course he could have done the other way.

And this is what comes out:

My name is Aegean. I am trapped in a hut. I don't know where I have a man named John who is against me, holding me. I need help. who are you? Can you scare me?

I stare at the computer and don't have the foggiest idea what to say. What is this, exactly?

I immediately forward the email to Officer Anderson. I don't know if it's real—boy, though, it sure seems real! Right? It seems pretty real to you, yeah?—but he's the only other person who has ever talked to Jonathan and he's a police officer and holy shit that email scared the shit out of me.

I type:

im sorry to keep bothering you but this is v v weird man. do you think maybe we should check on him again? should i keep emailing with him? can u call travis?

I stare at the email a little longer. The translation is off, but something is obviously up. If Jonathan is such a psycho that he is writing pretend notes from Ai-Chin and then sending them through Chinese Google Translate just for my benefit, would his English be THIS bad? That doesn't seem right at all, but then again, it doesn't seem right that he'd call the police confessing to crimes he didn't commit in the first place. The tone doesn't sound like Jonathan, but then again, who has a tone that sounds like Google Translate?

And what if she's really there?

I'm going to show Marjani the email, but not yet. We have our ritual Sunday walk first, and I want her to live in a world where she's not as bewildered by what's going on a little bit longer. Travis used to do something like this in college, never looking at his bank account or the receipts from the ATM so that he could have emotional deniability of just how broke he really was.

She always pushes me a little faster on Sundays. She has so much work to do that even though this is certainly the best part of her day—cleaning my dick and balls, putting me in clean underwear and whatever clothes she can find that will still hang on me, shoving eggs in my mouth, three-quarters of which is just going to fall out anyway, pushing my limp ass around campus, hauling me back into the same chair she just found me in, receiving no thanks other than my mean jokes about how bad she smells, of course this is the best part of her day—she has to rush through it. I don't mind the hurry. It's a cool afternoon, a sure 6 or 7 on the WIZometer, and the wind feels clean and crisp in my face.

"So you were with Travis at the game?" she says, with an odd lilt to her voice. "Was he with that girl? She is suddenly here a lot, I think." I don't say anything, because I have a very serious disease that atrophies my muscles to the point that they are too weak to make cogent, discernible words, a fact Marjani is aware of and a sign that this conversation is more for her than it is for me.

"I believe he needs a nice girl like that," she says. "Travis is a good boy, but he is old now. He is not a boy anymore. It is too much, with all the nights out, and all the music concerts, and the marijuana. He needs a good girl. He needs to grow up. He needs a house, his own house, for a family. He is no boy anymore."

Marjani often has these unsolicited thoughts on Travis's life, but they're usually more scolding than this, and more to the point, they're usually when Travis is standing right next to her.

"He has been such a good friend to you, for so long," she says as we turn the corner back onto Agriculture Drive and onward up to my house. "He was with you when you were children, always watching out for you. And he has been with you here now. He takes you where you need to go, he puts you in the back of that terrible truck of his, he comes to see you nearly every day. What a good friend he has been."

It is beginning to dawn on me that this conversation is not meant for Travis at all.

Marjani leans down to me as we approach my front porch.

"Daniel, this girl, I hope she is good for him," she says, staring into my eyes. I thought she was in a hurry? "But if it is not this girl, there will be another one. Someday a girl is going to show up, and she will never leave. They will start their own family. He will need to have his own life. He will always be there for you. But he will not always be able to be"—and here she raises her hand and spins it around—"*This*. Do you understand that?"

I do understand this. Why do you think I do not understand this? And why is this coming up now? Well, with any luck, I'll keel over in plenty of time for him to have that family you want for him.

"This is not a funny joke."

Poor Marjani. Only an exhausted Marjani would bring this up. Only a deeply exhausted Marjani would say something so undeniably true and final.

I grunt a little, and Marjani notices a tear coming out of my left eye: it was windy out there. She wipes it and brings me back to my room. I motion toward the computer.

Haven't you had about enough of that? Were you on that all night?

I have something I need to show you.
You know I do not like computers.
It is important. It is about what has been going on.

"Fine," she says. "But you know I must be quick."

She walks into the other room to get her glasses out of her purse. She places them on her nose and squints as she draws her face close to the screen. I see her mouth the words silently as she reads them. Then I show her the translation. Her face goes white.

"Oh, Daniel," she says. "This is very bad."

Is it?
Why are you still talking to this person?
He seemed lonely. I sort of . . . I guess we sort of understood each other? I am not sure.
Either this man is deeply disturbed and has taken his little game with you too far or . . . it's something worse. When did you get this email?
Last night, I guess. I slept a very long time.
Have you shown this email to anyone?
I forwarded it to the cop. I haven't heard back.
We need to call him.
It's very creepy.
We also need to call Travis. Right now.

"We need to call Travis," she says out loud, after she says it to me. "We need to call him right now."

44.

"Yes, yes, you need to check your email," Marjani says. "Right now."

After leaving a message to Travis telling him to come over *right this second*, Marjani called Officer Anderson, and now she's put him on speakerphone. "Ma'am, I'm on the road, I can't look at my phone right now," he says, faintly annoyed. No one in the disabled kid's house will stop bothering him.

"You need to pull over, this is important," she says.

"Can't you just tell me what's in the email?" he says.

"Daniel sent you an email that he got from Jonathan."

"He's still talking to Jonathan. I thought I told him Jonathan was full of it." I hear someone else, his partner I guess, chuckle in the background.

"Yes, but Jonathan has sent him some very disturbing emails."

"He's a disturbed person, ma'am."

"Yes, but Daniel got one that was in Chinese."

"Come again?"

"Jonathan sent an email that was in Chinese, and we translated it, and it looks like it is from Ai-Chin."

"What?"

"He says, wait, sorry, she says that he has her and that she needs help."

"He said it?"

"No, she said it." Marjani's patience is eroding. "Can you please just look at the email?"

Officer Anderson sighs deeply. "Hang on a second, I'm driving." I hear him say to his partner, "Open up my email." We hear a lot of scraping and fumbling and the partner mumbling "What am I looking for here?" Officer Anderson says he's looking for an email from me, and the partner makes a joke about there being nothing in here but Viagra spam. Marjani might throw this phone through the wall in a second.

"Oh, I see it," he says to Officer Anderson, and he begins to read the last email out loud. He stops when he gets to the Chinese. I hear them murmur to each other but cannot make out what they are saying. There's more fumbling, and then Officer Anderson picks back up.

"All right, we got what you sent us," he says. "That is . . . very odd. Even for him." He is silent for a few seconds. "OK. We've got a few more stops to make today, but we'll try to pop by his place before we check out tonight. The fact that he's bothering you so much is enough for us to want to have a little talk with him."

Marjani gives me a nervous thumbs-up.

What should I do?
What do you mean?
Should I keep emailing with him?

"Should he keep emailing with him?" she asks.

Officer Anderson consults with his partner again. I hope his partner is older and wiser than he is. Maybe he's Lenny from *Law & Order*. Or Columbo. Or just a particularly inquisitive dog. Maybe he's Hooch?

"It looks like he's been eager for you to respond," he finally says. "Go ahead and write him back, make him think everything's normal. Keep him talking."

Wait, I thought everything *was* normal?

"Can you maybe come by here too?" Marjani says. "We are a bit rattled over here." Marjani *does* look rattled. And this makes me worry that I'm perhaps not rattled enough. Should I be more rattled?

"I'm not sure we'll have time for that, but do have Daniel let us know if he makes any threats or anything," he says. "We'll try to check him out for you today, OK?"

Marjani thanks him and makes him promise he will answer if she calls again. He agrees, exhaustion in his voice.

Marjani hangs up and takes a towel to wipe my face. She then wipes her own and sits down at the kitchen table.

Thank you.
I do not like this. I do not like this one bit. Where is Travis?
You have to go. You're going to be late to do . . . everything.
I do not think you should be alone here.
It's fine. It's nothing. I forwarded the email to Travis, too.
This is very frightening. Is the officer sure this man is harmless?
Yes. You're overreacting. It's fine. I should have never showed that to you.

But I am not so certain.

"Look," Marjani says, and I catch her eyeing her jacket, hanging on the door. She can be worried all she wants, but she *does*

218

have hours and hours of work to do. She can't diddle around here much longer, and she knows it. And I know it too. "I will try to come by later tonight, when I have a break, after the press conference. But I am not sure: those often run late."

Another of Marjani's jobs is to serve sodas and snacks to the reporters who show up for Kirby Smart's weekly day-after press conferences. It's another crap job, but she does get to see Kirby.

"And," she says, pulling her phone out of her jacket, "Travis better be here by tonight anyway." She calls him, gets his voice mail, voice mail he will never check, and, after a deep breath, unloads on him:

"Travis. It is Marjani. Daniel needs you. You need to get over here as soon as possible. I have to leave, but he will be waiting. This is an emergency." She pauses. "Well, not an emergency. I did not mean to alarm you. It's not an emergency yet. But it could be. Just get here. Bring your girlfriend if you have to. I like her. Well, I don't really know her. But she seems nice. But I need you here now. Not an emergency. But please get here." She pauses again, and looks at me.

Hang up the phone, Marjani. He will never, ever hear any of that.

I have heard Marjani say more words in the last week, I think, than in the last year I've known her. The world is getting crazier. The center cannot hold. She's *shook*. Marjani being spooked and nervous and babbling scares me.

She leans down, lifts my chin, and puts my head in her hands. Staring straight into my eyes, she purses her lips and grits through her teeth: "*Be. Careful. Daniel.*"

I will be fine.

Then she wheels me over to my computer, because we both know I have to write him back.

"I will try to see you this evening," she says, but I'm already staring at the screen.

45.

I am not actually a detective, so I do not know what to think right now. Jonathan obviously has access to the same Google Translate that I do. But what would be the point of sending me an email in Chinese like that? Did he think that because I hadn't written him back, I didn't believe him or something? Why did he feel that he needs to sell *me* on this being real? He has no reason to think I don't believe him. He has no idea that I've talked to Officer Anderson and learned that he likes to make up stories about himself. As far as I know, in his eyes, everything he has said to me is on the level.

There is being lonely and needing attention and a friend. This feels like something different.

Like maybe he has her. He's had her the whole time.

And maybe our correspondence has put her more in danger. Officer Anderson said I could stay in contact with him. So I could just ask, straight up. *They'll never see that coming.* But if it turns out Ai-Chin *is* there, that will just put her in even more danger. Then again, he can see what emails his account has sent, right? Perhaps the middle ground: ignore the Chinese email, but put some cards on the table.

jon—

   i wanna be cool about this. ive liked our conversation. i really do think
we can help each other. but i was honest with you. so i want you to be
honest with me. i will be even more honest.

   i talked to a cop about you and he said you like to call them a lot and
say you did stuff like this. sorry about calling a cop but you understand of
course. i did really see ai-chin get taken. i assumed it was you when you
emailed me but when the cop already knew you that made sense to me
too. so you dont have to do this anymore. you dont have to pretend you
have her. if you are pretending.

   its ok. it really is. i think that you are right. i think that being alone
sucks. i think that not being able to talk to people is hard. i think that
feeling like everyone thinks youre stupid or an asshole is the worst. i get it
man. i too have felt like the guy from punch drunk love.

   so lets stop it ok and talk for real. you dont really have ai-chin. that
wasnt really her. you can tell me. i wont be like that cop. i wont make fun
of you. im on your side. just gimme the truth. im cool. i promise. shes not
there. right?

   right? right?

   Daniel

   I hit Send and am, not long after, alerted to fingers snapping in my face and the unmistakable odor of marijuana.

   "Uh . . . what have *you* been up to, man? You still talking to
that dipshit?"

"This is what happens when I leave you alone for the day, see,"
Travis says, popping several Zaxby's chicken nuggets in his
mouth at once. You know it's Sunday because no one in their
right mind would ever opt for Zaxby's over Chick-fil-A unless it
were Sunday and they had no choice.

Travis makes me a carrot banana smoothie, a combination he came up with a few years ago just to see if he could gross me out that ended up becoming a specialty, and puts the straw in my mouth as he scrolls past my Jonathan correspondence. He reads for a few seconds, shakes his head, reads for a few more, mouths a *What the fuck* a time or two, and reads a while longer. He finishes, whistles, puts down my smoothie cup, and looks me in the eye.

"I don't know if this guy is crazy or not," he says, "but he's definitely a fuckwit."

I laugh, and it feels good. Laughing hurts a little, but it makes me feel a little more awake.

Where the hell have you been, anyway?

Travis does something I have never seen him do before: he blushes. He stands up, takes my smoothie cup to the sink, rinses it out, makes me another one, rolls on the balls of his feet for a while, clicks his tongue, shuts off the blender, pours it in the glass, puts the straw in my mouth, heads to use the bathroom, stays in there a smidge too long, washes his hands slowly and meticulously, and then comes back and sits down.

He pauses again, and then breaks into a grin as wide as Texas.

"Dude, I've been with Jennifer, like, the whole time!" His voice gradually rises as he says this, like saying it aloud confirms that it's real, that telling another person assures him that he hasn't imagined the whole thing. "We just went back to her place after the game, and, well . . . I finally left her room about an hour ago. We didn't even look at our phones! I can never get girls not to stare at their phones!"

I glower at him. He had many messages from me when he finally got around to looking at his phone.

"Oh, yeah, uh, sorry about that," he says. "I suppose I should have been keeping a closer eye out after all that shit Friday."

It's cool. I'm fine.
Except for your lunatic email buddy. And that you look like shit. Have you slept at all?
A lot, actually.
Really?
I think so? I honestly have no idea.

I finish my second smoothie. I shake my head when Travis asks me if I want another, even though I do. If I have a third, I'll wake up constantly to pee. And I can't help but feel like I still need more sleep. I hadn't realized how desperately I needed sleep until I woke up after sleeping too long. I suppose that's how it works.

Travis wipes my chin, takes me to the bathroom, and then changes my clothes for pajamas. He actually wipes off some eye black that is still on me from my game-day costume the day before, which is embarrassing. He then carries me to bed.

I am not ready to sleep yet. Put me back in my chair. I want to see if he wrote back.
What exactly is the plan here?
I think he needs someone to talk to, and he's talking to me. And we've come this far, right?
So what, so you can arrest him and throw him in Daniel Jail?

Travis clicks the top of his tongue and looks at me skeptically.

"I think I should probably stay here tonight," he says.
I shake my head as hard as I can.

I'm fine. It's fine. We're just emailing. I'm going to see if he wrote back, and then I'm going to go to sleep. Charles or . . . the other guy will be here . . . later. Later? I think? What time is it?
It's early dinnertime. We just had early dinner. Are you OK?
I got this. The orderly will be here overnight, and Marjani will surely be here in the morning. Go get with your girl. I like her.

Travis frowns, looks down, clicks his tongue again, stands up, and pats me on the head. "You need to let me know what's going on, see," he says. "Forward me all those emails. And Skype me the second anything weird happens. I'll be back by tomorrow morning." He leans down and stares hard at me.

I am not sure you know what you are doing.
Who ever does?
But I got your back. You know that.
Always.

He wipes my sweaty brow, wheels me back to the computer, and eyes me warily as he backs out of the room. I hear him pass across my front porch, and I hear him open his car door, and before the engine even starts, I nod off in my chair, the glow of the computer taunting me, warmly, my friend till the end.

46

There's a woman, and she's looking at me, sadly, almost disappointed, like she wants me to catch up with her and can't
understand why I can't. She looks a little like Kim, actually, but
she's older. Not old, not a grandmother, not even Marjani, but
older, like she's aged twice as fast as I have in the last ten years:
she looks like she's lived well over the last twenty and wouldn't
change a thing but is still very tired. She beckons. She waves me
on. *Come here, you.*

I can always run in my dreams, and before you start thinking *How wonderful*, like it's some sort of wish fulfillment, that I
am freed of my earthly constraints, know that it is really not all
that exciting to be able to walk and is in fact rather hard. Walking is hard! It breaks down your knees and wrinkles your back
and destroys your feet. Every force of gravity that has existed on
the planet for eons and eons is doing everything it can to drag
you to the ground, and it is you, the walker, who must put forth
all the effort just to fight centuries of natural environmental
order. The world does not want you to walk. It wants you to
crumple. It wants you to look like me.

No. Screw walking. I should be able to *fly* in my dreams. I want to be free from all of it, my limbs floating off in all directions, lifting off with no constraints, no gravity, no force. I take it as a personal insult from my subconscious, an active reminder of my lack of imagination, that I can't fly in my dreams. I should be wafting toward Kim. I should be whooshing through the air, hair flapping behind me, my teeth chattering, the wind whipping through my toes, a supersonic surge—

WHOOOSH!

. . . until I am there, until I am with her, until she sees me for who I am, who I was then, not what I have become. Who is she now, this forty-five-year-old woman who has seen so much since we were teenagers and we could almost convince ourselves that we were the same, that this could be real, that we could be one in this little moment by this little pond in this little camp in this little town? Does she see me as a freak? Did she see me as one then? Does it matter? She is here now, and she wants me to come to her, and I can't make it. I'm just plodding along, the earth pulling me toward it, grabbing my feet tighter with each step I take. Why can't I fly? Why can't I fly to her? Why can't I now, in my dream, have this one goddamned thing?

She looks at me and frowns. I jump to fly to her and am yanked down harder. I am, as always, going nowhere. And, as always, she is gone.

I try to scream to her, and then there is a loud beep, and then another one, and then a louder chime, and then finally a blare. And then I am awake.

There is a blinking message on my screen.

Several.

You have been invited to a Google Hangout by user "aichinisnear2011" Please <u>click here</u> to accept the invitation to chat, or <u>click here</u> to block this user.

appear to have fallen asleep in the chair again. Time remains very confusing. It's dark. Sort of. Dusk? Or maybe the lights are just off.

This is the third time this week I have fallen asleep in this chair, an extremely dangerous activity for me. Sleeping upright requires more effort from my lungs, and it increases the possibility of a clot forming in my trachea, getting caught in there, and choking me on my own blood. It's the sort of offense that even Travis yells at me for. It's just a bad idea across the board.

But it's been an insane few days.

The Google Hangout requests have actually been coming in for the last hour. Jonathan is apparently not pleased by the fact that I was ignoring them, and him. There are five emails in my box, all one paragraph.

20:25 We should take this rare opportunity to chat, Daniel. I've built a Google Hangout for us. Here is the link: Let's Hang Out on Hangouts!

20:41 There is no need to worry. We don't have to video chat or anything like that. I just want to talk. Why wait for emails? You're right there! I'm right here! Let us be friends, Daniel. We should be friends. Let's Hang Out on Hangouts!

21:02 I do not know why I am putting forth such energy trying to get you to talk to me. It is an unnatural power that I have given you.

21:19 I am now concerned that you are trapped under a rock. Did a meteor hit you? Moments ago you were so eager to please, so hopeful that we could connect. And now: Bupkis. So I am worried for you. I would like you to tell me you are OK. We musn't waste this. Let's Hang Out on Hangouts!

21:38 Let's Hang Out on Hangouts! Let's Hang Out on Hangouts! Let's Hang Out on Hangouts! Let's Hang Out on Hangouts! Let's Hang Out on Hangouts! Let's Hang Out on Hangouts! Let's Hang Out on Hangouts! Let's Hang Out on Hangouts! Let's Hang Out on Hangouts! Let's Hang Out on Hangouts! Let's Hang Out on Hangouts!

I'm a semiregular on Google Hangouts. My boss at Spectrum Air corresponds with me throughout the day on there, checking in on how I'm doing, updating me on any particularly egregious delays, occasionally sending me weird right-wing memes. I only respond to him when it's necessary, or when I have to get approval for the official account to block someone: I'm not authorized to execute such a high-level corporate maneuver. There's also a Quentin Tarantino fan group in there that I used to play around with. Travis and I used to communicate through Gchat before they shut it down a few years ago, and sometimes I forget he doesn't use Google Hangouts anymore and send him a funny link or story—he usually responds, like, a year later, saying, "shit i forgot this was still here sorry hahahahahaha dude."

I only use the chat function, even though there's a video call and an audio call, for reasons I presume are obvious.

And now Jonathan wants to chat.

Let's Hang Out on Hangouts!

I check my phone. There are two texts from Marjani, checking in, seeing if Travis is here yet, and one from my mom, telling me she watched the game from Jamaica and GO DAWGS LOVE YOU. No texts from Travis. All quiet. Nothing to see here.

I could put you through a whole moral quandary here, if I wanted to. We could have a Socratic debate about the pros and cons of chatting with Jonathan. I could lay out the reasons it's a good idea, and the (much longer) list of reasons why it's a bad idea. You could tell me all the things I should do, how I should just block the guy and shut down my computer and maybe go back to sleep, and maybe I'll be able to fly this time. You would be right, whatever you said, and I would agree with you on all your points, but you have traveled with me this long so you know exactly what I'm going to do. I'm going to click that link and Hang Out on Hangouts.

48.

flagpolesitta1993

22:11 hello.

22:13 hello.

22:15 i am sorry. i was sleeping. its a sunday. its a good day to sleep hahahahahahaha.

Several minutes pass. I thought this guy was in a hurry. Another ten minutes. You know that feeling when you're particularly obsessed by something, and your heart is pounding, and you're sweating, and it's so intense and absorbing that it almost makes you fall asleep? Like, your body just decides *nope, too much for me, I'm checking out*, and engages Operation Shutdown? No? Just me?

Then a MEOW, the message alert sound on my computer. Whatever, I always wanted a cat.

aichinisnear2011

22:32 Well. Hello there. I was worried you had decided to end our chats just as they were beginning.

flagpolesitta1993

22:33 naw

22:34 naw man

22:35 im here. just took a little nap. whats up? new phone who dis hahahahahaahahaaha.

aichinisnear2011

22:36 Ha, yeah. Well, I think we both know why you are here.

flagpolesitta1993

22:37 oh? whys that?

aichinisnear2011

22:41 This is exciting, right? I think it might be sort of exciting. I like this. You like this. It honestly is pleasant to have someone to share this with, to find someone who understands what it feels like to be on the outside, someone who is not so terribly judgmental. You are not judgmental. Judgmental is so boring, Daniel.

flagpolesitta1993

22:42 im just trying to figure out whats going on.

aichinisnear2011

22:52 Oh, stop.

22:52 I'll confess I have no idea how I missed you. It is weird that I missed you. But that makes no difference now. You saw me. It has been more than a week since Ai-Chin got in my car, and no one knows anything about it but you . . . well, other than me, of course.

22:53 And now you are running this game, acting like you don't know what's going on. You know. YOU KNOW.

22:54 Are you scared of me? That makes a certain amount of sense. I have proven myself capable of, at the minimum, kidnapping, and that

232

alone is more than I suspect you are accustomed to. And frankly more than I am accustomed to. And as far as you know, that is only the start of it. What more might I be capable of?

flagpolesitta1993
23:00 thats what im trying to figure out.
23:00 but go on

aichinisnear2011
23:06 I think, Daniel, that you are restless. Like me! I think you have seen enough of this town, and this world, and its relentless sameness, and when you were confronted with something different, something new, something REAL, you found it irresistible.
23:07 And I think you understand where I am coming from. I think we're not so different. I think you are alone. Isn't that all we keep talking about? Being alone? Not a lot of people understand, truly understand, what that is like. You do. Don't get me wrong: I don't think you were out getting girls in your car or anything. But that's why we could talk. I think that's why you saw me in the first place. I think it was fate.
23:12 It's lonely out here. I think it's lonely for you too. I think you only wish you could do what I did.

flagpolesitta1993
23:14 you are wrong

aichinisnear2011
23:21 Am I, Daniel? You want to know what it is like to do something like I have. To go out and change the world, to make something beautiful, to upset what you all sleepwalk through every day of your lives. To get someone who <u>understands</u>. To see someone who will finally fucking listen. You see it, don't you, Daniel? You see that what I did has value. That I am not like other people. Because you are not like other people either, Daniel.

You recognize this. You might not be like me. But you wish you were. You wish you could do what I do.

flagpolesitta1993
23:26 what did you do?

aichinisnear2011
23:31 That is why we are here, no? It is why you responded to my email, why you are chatting with me now. You want to know what I could do that you could not, what no one else could even imagine. You want to know what they all want to know, the cool guys and talking heads on the television, titillated beyond their greatest hopes, elated that they at last have a missing girl, they need a missing girl, if only they could have a missing girl every day of the week and perhaps twice on Sunday when it's Sweeps Week. They live for the missing girls. I gave them a missing girl.
23:35 But that is not why I gave them a missing girl, Daniel. I just wanted someone who would <u>listen.</u> I knew she would eventually come walking down Agriculture Drive, and I knew, if I arrived early enough, I would be able to find a time with no one awake and walking around.
23:35 Well. Almost no one, I suppose.
23:41 I needed the right person to come along at the right time. But I needed more than that.
23:42 I needed someone who was innocent. I needed someone who was isolated, alone, lost, confused and—and this is what was most important, Daniel—hopeful. I did not pull a gun on her. I did not threaten her. I saw her, I pulled along beside her, I opened the car door, I offered her a ride and . . . she just got in.
23:43 Because she believes. She believes that there are good people out there. That's what she was searching for, even if she didn't realize it. That's what was so great about her then, what's honestly so wonderful about her now: She <u>listens.</u> We just want someone to listen.

23:44 So now I'm listening to you. And you're listening to me. You are listening to me, yes?

flagpolesitta1993

23:45 yes

23:45 i get it

23:45 but i still dont understand your game.

23:46 i talked to the cop.

23:46 he says you are full of shit.

23:46 he says you call them all the time saying you did things you didnt.

aichinisnear2011

23:47 I was wondering when your tone began to change. It was when you talked to the cop.

23:47 I had been thinking that you got it.

23:47 But you don't. You don't get anything.

23:47 That guy didn't take a second to learn anything about me. He's just an oaf.

23:48 He was an oaf again tonight, you know.

23:48 He came by.

23:48 Just a couple of hours ago.

23:48 It could have taken me off guard, him and his partner, in the midst of The Great Ai-Chin Search, showing up at my house out of nowhere.

23:48 But it wasn't out of nowhere. You warned me. In your last email. You warned me that you'd talked to them. And it looks like you sent them my way again. But I was ready.

23:48 Ai-Chin was safely out of sight. I told them I was just messing with some kid on the internet and that I was sorry. They told me to knock it off and that next time I pulled this stunt they'd bring me in.

23:48 They know nothing. They never do. What oafs.

23:48 He's the problem, Daniel. Guys like him. Because he's big and has a uniform, he gets to do whatever he wants.

23:48 But he doesn't know anything.

23:49 Honestly, I'm disappointed in you.

23:49 I think that maybe you don't get it at all.

That email in Chinese sure isn't sounding like a joke right now. This is all sounding pretty fucking real.

flagpolesitta1993

23:50 so what do you want?

23:50 whether you did take her or you didnt what do you want from me?

aichinisnear2011

23:50 I thought you were listening.

23:50 <u>I THOUGHT YOU WERE MY FRIEND.</u>

23:50 But you don't listen to me any more than anyone else does.

23:50 Not like her.

23:50 She listens. You're just another one of them. You only think about yourself.

Sweat drips down my neck. I've started to slink slowly down in my chair to the point that I can barely see the screen.

flagpolesitta1993

23:52 is she OK?

aichinisnear2011

23:52 Oh, she is right here. Hello, Ai-Chin. Say hello.

23:52 She might not understand all this just yet. It's been quite a lot to take in, for both of us. Frankly, we had to have a very serious talk when I discovered her little email to you.

23:52 That is what I get for leaving my laptop open when I go to the bathroom. She is resourceful.

23:52 We have that resolved now.

23:52 We are now back on the same page.

23:52 They're all going to feel very silly when she comes around, fully, when she tells all these people that she wants to be with me, that while what initially happened might be technically thought of as "kidnapping," it was more like a charming introduction. It'll be our story! She'll tell them she's where she needed to be all along.

23:52 That she found her place. And I found mine.

flagpolesitta1993

23:52 if she really wants to stay, then you should tell her she can leave.

23:53 can she leave?

23:53 she cant.

aichinisnear2011

23:56 The thing that you're missing here, Daniel. You're the one who got me to this place.

23:56 I wasn't sure what the purpose of this was at first. I enjoyed talking to her, but then she got in the car, and then she was at my place, and then I asked her to stay, and then she wanted to leave, but I wasn't ready for her to leave yet. What if she never came back? What if she was lying like the rest of them?

23:57 But the thing is now that I realize, thanks to you, that this is all part of a larger story. Her getting in my car. Her in my basement. Me meeting you, my fellow outcast, my fellow traveler. You're the one who helped me understand that I wasn't alone here. That there are people who feel like I do, who are lost just like I am. I think you are confused. I think the cop has confused you. This is still something we can share.

23:58 And that there is hope. And that this is going to end well.

23:58 I just need some time. And I need you not to stand in my way.

23:58 You're just a guy who sits on your porch and does nothing.

23:58 Yes. I've seen you. I know who you are now. You were paying too close attention to yourself, and you didn't notice that I've been watching you the whole time. You are very easy to find. Did you think I wouldn't be able to find you? There are not very many houses in your neighborhood. And definitely not very many with people living in them who stay inside all day.

With most of the energy I have left, I pull myself back up in my chair.

flagpolesitta1993
23:58 what
23:58 what
23:58 youre crazy.
23:58 youre just a creep.
23:58 i dont want to be a part of your sickness dude.
23:58 i just want to see you in jail.
23:58 but first i want to kick your ass.

aichinisnear2011
23:58 No you don't. You're not going to kick anyone's ass.
23:59 Because you can't even get out of that chair.

There is a loud *crack*, a brief flicker of intense light, and then I fall.

MONDAY

49.

My dad left before I knew him. I'm not even mad about it. I didn't know him enough to miss him, or even know what I was supposed to be missing. I do not think about him.

Mom never said a bad word about him because she never said any word about him. Her strategy was to hide him from me, not to even mention him, the way you wouldn't mention a random schoolteacher in South Dakota you'd never heard of, or an extra in a Norwegian kids' TV show that you couldn't watch even if you wanted to. To discuss him would be to give him a power that he didn't deserve. He was just a guy. She didn't seem curious about him, so I wasn't either.

I finally asked her about him a few years ago, once it was safe, once it was clear that I had turned out just fine after all and that I wasn't going to start searching for him or anything. I was just sort of curious, the way you wonder what your parents were like before you were born—I kind of cared, but it wasn't urgent or anything. She said she had no idea where he was, that the last she heard he was selling cell phones somewhere in Northern California, but that was twenty years ago, he could be on the moon by now.

"I didn't really have time to worry about your father," she told me. "I was too busy grieving my mom."

About six months after my diagnosis and about three years after my father left, my grandmother, Rosemary Whightsel Lamm, was plucking flowers with her best friend, Elizabeth. Rosemary was recently widowed: Otis, her second husband, had died of prostate cancer after a long, grueling illness, one that required Rosemary to quit her job and tend to him for the final ten years of his life. She had been a semi-successful real estate agent in Ohio, but when Otis got too sick to work, and then too sick to leave the house, she quit to be his full-time caretaker. It was brutal, Mom says, just a sad empty house where nothing was happening but a man's slow, painful death, waited on solemnly by the woman who loved him but didn't necessarily sign up for a decade spent cleaning his bedpan, draining boils, and listening to him groan in pain. Mom said it was too much for her to handle—she went three full years without visiting. "I feel so ashamed," she told me, starting to cry. "I didn't even take you to see her when you were born. It was too horrible in there."

Just after my diagnosis Otis at last died. Mom said that after the funeral, Rosemary immediately blossomed into the woman Mom remembered: fanciful and goofy and voraciously curious about the world. Freed of having to tend to her dying husband, she returned to life. She made plans to sell her house, to take a cruise to Alaska, to maybe see London; she'd always wanted to see London, but she'd never even left the United States. She came to Illinois and she spent a month with us, enjoying her grandson and her daughter, planning all her trips and what she was going to do with her life now that she at last would be allowed to enjoy it. "I miss Otis," Mom said she'd told her. "But I'm glad it's over." She returned to Ohio. We were all going to visit that summer.

It was a brisk, comfortable April late afternoon when Rosemary and Elizabeth took their weekly visit to their friend's garden, across the bridge in Kentucky, about twenty minutes outside Cincinnati, where you left suburbia and hit the long, flat, empty lands of rural Kentucky, where there is one stop sign to be seen for miles on end, where there are 55 mph two-lane roads with names like 44 RR 2 E. They had an isolated spot at the end of a long blind curve but miles and miles from the nearest freeway, a place you could just wander around, looking at flowers, listening to birds, finding some peace away from the madness.

Elizabeth told Mom later that Rosemary was just lost in thought, walking across the road toward a new garden where some lilies had blossomed suddenly, unexpectedly, off in her own little world, a space that was just hers, at last. She didn't see the truck barreling around the curve, and he didn't see her until it was too late for either of them. He was speeding. She was in the middle of the road. There usually weren't any other people for miles. Elizabeth said Rosemary was facing away from her when she was hit. She didn't know if Rosemary was smiling, or sad, or wistful, or just walking blankly along the way we all walk blankly along every day, just going where we want to go.

Elizabeth said she watched Rosemary fly through the air. That's when Mom asked her to stop talking.

Rosemary Whightsel Lamm, aged fifty-six, after a life spent caring for others and cut short right at the moment she no longer was required to, was buried in Illinois even though that month she spent with us was the longest she'd ever set foot in the state. Mom just said she needed her close by.

My mother, a young mom who had lost her husband, then her mother, mere months after learning that her only son would spend his entire short life, as far as she knew, crumbling and decaying in front of her, felt as if several airplanes had landed on her at once. "I'd lived such a lucky life," she told me. "I realized right then just how fortunate I had been. I mean, nothing all that bad had ever happened to me. Dad died before I ever got to know him. I didn't have any close friends die, I was never assaulted or raped, people had always been nice to me. I had no real complaints about the world.

"You don't really know anything about yourself until you've been forced to deal with pain, real pain. My life before all that happened feels now like a hazy, vague summer where I was protected and sheltered and completely lacking in understanding about how the world worked. I'm better because of it. I learned I wasn't exempt from suffering, because no one is. There was nothing special about me. I had to go through it like everyone else."

It was losing her mother that almost broke her. My father, well, she'd always suspected he was a bit of a shithead. And as sad as she was about my diagnosis, that mostly made her dig in her heels. I was someone who needed help. What mother doesn't want to help her child? I gave her focus and purpose and determination. I required effort and grit and fight, I required fortitude and strength she didn't know she had. SMA and what it took from me gave her an enemy to tussle with, a target at which to launch all her energy and focus. I gave her a cause.

But losing Rosemary, there was no target to aim at there. It was just loss, pure loss, someone she loved and needed, someone she regretted not being a better daughter to, someone she wished had been given a better life, someone who was just about to become the person she was always supposed to be before it was taken away from her . . . someone who was there one day, and then the next day was not.

Grief, Mom discovered, was not a problem you could fix, a

loose screw you could tighten, a math problem you could solve, a child whose pain you could comfort. It just sat there in your stomach and didn't move. Sometimes it grew, sometimes it shrank, but it was always, always there.

That was the hardest part, she said, harder than anything else, before or after. The grief doesn't leave. It becomes a part of you. Either you learn to live with it or you die.

You can deal with a disease you can research and attack. You can deal with an ex-husband you can pretend never existed. These are problems with clear forms, straightforward parameters, problems you can whittle away at until they are more manageable, small enough to get your arms around.

But grief just sits there.

The part I always go back to is that Mom felt lucky until her mother died.

She was just wandering through the world, lah-dee-dah, thinking life was just this happy sandbox she got to play around in, and then the reality hit her, and her life was just not the same again. She could experience joy, and she could embrace life. All the travel she does now, the exotic trips with various companions lingering in the background of the Skype shots, that's a direct response to Rosemary: she's living the way she wishes her mother could have had the opportunity to live, a way of honoring her. (I bet the hotel massages aren't bad either.)

But this new life came after. It was all in the wake of that realization that life is pain, that everything you love can and will be taken away from you, that the only way to keep going is to accept that that big black grief is going to fester there in your stomach forever—that it's never going to get better.

This is what made me realize that I am lucky. Right now.

My whole life up to this point, I've never lost anyone. Not Mom. Not Travis. Not Kim, really. Not Marjani. And I am blessed. I am blessed because I am going to go long before any of them do. I am not going to have to grieve for them, because they are going to have to grieve for me.

I know that this is selfish, this solace in the fact that my loved ones will miss me and thus have to experience pain that I never will. But I cannot deny that it is true.

I am the lucky one in this regard. I get to go first. I get to leave before grief ever becomes the house guest that never leaves. I get to prance around this world, how lucky, not having to live with the ache of saying goodbye. That's for them. I'm sad for them that they'll grieve when I die. But I'm glad I won't. I'm lucky. I'm lucky I'll leave before the grief gets here. I'm lucky to get to go alone. I'm lucky, I'm lucky, I'm so, so lucky.

50.

force my eyes open. I'm on the floor, out of my chair. My shirt is ripped and wet. I see a pair of chrome-tipped boots. They look sharper up close. I lift my head up.

Jonathan is dressed all in black. There is no Atlanta Thrashers hat. He is clean-shaven, and it is not a good look for him; he should definitely grow a beard to hide that weak chin. He is holding a small flashlight. He leans down and shines it in my face.

He laughs. "You are a more formidable opponent online than in all three dimensions. Your house was easy to find, but I hadn't known until yesterday that you were . . . this. The world is just a cavalcade of surprises." He flicks the light off, and I nod back out.

don't know how long it has been, but I'm still on the floor. All the lights are on in my room, and now the kitchen light is on too. I think I can smell bacon cooking in there? Maybe I'm having a heart attack. They say you experience all sorts of weird smells when you're having a heart attack. Or is that a stroke? I can't remember.

I must look like someone shuffled all my body parts like a deck of cards and then just randomly splayed them across the floor. It takes me a second to realize that the chewed-up wad of gum on the floor a few feet in front of my face is, in fact, my left foot. My hair is sopping wet, and it could be from any number of things, none of them good. I can't open my left eye, I can see dust bunnies kick up around my nose every time I breathe, and I honestly have no idea where my left arm is.

A vague, unsettling pocket of air begins to settle in my chest. I know this feeling. All this jostling has dislodged some junk in my lungs, and once I get up, it's going to keep rattling around in there. I have no idea how it's going to get out.

This is not a good situation.

I hear rustling from the kitchen. I have a brief moment where

I think maybe I made all this up. One of the orderlies tucked me in poorly last night. I've just fallen out of bed. Marjani's about to come in. She's going to yell so loud when she sees me. She's going to clean me off. Then she'll laugh. We'll eat breakfast. I'll ask her why she made bacon. She knows I can't eat bacon. She'll just say, "It felt like a bacon day!" I will laugh, even though I don't understand. It's another beautiful day in Athens.

I shut my eyes. Then WHOMP, my stomach explodes as Jonathan—holding a plate of bacon, apparently—kicks me. Hard. I scream, then roll over to my side, where my ribs make a sound that's vaguely similar to crunching a bunch of croutons with your fist. It hurts beyond words.

"Wake up, Daniel!" Jonathan yells. "We're finally getting to know each other." Air is slowly expelling out of all parts of my body, all of which are slightly obstructed in one way or another, for one reason or another, which means I'm currently a symphony of balloons slowly being deflated. I feel like I'm being propelled, gliding from the air slightly across the floor.

This is definitely the worst pain I've ever felt, and that's saying something. Jonathan bends down on one knee, seriously, still holding that stupid plate of bacon, and leans close to my face. "You must get up, Daniel," he says. "It's extremely difficult to have any sort of conversation with you in this condition."

He finally sets the plate down in the living room and tries to pick me up again. He is not good at it. He jams his left arm into my already broken rib cage and absentmindedly bashes my face with his right elbow. Just about all the air I have left escapes my throat and mouth with a sad wail.

"Shit, what's the best way do to this?" he says. "This is harder than I had realized. You must need a lot of help around here, Daniel!" He lies flat on the floor and puts his nose up to mine. He has a pasty, flabby face, with stupid round rosy cheeks and that soft chin. He also has the breath of a cadaver. "How do you usually get yourself up, man?"

He stares at me for a good ten seconds. What's most disturbing about him is how he looks like just like every postgrad dope I see around campus every day. He doesn't look deranged. He's not frothing at the mouth. He doesn't have a swastika tattoo on his eyeball. He's not scary at all. If anything, he looks a little bewildered to find himself here, even afraid.

"You don't talk either? Come on." He stands back up. "Well, let's try this again," and he leans over, and I prepare myself to scream again.

And then I hear rapid footsteps from the kitchen, and I see a blur above my head, and then I hear another scream, and then grunts and gasps and growls, and then a crash into the bookshelf just to the left of me. It falls. Down come the books and an old EIU Panthers novelty coffee mug my mom bought so I'd remember home, on top of me and Jonathan and whoever the hell this is, and here we go again, I'm out—

52.

Terry! That's the other night orderly's name! I knew it would come to me eventually.

Terry is right above me. And he knows how to pick me up.

"Who the *fuck* was that guy?" says Terry, who has a tattoo on his neck and a pack of smokes in his shirt pocket, as he straightens up my chair, which was knocked over in the melee, and takes a rag to wipe off my forehead. I look at the rag: yep, it's blood up there. "I come in for my rounds, and . . . shit. Do you know that guy?" I think Terry has forgotten I can't speak, and he hasn't worked here long enough for us to be able to talk with our eyes yet. He looks at me, sighs, grunts, and says, "Let's get you back in your chair."

I start to pant, and panic. "It'll be all right, man, I know he banged you up pretty good," he says. "I'll be gentle. But you gotta get up off the floor."

He is very gentle. He caresses the top of my head, massages his left hand behind my neck and cradles his right hand under my knees. It's excruciating, but it at least gets my body straightened out: I am at least in the shape that I was in the first place. I feel the croutons crumbling in my chest as he lifts me, and more air is leaving my body at every orifice and crevice, but: I am not on the floor. He puts me in my chair, and I moan as he straps me in. He pushes me into the kitchen.

"So, Daniel, what the hell happened?" he says, a wild look in his eye. Tonight is a lot more than he signed up for. "How'd that guy get in here?" He stands up and begins to pace around, working through what just happened.

"I come in here, a few minutes late, and all the lights are on, and I'm like, 'Yeah, that's a little weird, but whatever,' and then there's some dude cooking? And then he walks in here, and you're on the floor, and he's trying to pick you up? We scuffled around a bit, and then I punched him and then he ran off. Who is that guy? Like, what the fuck?"

I try to make eye contact from my chair.

Call the police.
Call the police.
The phone is right there on the wall.
Call the police.
Call 911.
Call 911.

I try to move my eyes back and forth between him and the phone, but I'm moving slowly because everything hurts so, so much.

We need help.
Call 911.

He's not getting the hint.

"That's not your friend, is it? I met that guy once, he wasn't anything like that. Why is there some dude in here in the middle

252

of the night? And he's knocked you over? What the hell?" He has stopped pacing and is now looking up at the ceiling in bafflement. I sympathize.

And then I see Jonathan. He must have come in the front door while Terry was putting me back in my chair. He is creeping up behind Terry, holding something in his right hand. I attempt to scream, to warn Terry, but I can make no sound other than a faint wisp of sad, saggy air dribbling out of my nose. I am even more useless than usual.

"Man, we gotta call the cops," Terry says, catching on a bit too late to help me or himself. I can do nothing as he turns to his right, toward the phone, and he is met with Jonathan hitting him square in the face with an aluminum baseball bat. He falls, banging his head on the kitchen table. Jonathan stands above him, and hits him again, and again. After the third hit, Terry is no longer making any noise. But Jonathan hits him one more time. His face is a lot less slack now. He looks a lot less normal now. He looks . . . at peace.

floor it. Seeing Jonathan's trance, the narrowing of his eyes, the blaring of his nostrils, the way his forehead seemed to find all sorts of new veins with every swing, seeing all that while he was beating in the brains of Terry with a baseball bat—it was horrifying, but it was also clarifying: this situation is incredibly real, and I have to get out of here, right now. The last thing Terry may have ever done was put me in my chair, and it's my responsibility to make sure that act saves my life.

So in between his third and fourth swing, when Jonathan is looking away from me, I jam the accelerator on my chair forward and make a beeline through the kitchen and toward the front door. The mere act of moving makes every one of my nerves burst into flames. But it's that or the bat.

I run into one of the chairs at the kitchen table, causing a loud screech across the linoleum that breaks Jonathan out of his trance. He turns around. He is not calm. "Where do you think *you're* going?" he roars. I have roughly one second for this to work.

But: my chair gets caught on the thick refrigerator cord, and suddenly, I'm not moving. I sit there for a millisecond or five hundred, spinning my wheels, caught on the refrigerator cord as Jonathan sprints around the table toward me.

I push the accelerator with every tiny bit of strength I have.

Come on. Come on.

Then another screech. The refrigerator yanks loose from its moorings on the wall and pushes right in between Jonathan and my chair. My wheels get free of the cord, and he's stuck behind the refrigerator. I hear him yell behind me, not in a murderous rage but in frustration, woe-is-me self-pity. But I am out the door, and down the ramp, and onto Agriculture Drive.

It is still dark. No one is on the road, and no lights are on. I would have thought the ruckus at my place would have woken someone up, but apparently not. It's just me in my pajamas, with blood all over me, and my chair, wheeling me away from my home, where there is possibly a dead man, a maniac the whole state's looking for, and a refrigerator sitting in the middle of the kitchen.

I check to make sure the phone hookup on my chair is working. I Skype Travis.

"*Mmmmmmphhhhhhhhh,*" I say when I get his voice mail.

And then I hear what sounds like my front door opening, and I turn right onto Agriculture, and I go as fast as I can, away, away from all of it. I hear a brief scream, and then it fades, and the farther away I get, the less I can hear. Which only makes me want to go faster.

've never crashed. Pretty proud of that. My chair's industrial, a tank: Its wheels are wider than my waist. If you see me on the street, you should be more worried for yourself than you are for me. I'll run your ass over.

I have no idea where to go. Travis could be anywhere, Marjani's house is way out in Winterville, twenty miles away, and it's not like any school buildings are open at three on a Monday morning. I could go knock on one of my neighbors' doors, but none of their porches are wheelchair accessible, and also there is the problem of the actual physical knocking. I've gotten out of my house and away from Jonathan, and that's a victory. That situation was not going to turn out well. But now what am I supposed to do?

I come to the end of Agriculture, on Carlton Street. I stop to think. Stegeman Coliseum is just a couple of blocks to my left. Maybe there's security in there or something? The police? The closest police station is all the way downtown, which isn't that far, but particularly perilous when it's pitch-dark outside. The closest hospital is even farther away from the police station. I dial Travis again. Nothing.

I sit there for another second. Slowing down for the first time since I woke up has allowed me to take stock of the current physical situation. My breaths are short and rattling, the croutons in my chest have broken into even smaller pieces and are floating around loose and dangerous in there, and it's a good thing it's dark, because I'm pretty sure what's left of my pajamas is drenched in blood.

Look at me. Look at me, Mr. Tough Guy, Mr. I Can Do This on My Own, Mr. Don't Worry, Mom, I Want You to Go Live Your Life without Having to Care for Me, Mr. Travis and I Will Be Fine. Look at me now. It's the dead of night, Terry might be murdered in my home, I'm by myself in the middle of the street, liable to stop breathing at any moment, which might not matter because I'm pretty certain my rib cage is shattered and my skull is cracked. If I even make it out of this, none of these wounds are ever going to heal.

This is serious. I was hanging by a thread before a madman barged into my house and kicked the shit out of me. You prepare yourself for what might be coming, what *is* coming. You're taught to appreciate every moment, from a very young age, because life is short, but it is unusually short for you. You have to drink it in, lap it up, embrace all of it, because it's going to be taken away from you quicker than it's going to be taken away from the rest of them. So you have to be ready. You have to accept it.

But I realize now, at the moment of truth, at the last, worst possible second, that I'm not ready. I don't know if this is it or not. I don't know how much is left. But now that it is staring me straight in the face, I won't kid myself: I'm not ready. I want to keep going. I want to live a long time. I want to see if Travis and that girl get together or if he fucks it up. I want to see if Marjani can ever get out of this endless cycle of constant labor, and maybe help her do it somehow. I want to beat Todd in that game someday. I want to see a picture of Kim's kids, if she ever has them, they'll be so cute. I want to see who wins the next election (I think). I want to see if Georgia football ever wins a national championship. I want to find out where D. B. Cooper ended up. I want to see if Glenn Close is ever going to get an Oscar.

I want to see my mom. *I want to see my mom.* I want to keep going. I want to stay here.

I've never wanted any of that more than I want it right now. You're never ready. How could you be?

I am alive. Just barely. But: I am.

The hospital. That's where I have to go. Everything that's going to happen has to start there. I can't do anything else until I take care of myself. You gotta give yourself oxygen before you can give it to anyone else. I have to put my own mask on first.

I turn left on Carlton. If I can make it to Lumpkin, I can turn left on Baxter and make it to the St. Mary's emergency room. I was just there a few days ago. If I can make it there, we'll figure out the rest.

It is a plan.

I'm coming up on Stegeman, booking pretty good up the sidewalk, when I hear a horn.

55

Of course it's Jonathan. He's in the Camaro. I am fast, but I am not faster than a Camaro. He slows down to drive alongside me. The morning is chilly and windless. He is smiling. He looks happy. He has a glow to him. He looks like he has, at last, figured out who he is.

"Hey, buddy," he says. "Need a ride?"

He then speeds up the Camaro and pulls in front of me on the sidewalk. How is there *nobody* up at this hour? I pull back on my controller to slam on the brakes, and shift into reverse. Jonathan leaps out of the car and begins sprinting toward me. I floor it backward, my cheeks flapping and chattering, my heart pushing little pieces of ribs all around my chest.

And then I plow straight into a street sign, and hard. This thing really needs a backup camera.

My chair flips on its side, and I land on the Carlton Street asphalt. There is a crunch, and when I open my eyes, two of my teeth are lying on the concrete in front of me. A little part of me that had been with me my whole life, now gone, out there in the world, just two more bits of trash on the ground.

I look at them. They're larger than I realized. We had a good run, boys.

Jonathan's boots approach. Lit from behind by his headlights, he looks like an alien, distorted in shadow and massive, infinite. He has come to take E.T. home.

"You are a persistent fellow, Daniel, I will give you that," Jonathan says as he bends down again, right there on Carlton Street, to look me in the eye. His face has a halo of blood around it, somebody's, maybe his, maybe Terry's, maybe mine, like he tried to wipe a coat of it off but did it in a hurry and mostly just pushed it out of his eyes.

"You know what's wild, man?" His eyebrows are at the top of his forehead. He looks like he's going to bite the head off a bat. He hisses directly into my ear. "I didn't know what I was going to do when I got over here. You know I've never punched someone in my life until now? I didn't know it would feel so . . . good. It feels so good! It makes you understand why people are always hitting people." He pauses. "I'm sorry it had to be you. I really am. But it turns out you don't understand any more than the rest of them do. I'm not sure you ever did."

He rests his elbow on the turned-over wheel in front of my face.

"This chair of yours is rather formidable. I am impressed."

He takes my left hand in his.

"It is remarkable how much this chair can do, I have to say," he says, his face contorting into a smirk. "And it's all controlled by this little lever, yes?"

He places his right hand on my controller and jiggles it around like a video game joystick. He chuckles. "Vroom, vroom."

He then looks me in the eye.

"And all it takes is these little fingers to move so fast," he says. "What can't technology do anymore?"

And then he squeezes, and I scream again. It is my loudest scream yet. Maybe I've got a little bit more left in me than I thought.

"Probably a lot harder to drive now, though," he says.

56.

If I'd been born ten years later, I'd have had a real chance. You would never believe the advancements they've made with SMA just over the last ten years alone. The death sentence my mother had to deal with, learning that your smiling, bouncing toddler probably isn't going to make it to his twenties, parents don't have to deal with that today. Remember the Ice Bucket Challenge? We talked about the Ice Bucket Challenge. When millions of people all across the world dumped ice water on their heads and posted the video to social media? Even the president did it!

I know memes are silly and a waste of time, but it is worth noting that this silly meme did some real good. The Ice Bucket Challenge was in support of fighting ALS, or Lou Gehrig's disease. As we've established, SMA is, kind of, ALS for kids; they found back in 2012 there's even a genetic link at a molecular level. Which means a lot of that money and attention ALS got because of the Ice Bucket Challenge back in 2014, $115 million over the span of *eight weeks*, ended up helping fight SMA too. Since 2014, thusly, there have been dramatic breakthroughs in the treatment of SMA, specifically among babies. In the last few years they've developed a drug called Spinraza, and it has changed the whole game. You know back when my parents discovered I couldn't roll over, or hold weight on my legs, and when they took me to the doctor, and the doctor said, "Yeah, he has this disease you've never heard of, and he'll never be able to walk and it'll kill him when he's a teenager. Now, please sign here." Yeah, I told you about that.

Well, now you can give them Spinraza, simply by injecting it right into their cerebrospinal fluid. (Simply.) In some clinical trials, it has actually halted the disease entirely, and a majority of kids have experienced improved motor function within months. There are side effects, many involving respiration issues (it's always that with us), and nobody knows for sure what the long-term ramifications of the drug are. But it's tough to come up with a worse long-term ramification than "death by your early twenties." Kids have hope now. Their parents aren't told that it's twenty-one or bust, and that's only if you catch a break. They get the bare minimum: they get a chance.

I am not bitter about coming around too late for this. I am happy for them! And anyway, it's not like Spinraza suddenly makes their life easy or anything. All Spinraza does is give them a modicum of hope that someday they might have an outside shot at something resembling the vague outlines of a normal life. Spinraza comes with its own issues too, not least of which is that you can only get Spinraza if you're SMA-1 or SMA-2, the most severe forms, and every injection is going to run you $125,000 apiece. You get five injections your first year, and three every year after that, which means that over the first ten years of your life, it costs $4 million just to give you a chance at maybe possibly staying alive. You thought my mom's life was hard enough raising me? Now imagine what insurance looks like when you have to fight for four million bucks' worth of injections.

I wouldn't change anything, all told. I'm glad they've made

advancements. I'm glad they know more. I'm glad SMA is not an obvious death sentence anymore. I'm glad a bunch of people dumping water on their heads and posting it to Instagram made an actual difference in the world. It's only a few years later, but you would never see an Ice Bucket Challenge now. We don't trust or believe anything online anymore. I'm glad that happened at the exact last moment it could have meant anything. It doesn't seem like things are getting better, but sometimes they are, they really are.

But my life is mine. I had an opportunity to live as close to a "normal" life as I possibly could have. That's not nothing. I will take it. I have taken it.

But yeah.

When you know you're going to die young before you ever know what "dying" or "being young" even means, you're an odd combination. You can be incredibly cautious (what if right now is when it happens?) and stupidly reckless (what if tomorrow is when it happens?). I've spent my life with death sitting right next to me, silently observing, taking its time, happy to scoop me up on a whim. I had to take advantage of the little time I had. For me, it manifested itself in taking big risks, like moving to Athens, far away from my mom and almost everything I knew.

I wonder what it would have been like if I hadn't always known I was gonna die. I wonder if I'd be sitting in this chair right now, in Georgia, in the middle of the night, with crumpled bones and a maniac pushing me down the street while muttering to himself about how heavy this "gimp" is, with no one knowing where I am, with no one who can help me. I put myself in this predicament, I think, because I felt both fragile and immortal. I cheated death for a long time. And yet here I am. All because the end always felt around the corner.

Don't judge. It's just around the corner for you too.

'm sorry about all that, Daniel," he says. "Ai-Chin will be disappointed in me. She says she liked you. She didn't tell me about the chair, though. We're going to have some words over that."

He inhales deeply. "Ahhhh . . . Now let's get back to this bacon."

Jonathan is making bacon again. At four in the morning. In my kitchen. He wheeled me back home, panting and cursing all the way because I had the emergency brake on and he didn't know how to click it off, pushed me up my ramp, brought me inside, stashed me in the corner, kicked Terry to make sure he wasn't moving (he wasn't, though I think I saw his chest move a couple of times), washed the blood off his hands in the sink, picked up the bacon he had been eating off the floor, put a piece of it in his mouth, scowled and grimaced, placed it in the trash, walked up to me, looked me in the eye, apologized, mentioned that Ai-Chin hadn't told him about the chair, and then said, "Now let's get back to this bacon."

Nothing hurts anymore. This is a gift, I suppose, like at the end of *Brazil*, when Jonathan Pryce is in so much pain while he's being tortured that he leaves his body and imagines a future where he makes a hero's escape and runs off with the woman he loves. I am just curled up in the chair, tucked into this corner, and the pain of my broken bones and my gasping lungs and whatever is causing my hair to be dripping blood from its wet tips, it's all somewhere else. I appreciate the break. I must look like I've been dribbled down multiple staircases, but I'm alert, lucid, even a little calm. And the bacon still smells terrific.

In the light, Jonathan doesn't look crazy anymore. He's just the same postgraduate doof I thought he was in the first place, doughy, pasty, entirely unremarkable. Amusingly, he has put on Marjani's apron to cook the bacon.

My mind drifts. My mother loved bacon, and Travis loves bacon, which may be why Marjani always makes it. Mom's a midwestern girl, and she used to fry up bologna for me. You ever had fried bologna? I know it's a little trashy, but I'd eat fried bologna sandwiches on Wonder Bread, covered in ketchup, as long as she'd keep putting them in front of me. It's the ultimate white people food: spiceless, flavorless. But hearty. There are twenty slices of bologna in an Oscar Meyer package. That used to feed me for a week. I always liked that old house. Mom sold it when she decided to leave the EIU job, and then when I moved, we just—

Jonathan is sitting at the table, eating his bacon and staring intently at the wall. What was this all about again?

Ai-Chin. The pain slowly returns, which makes me feel urgent, insistent. *What was all this for?*

I conjure up what I can, and from somewhere deep, I make a sound.

"*Aiiiiiiiiiiii.*"

Jonathan snaps out of his trance. "Oh, look at you," he says, smiling. "You're a piece of work, Daniel. Full of surprises."

Rather than get up, he scooches his chair toward me, still seated, scraping it against the floor and leaving scuff marks all over the linoleum. He positions it across from me and once again puts his face up close to mine. He always looks at me like I'm a toy he can't decide if he should play with.

"What are you trying to tell me, Daniel?"

"*Aiiiiiiiiiiiii.*" A deep, extremely painful breath. "*Chhhhhh-hhhhh.*" Another. Some sort of liquid drips down my nose, and Jonathan, not insensitively, wipes it off with his shirt cuff. "*Nn-nnnnnnnn.*"

He jumps up from his chair as if he just sat in something. "Daniel! Are you asking me about Ai-Chin?" He walks over to the refrigerator, still looking at me with something resembling awe. He takes out a beer, a stray Terrapin Golden that Travis left in there. "You are nothing if not persistent. She was right about you. You really are sweet."

He takes the bottle and pops it open against the edge of my dinner table, leaving a nick in the wood that's going to irritate Marjani. He pours it into a pint class and lifts it to me.

"Cheers, Daniel," he says. "Cheers to the one guy I can talk to."

And then he begins to talk.

This was all I wanted, all along. I wanted to know if it was him. I wanted to know why he took her. I wanted to know where she was. I wanted to know if she was safe. I wanted to know why this was all happening. I wanted to know if it was all real.

Jonathan talks. He talks and talks and talks and talks.

And I am unable to listen. The pain has ended its sabbatical and overtaken me again, and I find myself passing out, waking up, passing out again, waking up again. My ears have begun to ring so loudly that I wouldn't be able to make out what he was saying even if I were awake for the whole thing. It is all just droning noise. I have no idea what he's saying. I can barely tell if he's still here.

None of it matters. Maybe he said he took her because he was lonely, and it's something that we shared, and maybe he thinks Ai-Chin really loves him because he's a sad pathetic man with no social skills who blames everyone else for all his problems and lashes out because he can't handle the real world. Maybe it was a master plan. Maybe it was all an accident. I have no idea. I am only barely conscious. It doesn't matter what he's saying. None of it matters at all. All that matters is that he has her. And that now he has me.

I'm sure he hasn't noticed. To him, I look the same awake or asleep, alive or dead. He just keeps talking, just to himself. As always, and probably as forever.

We went through this whole thing to find out the truth of what happened, to find out what was real, and he's sitting here right in front of me, in my kitchen, telling me the whole thing.

And I can't keep my eyes open.

Jonathan lightly slaps me across my left cheek with his phone. He finally noticed I was asleep.

"You are a little too captive of an audience, it seems, Daniel," he says. "To be fair, we have been through a lot."

My eyes focus and look up at him. I feel a surge of strength, and the pain fades for a moment. It occurs to me that I truly hate this motherfucker in front of me right now and would like to see him run over by a truck.

"But you will want to see this."

His phone is showing a grainy video I can't entirely make out, but appears to be some sort of security footage. It is. It is security footage. I see a dark figure, pixelated and hazy, and then it moves, slowly at first, and then quickly, jutting left and right but locked in place at its center. There is no sound, but the figure is looking toward the sky, no, toward the camera, and screaming. I think it's a scream. Where I'm guessing the mouth is, it's opening wide for a few seconds at a time. A scream is as good a guess as any.

"See?" Jonathan says. "She's fine! She was always fine! We're friends. She finally likes me."

I pass out again.

When I wake up, Jonathan has stopped talking. He has stopped paying attention to me. He has stopped doing anything at all. He is sitting in the chair in front of the television in the living room, where Travis is usually playing video games and occasionally passing out when he doesn't feel like driving home. One weekend, I think he was depressed about a girl or something, he didn't leave that chair other than to use the bathroom or open the refrigerator for about sixty hours.

Jonathan is not playing video games, or watching anything. He looks exhausted. It's still dark, but I'm starting to hear birds chirp outside. I realize it'll still be hours before Marjani arrives. Jonathan has been up all night. I've been up all night. As far as he knows, there's a man he killed in the kitchen, an act, it's becoming increasingly clear, he's never done before, and one he's struggling with. He just stares into space. He'll blink heavily every few seconds, sometimes put his head in his hands, sometimes put his chin into his shoulder, maybe nod off for a bit before snapping himself alert, muttering to himself.

I watch him trying to calculate all this.

It all just got out of hand. You took Ai-Chin, and that was

bad, that was very bad. But you haven't killed her. You locked her in your home and put a camera on her, but, if I can piece together at least *some* of what you were trying to tell me, you haven't beaten her or raped her or done much of anything to her. You just . . . *had* her. She wanted a ride, she got in your car, you didn't take her to where she wanted to go, you took her to your place and then before you knew it, here you were, with the whole South searching for her, her whereabouts leading every newscast, mass vigils all across the town, with all kinds of different people gathering to try to find her, to help her. All because of you! You went out to breathe it all in, because how could you not? This was happening as a result of a series of decisions you made. You made the world happen! You had been invisible, and then you weren't. Then you mattered. This made you feel connected. This made you feel important. This made you feel *seen*.

I position my mangled left hand so that I can say something. I can still say something. It hurts. But I can say something.

"Jonathan."

He slowly lifts his head up and turns it to me.

"It. Is. Not. Too. Late."

He gives me a tired, sad grin. "Look, you can talk," he says. "Good for you. We should have been talking this whole time. But you're not gonna trick me. I'm"—he puts his head down on his chest—"I'm on to you."

He closes his eyes and succumbs to sleep. I get it.

He sits there, for five minutes, for ten minutes, not moving. And then I notice.

His phone.

It's sitting next to him in the chair, on the armrest, the same place Travis's phone always sits when he conks out. I can still make out the figure of Ai-Chin on the Nest cam on Jonathan's phone, glowing from the iPhone screen. I can even tell she's sleeping too.

I turn my head to my left. My wrist has some feeling in it; it has throbbed constantly since typing Jonathan that message. I can move it, slightly. More to the point: I can jut it forward enough to make my chair move. I can't control my chair: I need my fingers for that.

But I can push forward.

And then what? I can't pick up the phone. I can't dial it.

But what else? Am I just going to sit here and choke on my own blood? That's what's going to happen if I don't do something. Oblivion is just around the corner.

But.

I'm not ready for it.

I'm not ready for the last thing I ever see to be this shithead sleeping in Travis's chair as the girl he kidnapped starves right there in front of him on his phone.

This is not how this ends.

I don't know how this will work.

But this is it. I've got some kick left in me. You can smash my bones, you can crush my lungs, you can bloody my skull, you can even drink Travis's beer out of my goddamned fridge.

You cannot, however, make me just sit here and take it. Not anymore.

The plan? There is no plan. Is there ever a plan? Just go forward. Just go forward, and see what happens.

They'll never see it coming. I wedge my wrist behind my joystick. There is a possibility that if I plunge my wrist forward and I'm at a bad angle in a confined space, I will just spin around in circles really fast until I fall over. Maybe the chair will just land on me at that point and finish the job. That'd be an appropriately dignified way to go out.

Not a lot of options here. No precision. No control. No plan. Just forward. Just floor it.

JUST FLOOR IT.

This.

This is for everyone who was born with this terrible disease decades ago. We are everywhere, and we are strong, and we are not just objects of your pity. For every one of you who talked to me like I was a moron, like my brain was malformed just because I used this chair and because I couldn't wipe cheese from the side of my mouth, know that I forgive you. You just don't know.

This. This is for my mom. You did everything you could have done and more. You put your life aside for me, and you gave me what I needed to survive, and to be autonomous, to have my own life. You are the reason I am anything. I love you.

This. This is for Kim. Another life, another time, another body.

This. This is for Marjani. You have always understood me better than anyone else, and I have understood you. You are frisky and clever and smarter than all the idiots who take you for granted. You have a strength none of them will ever have. I do not know if there is justice in this world. I do not know what happens next. But if there is ever a reward for all this, it will be reserved for you. You should be president. You should be queen. You should be God.

This. This is for Travis. Big, dumb, wonderful Travis. I'd never have had the courage to do any of this without you. You did the one thing I wanted everyone to do but never could get them to: you treated me just like every other dope, no better, no worse. There's greatness in your future, Travis, because you have the only character trait that matters: you are kind. Go be fearless and mad and wild and free.

This. This is for Ai-Chin. I couldn't do much in this world. But maybe I can still do this for you.

I take a deep breath. I glance at Jonathan. Still asleep. Maybe this will be a straight shot to his chair. Maybe I'll go flying out the door and off the porch. Maybe none of this means a goddamned thing. But you have to do something. You gotta do something.

I'm ready.

Then I see it. My chair iPad flashes Travis's face. There is a message.

We are here. I see you. We got you. Let's do this.

I grin.

I am not alone. I never was.

With every whit of strength I have left, I slam my wrist against the joystick.

slam straight into the kitchen table. I moved about three feet.

   My dramatic escape.

But this sets into motion a series of events. I am dimly aware of most of them. But here's what I can reconstruct.

The crash knocks over a vase with a tulip that Marjani put down as a sad little centerpiece and a cup of coffee that Jonathan apparently made but forgot about.

Liquid spills all over the place. The coffee begins pouring off the table, and a large splash of it lands on Terry, who is not in fact dead. He groans.

The noise from my chair ramming into the table wakes up Jonathan, who then hears Terry moan and leaps out of his chair, yelling, "Oh, no, oh no, oh noooooooo!" He runs into the kitchen and grabs the baseball bat.

But before he can do anything with it, there is a jiggling of keys at the door.

Marjani walks in.

My God, Marjani. But she does not look surprised to see Jonathan, or the orderly, or even me, now jammed between the table and the refrigerator with tires spinning. And she certainly does not look scared.

She does the strangest thing: she smiles. There is a tremble of her bottom lip. But still, she smiles.

"Well, hello," she says, as Jonathan stands there, bat in his hand, jaw dropped, a look of astonishment on his face. "My name is Marjani. I work here with Daniel." She surveys the room.

"I see you found the bacon," she says.

Jonathan looks at me, dumbstruck. I try to shrug. I don't know if it comes across.

She looks at me and, for the first time since she came into the room, briefly loses her composure, stepping back, startled. I must look awful. But she straightens herself and looks me right in the eye.

Hello, Marjani.
I am here, Daniel. This is almost over.
Marjani, I was right. That's him. He's here. You have to be careful. He is very dangerous.
We know who he is. We are here to help you. You have been so brave.
I'm scared.
I am scared too. But you are so strong. So we will be strong too.

She winks at me. *She winks at me.* She then turns back toward Jonathan. "So," she says, utterly calm, "is there any coffee?"

Jonathan stands there, flabbergasted, and takes a short step toward her. "Lady, you need to—"

Then there is a flash, and an explosion, and suddenly the room is full of smoke and sparks and many, many booming voices. "GET DOWN EVERYBODY DOWN EVERYBODY

DOWN GET THE FUCK DOWN DOWN DOWN DOWN DOWN." I hear something awfully loud, and then something rams into the table, spinning me around to where I am lodged against the refrigerator, staring up at the ceiling.

The smoke burns a little, and it's becoming harder and harder to breathe. I shut my eyes, still sure I'm fading out, still sure these are the last moments, still all right with it, all right with all of it.

I open them when a figure slams up against my chair, and then slides down, then gets up and tries to run across the room.

There is another bang. The figure stops. I close my eyes again.

It is quieter. It is calm. It is all going to be OK.

I open my eyes. The ceiling fan is slowly turning above me. The shadows of the early-morning sun flicker in and out. If the final thing I see is this kitchen, well, it's my kitchen. It's my home. I made it mine. People say goodbye to worse. I always liked this kitchen.

But it doesn't fade to black, or light. The smoke clears. The noise dims. My eyes sharpen. I see a police officer in the corner of the room. He walks into the kitchen and leans down to attend to Terry. My eyes focus on his nameplate: ANDERSON. Back in this home again. His face is ashen and ruddy, and he is wiping his nose with the back of his hand. He looks at me, blinks, and looks away.

I roll back over and stare at the ceiling fan again.

And then Marjani and Travis are here.

Marjani wipes my face. Travis is weeping. And they're here and we are together and we're not alone and it's the best feeling I've ever had, I'm telling you, there is nowhere else I've been or am going that will ever be better than right here and right now.

AFTER

She sits in the corner, a little nervous to look at me, a little cautious, but not too cautious, to come in. I understand. I'd be afraid of me right now too.

But she is strong. A security guard puts an arm around her, but she pushes it off gently. The nurse next to her, young, so young, offers her a glass of water and a chair.

This nurse is very sweet, but she makes me antsy, regardless. The whole week I've been here, when she finishes her rounds, she doesn't go back to the nurse's station to gossip with the staff or complain about one of the doctors. She comes back here, and she sits down next to me, and she holds my hand. She works the night shift, after all my visitors have left for the day, and she's in that chair every spare moment, wiping my brow, fidgeting with my monitors, praying.

This nurse has been in my room too much, man. Most medical professionals, nurses, doctors, paramedics, they have a certain studied remove that's a job requirement, a callousness that develops after years of watching person after person die and person after person weep after them like they've lost the only person on earth who ever mattered. Death happens constantly, thousands of times every second, and there is nothing special about it. If you are close to the person who has died, it's devastating. But if you're not, it's . . . not. More people than you have ever known in your life just died in the last five minutes. Does that make you sad?

No, mourning is a luxury of the emotionally committed, and when we're not, death is just one more line item you can't do anything about. The experienced medical professional knows this. They are sad for you, and sympathetic for you, and there to help guide you through the grieving process. But then they will do it again tomorrow, with somebody else, and again the day after that, and the day after that, over and over until they grow too old to be of much help to anybody anymore. (And then *they* die.)

This nurse is handling this whole scene now, though, and I'm realizing there are some advantages to having a medical professional with an emotional investment. She shooshes off the security guard, who waits outside the door, and the nurse whispers, "I'll be right here" in my ear, and then in the ear of the woman next to her. The nurse then sits down next to her and rubs the woman's back.

Ai-Chin sits and looks at me. She's older than I realized. Well, not older, exactly. Stronger. In my mind I had thought of her as a babe in the woods, swept up by the big bad wolf. But that is not right, and the fact that I thought that says more about my own preconceived notions than anything about her. I see her looking around the room, absorbing everything, calculating, figuring out the lay of the land. Her eyes flame with intelligence. This is not a scared little lamb.

And then, just as quickly as I notice all of this, she chokes back a tear and looks away from me.

I get it. I'm quite a sight. The first three nights were touch-and-go, from what I'm told. Travis told me I nearly died around four times before my mom's flight even landed, but I have no recollection of any of that. I wasn't dreaming of Kim, or that I could fly, or of fighting my way toward the light. I was just out. I wonder if that's what it's really like. Just out. I bet it is. That's not so bad, if that's what it is. I can deal with just out.

I'm still in critical condition, and I've been lying in this bed for a week, and I suspect I look like a wadded-up ball of yellow construction paper. But I am still in here.

I want Ai-Chin to know I am still in here. Using all the might I can muster, I strain to move my left hand. It doesn't really work. I grunt and pull and groan, and my index and middle fingers only barely move. But Ai-Chin hears the grunting and pulls her head back in my direction. She looks at me. I look at her.

Hello.
Hello.
I know what I look like. But you need to know I'm in here.

She needs to know that it is not as bad as it looks. She needs to know that I am stronger, not weaker, because of her. On the surface, she sees a void where there is a soul; she sees a victim where there is power; she sees weakness where there is strength; she sees death where there is so much life. Look what I can *do*!

I can do so much.

I know that Ai-Chin Liao is alive because of me. According

to what Travis told me, she had been locked in a storage shed behind Jonathan's duplex all week, ever since she got in his car because she wasn't sure where she was going and it was a little dark and she thought the man in the car looked like the one down the hall in her student housing complex and he had a kind face and America is supposed to be a place of nice people who will help you when you need their help. When the police found her, she was terrified, hungry, but otherwise unharmed. Whatever he was going to do with her, he hadn't done it yet. His first taste of ultraviolence appears to have been with me and Terry. Jonathan turned out to be rather bad at being a criminal, as long as his victim wasn't confined to a wheelchair. Terry not only didn't die, all he ended up with was a broken jaw and a concussion. Travis said Terry even got a few blows in on Jonathan when he was lying on the floor of my hallway, and while I think Travis might be pulling my leg, I like the story enough that I decide to believe him. Good for him.

Ai-Chin takes my hand. In it, she puts a letter. It is in Chinese.

"I . . . letter," she says. "For you."

I will read it. I know how to translate these things.

I can do so much.

Jonathan is in the Athens Correctional Center because of me, arraigned on felony kidnapping, aggravated assault, attempted murder, and a bunch of other charges they hurled at him because, honestly, screw that guy. When Travis got my message when I was trying to escape the house, he called 911 and told them that a disabled man was being attacked at his home. He then called Marjani, who called Officer Anderson, and they all arrived at the house at the same time, along with a phalanx of officers. Marjani somehow talked them into letting her serve as a distraction ("Is there any coffee?") as they busted in the back door. Jonathan tried to run away, but they shot him in the leg and cuffed him right there.

I hope getting shot hurt. I hope it still hurts.

Now Jonathan is going to be away for a long time. I feel no bond to him, none of the special connection he so desperately wanted. He's just a sad, sick guy who needs to be kept away from the rest of us from now on. I wanted to share his loneliness because I felt it too. But his isolation is not my isolation. He sees the world as a place that rejects him. I see the world as a place that can welcome everyone. His rejection is not because of isolation; it is because of stupid fear and sadism. If we hadn't come across each other, maybe Ai-Chin would be dead. Maybe he'd do it again. Or maybe he'd let her go and hope she was too scared and confused to identify him. I don't think Jonathan knew himself what was going to happen. It doesn't matter. It's over now. With any luck, Jonathan, none of us will ever see you again. You turned out to be nothing at all.

That is not what is important right now, Ai-Chin, now that you are here. What is important is that I am the lucky one.

I have power. I have strength. I have the security of knowing that even though I needed to use this chair, even though I could not just reach out and grab this world by the collar, I have changed this world. I have found my place. The world is different because I was in it. This is what we should all want.

This is what we should all want.
I know.

I have the certainty that I took part in this life. I was an active participant. I did not just sit at my computer and let it all pass me by.

I have people who love me. I have people who will be with

285

me until the absolute end. I have the warmth of knowing that when I am gone, no matter when that is, the people near me will speak of me and remember me and keep me in their souls for the rest of their lives. I have helped people, and I have people who have helped me. Letting someone help you is the nicest thing you can do for anyone.

Do you understand?
I do. There has been such pain. You have suffered too much.
I have not suffered. I have lived!

I have lived!

Ai-Chin begins to stroke my left cheek with her hand. She is lovely. She is strong. The world is so much better because she is in it. I can see that. And I know that she can too.

"Thank you," she says.

I take a deep breath.

"You. Are. Well. Come."

She smiles. She then stands up, takes the nurse's hand, and walks out of the room.

I have brought light into this world, and I have been given light from this world. And what light it is! I can say that I have lived. Can you say that you have lived? You must be able to say you have lived. I have loved, and I have been loved.

That is all we should want. This is all you have to do right now. It's right in front of you.

So just take it. I know I plan to.

ACKNOWLEDGMENTS

Like most people, I had never heard of spinal muscular atrophy until it touched my life. My son William was two years old when his close friend Miller was diagnosed with the neuromuscular disorder. He and my son are now nine years old, and still best pals: Their Madden battles get a little more intense every year. Being close to Miller, along with his parents, Lindsay David (whose help was consistently invaluable, and without whom none of this would have happened) and Eason David, introduced me to the world of SMA and, more to the point, all the families and individuals who live, and thrive, with it every day. Their warmth and good cheer sparked the initial notion to write this book, and their guidance lit my path throughout. I hope I've honored their strength. Thank you. I also must thank all the people who allowed me to listen to them about their experiences with SMA and disability. I'll never know as much as you, but I know so much more because of you.

Even though I hadn't written a book for him in nearly a decade, my agent, David Gernert, still met me for dinner one night two years ago in the West Village, where I surprised him with a completed first draft of a book he had no idea I had been writing. His enthusiasm for this project, his faith in its voice, and his dogged persistence at making sure people saw it are the primary reason you're holding it in your hand right now. I don't know if your agent is supposed to be your friend, but I am glad he is mine. And I could not have imagined a better steward and shepherd for this book than Noah Eaker, my editor at Harper. He is brilliant and funny and incisive and is blessed with the best possible attribute an editor can have: He's always right about everything but, you know, he's cool about it. He is also my favorite person I met during the pandemic: We will be drinking much bourbon together at the earliest opportunity. I also can't thank the whole Harper crew enough: Elina Cohen, Kate D'Esmond, Mary Gaule, Erin Kibby, David Koral, Lainey Mays, Joanne O'Neil, Virginia Stanley, and the rest of the gang.

I wrote this whole book before I showed it to anyone and had no idea if it even made sense, let alone whether or not it was any good. I was fortunate to have intelligent friends to run it by: Their handiwork is all over it, whether they realize it or not. So, thank you to A. J. Daulerio, Aileen Gallagher, Tim Grierson, and Edith Zimmerman for their feedback and advice.

I also must thank my editors and colleagues at all the various publications I regularly soil with my words, for their willingness to give me the opportunity to do so and the patience they had with me as I wrote this book in between all my assignments for them: Matt Meyers, Gregg Klayman, Matthew Leach, Jenifer Langosch, and Mike Petriello at MLB.com; David Wallace-Wells, Benjamin Hart, Ray Rahman, and Ann Clarke at *New York* magazine; Jon Gluck and Brendan Vaughan at Medium; Meredith Bennett-Smith at NBC News; and Ben Williams and Sam Schube at *GQ*.

Special thanks also must go to Jami Attenberg, Chris Bergeron, Amy Blair, Mike Bruno, Joan Cetera, Mike Cetera, Jim Cooke, Tommy Craggs, Joe DeLessio, Denny Dooley, Jason Fry, Julia Furay, Derrick Goold, David Hirshey, Jenny Jackson, Kim Keniley, Andy Kuhns, Keith Law, Jill Leitch, Mark Lisanti, Bernie Miklasz, Adam Moss, Matt Pitzer, Keri Potts, Lindsay Robertson, Sue Rosenstock, Joe Sheehan, Trevor Stevenson, Susan Stoebner, Mark Tavani, and Kevin Wiegert. And thank you to my crew here in Georgia. I knew no one in Athens until I moved here in 2013, but now, thanks to so many of the people I met along the way, it is my home. Thank you to Matt Adair, April Allen, David Allen, Josh Brooks, Lillie Brooks, Hailey Campbell, Bertis Downs, Scott Duvall, Elizabeth Earl, Michael Earl, Seth Emerson, Kelly Girtz, Haley Graber, Will Haraway, Bryan Harris, Carrie Kelly, Tim Kelly, Kerri Loudis, Vicki Michaelis, John Parker, Michael Ripps, J. E. Skeets, and Tony Waller.

One of the best parts of living in Georgia has been the presence of my parents, Bryan and Sally: They moved down from Illinois to be closer to their grandchildren, but for me to have them here has been a lifesaver for me, personally (even before the pandemic). Thank you for everything you have done for me: I'm so happy and fortunate to get to spend this time with you. Also, thank you to Wynne Stevenson for being the sort of mother-in-law I am elated to have part of my pandemic pod. (She's a great copy editor, too.) And, man oh man, do I love the two little boys who live in this house with me. William and Wynn, you are the center of everything in my world, and just looking at you makes me feel like everything is going to be OK.

And, lastly, to Alexa: You were the first person to read this book because you are the first person I want to do everything.

You know more about books than I do, but you know more about everything than I do. (She even solved this book's biggest plot hole!) You are brilliant and talented and should probably just be in charge of everything on the planet. Being with you is the greatest privilege of my life. I love you, and thank you.

ABOUT THE AUTHOR

WILL LEITCH is a contributing editor at *New York* magazine. He also writes regularly for the *New York Times*, the *Washington Post*, NBC News, *Medium*, and MLB.com, and is the founder of the late sports website Deadspin. He lives in Athens, Georgia, with his wife and two sons.